I0681060

Cathryn Grant

The Hallelujah Horror Show

A Novel

D2C Perspectives

Email Cathryn at Cathryn@SuburbanNoir.com or visit her online at SuburbanNoir.com

Cover design by Lydia Schufreider.

ISBN: 978-0-9888241-9-5

For Grandpa Denaro
who dared to question *God.*

Before it began

HE HATED HER from the moment he first saw her. Maybe what he hated was the sheer size of her — easily as tall as him. In general, the immensity of women overwhelmed him, physically and emotionally, their power to consume your life and your thoughts. Their absolute certainty about everything.

One

BOB LAMBERT STOOD on the sidewalk. He held his silver lighter to the tip of a cigarette and flicked the wheel. His eyes crossed slightly as the flame shot up. The tobacco and paper caught fire, flared, then settled into a calm glow. Smoking on Sunday mornings satisfied him. It defied god on two levels — replacing his attendance at mass and the act of smoking itself. Not that smoking was considered a sin, but there was something rebellious about it.

A thread of smoke rose past his face. Through it, he observed the church across the street.

It was peach — the color of a baby's room. The roof was flat with a white overhang that wrapped around the stucco sides as if it held the structure together. In place of the traditional wooden doors of a proper church, double glass doors like those on a store at a strip mall opened into the small lobby. Bob had never seen past the lobby, he hadn't even seen inside the lobby, because he'd never stepped foot on the property. He hated those people. More for what they represented than their individual presence in the scenery of his life. As far as he was concerned, god was a masochist. He carved a hole of desire into your heart, then left it empty.

Alongside the front doors were four white pillars that should have belonged to a classical building. The sign read — *Triumphant Life Tabernacle.* A white bench faced the glass doors. It was as if they knew they were putting on a show and the bench stood waiting for an audience. No one ever sat on the bench.

To the right of the building was a parking lot that accommodated fifteen cars, forcing some of the members to park along the street.

Everything about the building screamed shabby, no sense of design. If those people thought their god was almighty, you would think they'd construct something fitting for their image of their creator and caretaker. But no, they'd thrown up a building that made them look as if they were gathering inside a dollar store on Sunday mornings.

When he was a kid, a church was considered the house of god. But this brand of religion was focused on god living inside of people, flaming out with strange languages and wild gyrations, clapping and dancing, and supposed miracles of healing. The building didn't matter to them.

He knew about the clapping and shouting because the noise seeped out through the poorly sealed doors while his cigarette burned every Sunday. It sounded like a free-for-all in there. If he hadn't inherited the house from his grandparents, he never would have chosen to live across the street from those unhinged women and men. Several times he'd considered moving, but Dana loved their old house with its wide front and back porches, a distinct sitting room, living room, and dining room — features you didn't find in newer homes.

Dana had hung wallpaper and ripped up carpet to reveal hardwood floors, making over every piece of the house to her liking. The only thing missing, she said, was a remodeled bathroom. She really wanted one of those big step-in tubs and fancy fixtures, a slate floor and a spacious, separate shower. So far, he hadn't gotten around to it. He'd been promising *soon* for nearly six years now. Amazingly, she still believed him, although he wasn't sure he believed himself.

The cigarette was half gone when the red Buick careened around the corner from Iowa Street onto Calliope Avenue. The driver gunned the car unnecessarily. As she pulled to the side, the right front tire hit the curb and the car lurched to a stop. The front end was a foot past the edge of Bob's driveway, the tail a good four feet from the gutter. She parked as if the street were an extension of the church property. He wasn't going to let her get away with it anymore. There weren't many things you could control in life, but making sure your neighborhood was treated with respect was one of them.

The woman shut off the engine and flung open the door.

As she climbed out, she looked like she was unfolding her tall, thin body. She had short light brown hair, pale skin, and eyebrows that were barely visible from where he stood. She wore a cotton smock with tiny blue flowers and a white t-shirt that reminded him of long underwear, waffled sleeves and tight cuffs at the wrists.

Although she looked familiar, he was never able to place her in any of the prominent scenes of his life. Maybe she reminded him of someone. As he got older, a lot of people did. It seemed there might be limited blueprints for human beings, and the longer you walked on the planet, the less variation you observed. Still, he couldn't shake the feeling he'd met her before, and not just in passing. For whatever reason, either that previous knowledge, or her horrendous driving, or the fact she represented what he hated about religion, she stirred in him a desire to correct her bad behavior.

"Hey!" He tapped his cigarette and let the ash fall on the sidewalk.

"Good morning." She smiled.

"You need to slow down."

"I wasn't speeding."

"You hit the curb."

She laughed. "I guess I didn't notice. I was praising the Lord."

"Cut the crap."

She looked shocked. He could have said far worse. He was

pleased with his restraint. "This is a residential area, speed limit twenty-five."

"I wasn't going that fast."

"You were."

"Well I hope you'll forgive me." She opened the back door of the car and reached inside. She emerged holding a red leather Bible.

"So you can do whatever the hell you want and you'll be forgiven?"

"It's true."

"Slow down or I'll request a traffic cop out here."

"I said I was sorry."

He drew on his cigarette and let the smoke out slowly. A thin cloud hung in the air then floated away. "Actually, you didn't. You said I should forgive you."

"Sorry.

"I'm sick and tired of it. Don't let it happen again."

"I can't promise that. I get so excited when I'm singing, I lose myself." She stepped into the street. "You should join us. It might make you less grouchy."

"Doesn't the bible require you to obey the law?" He knew it did, but he felt excited by the conversation, the anticipation that she might get angry, might curse at him or otherwise lose her goofy smile. She might even tell him he was damned. He loved it when they got overwrought.

"I wasn't actually speeding."

She lifted her arm and pulled back the white sleeve to look

at a small wristwatch with a pink strap.

"You were going too fast and you weren't watching. There are kids and animals around here."

"O-*kay! Sorry.* Jesus forgives *you too,* you know."

"I don't need forgiveness."

"We all need it."

The excitement drained out of him like ice cream melting down the sides of a cone. Why had he thought he'd get her to lose her cool? They always won, always had an answer for everything. Even though their answers were simplistic. It must be nice to have everything all worked out, to feel as if you had life by the balls. But you didn't. He had a sudden urge to continue the conversation, to invite her into his house and initiate a debate that would leave her crying, realizing she was stupid and all alone in the world. There was no one watching over her, taking care of her, ready to help, giving her whatever her tiny heart desired. "You only need it if you're guilty."

She licked her lips, her tongue purplish from the effort of shooting it out of her mouth. It ran along her pale lips, thick and ugly. "Well, Mr. . . . . What's your name?"

"Doesn't matter."

"Yes it does. I'm Melody."

He sucked on his cigarette.

"Well, everyone is guilty. If you think you're not, you're lying to yourself." She looked at her watch again. "I don't want to be late."

"You're already late. I heard them in there rockin' and rollin' forty minutes ago."

"I have a special prayer meeting this morning. After the service."

He dropped his cigarette on the sidewalk. He didn't step on it, but let it burn slowly. "Watch where you're going from now on. Because I'll be watching you."

She smiled and licked her lips again. She turned and crossed the street without bothering to look for oncoming traffic, as if angels stood on either side of her.

He reached into his shirt pocket and pulled out his pack of Marlboro reds. Usually he only had one cigarette on Sunday mornings. In fact, it was his only cigarette of the week. But he'd felt unsettled all morning.

He'd been up early, wasted thirty minutes on Facebook — a poor addition to society, all it did was show you what was missing in your life, but somehow irresistible. He tried to stay away from Ashley's page, not wanting to be one of those fathers trying too hard to be a friend with his kid. It was a good method for keeping up with family. He saw a flood of photographs uploaded from a trip his nephew and brother had taken to Germany. Strings of comments were attached to each image, the final one a sunset view of their stop at Regensburg. Bob's brother had posted a comment — *Thanks for letting your old man tag along. Watching you grow into a fine young man makes me the wealthiest guy on the planet. Cheers!*

His brother crowed all over his sons' Facebook pages. He

should show a little dignity, a little concern for the kids' social lives. Four sons. The guy couldn't seem to stop reproducing himself. Bob put the cigarette in his mouth and flicked the cap of his lighter open and closed.

The red LeSabre mocked him from its crooked position near the curb. She hadn't even asked if her car was preventing him from backing out of his driveway. She didn't know the Chevy truck parked in front of the house belonged to him. He could call the police and have her towed, but it really was only a foot or so past the dip in the apron of the driveway.

He stared at the unlit tip of the cigarette. Bits of tobacco pressed against each other. He rolled it across his palm and a piece of tobacco fell out and stuck on the webbing between his thumb and forefinger. He put the cigarette in his mouth and brushed the tobacco off his hand. He touched the side of his face and raked his fingertips down his sideburns. They needed a trim. Ashley hated his sideburns, said they made him look like he was stuck in the seventies. Well maybe he was. In the seventies, his whole life had been in front of him. Smoking hadn't seemed risky, and god was only a small irritant, a steady, low-grade whisper of guilt, but someone who was there when Bob was desperate. Over the years, he'd realized the mass of humanity was brainwashed into thinking there was some entity watching over them, lending a hand, giving them a shoulder to cry on, answering their prayers. He laughed, a dry sound more like a cough.

There weren't any *answers*. What made people think a being

powerful enough to create galaxies was intimately concerned about their ability to get a parking space at the mall? It was beyond funny. He laughed again, louder this time. He glanced quickly across the street and at the houses on either side to be sure no one noticed him standing on the sidewalk, an unlit cigarette in his mouth, rubbing his sideburns, and laughing at nothing in particular. He snapped his lighter at the tip of the cigarette.

Dana didn't understand why he stood on the sidewalk smoking every Sunday, brooding, as she put it. *If they annoy you so much, why do you expose yourself to that? Stay inside and read the paper or work in the backyard. They'll be gone soon enough.*

He took a drag on his cigarette, held the smoke in longer than usual, then let it out in a tight, narrow stream. To be honest, he didn't understand either. Brooding. That was a good word for it.

Two

MELODY WALKED ACROSS the street, her navy blue ballet-style shoes caressed her feet, making her steps lighter, as if she were skipping over the surface of the blacktop. The delicate shoes made her feel lithe instead of too clunky, towering over the average woman, her hands and feet as large as a man's.

The service was still in progress. She turned and went into the prayer room. It was furnished with a small flowered couch and two armchairs surrounding a glossy caramel-colored coffee table. She sat on the couch and put her bag on the coffee table.

Her pulse jittered from that man lashing out at her for driving too fast. She'd parked near his house every Sunday for weeks. Why did he have to choose today for his lecture? Even after she'd crossed the street, she smelled him fouling up the air. Smoking was a filthy habit. The human body was created to be filled with the Spirit of God, not tobacco and tar and all kinds of carcinogens. Her heart ached, thinking about the damaged state of his soul.

If she hadn't been anxious about what might unfold at this morning's prayer meeting, she would have talked to him longer. Or rather, tried to get him talking. It was always better to let the other person talk, especially someone who was as deeply wounded as that man obviously was. Listening allowed the poison inside to seep out, her ears a vessel for the waste. If a man could know, often for the first time in his life, that someone was listening, if he could see that God Himself was listening through her, then there might be an opportunity to guide him to the truth.

It wasn't that she had an agenda. He wasn't a project. He looked like a nice man, a little lonely, a little sad about how the world had treated him. She hated seeing people beaten down by life. People who had tried so hard to be good, to do the right things. It wasn't fair how harsh life could be sometimes. She knew.

She set her Bible on her lap. The leather was worn off in spots along the spine, the tissue-thin pages thickened by slight crumples, many passages carefully underlined in blue ink. She'd used a cardboard bookmark to ensure the underlining was straight. She didn't want the words obscured, even though she'd memorized most of the marked passages.

Today was a frightening and wonderful day. Each time she thought about it, when she pictured what lay ahead, her hands trembled along with her pulse. After the morning service, three women would meet with her in this room to place their hands on her and pray. Her life would be transformed.

She'd skipped the morning service. It was the first time since she'd started attending Triumphant Life Tabernacle two months ago. A long and lonely two months it had been. She'd spent extra hours every day kneeling on her bedroom floor, bare knees pressed against the concrete slab below the carpet until the skin of her kneecaps turned bright red, until her feet grew numb, and needles of pain raced up her shins.

The gathering today was something she had to be prepared for. She couldn't get caught up in her ego, in worrying about what the others were thinking. Most of all, she had to put her experience at her last church out of her mind. She had to believe with all her heart. When God granted her the gift of speaking in tongues, she would know without a doubt that He loved her as much as she loved Him. She'd finally receive proof that she belonged.

The service was running late, as it usually did. She opened her Bible to the book of Hebrews. Her fingers continued to shake as she turned the pages, reading but hardly absorbing the words. The fluttery rhythm in her heart coursed through her whole body so she felt like her blood vessels were vibrating. It wasn't good to be nervous, but she was terrified something would go wrong. That they would place their hands on her and the gift would refuse to materialize.

Her stomach grumbled, churning with too much coffee,

already having digested her two pieces of toast with butter and orange marmalade and the apple she'd consumed hours ago.

Bass guitar and drums thumped through the walls. The clapping was loud, revealing the complete abandon of the worshippers in the main hall, a cluster of people in front of the stage, eyes closed, chins lifted so their faces pointed toward heaven, waving their hands over their heads when they slipped off the beat, lost in the ecstasy of the moment, the words of the Spirit bubbling out of their mouths.

She experienced that same recklessness when she attended a service. Almost. She loved the songs. It was so easy to move with the beat. Now, sitting here alone, trying to comprehend the passage in front of her, she felt disconnected from the music. It was too loud. The voices were blurred, the lyrics indecipherable, although she knew the words to most of the songs, so her mind filled in the blank spaces. The clapping was rough, childish, and slightly disconnected from the rhythm.

She closed the Bible and placed it on the table. She stood and walked to the window and looked out. A narrow strip of grass ran between the side of the building and the sidewalk. It was too bad they hadn't planted shrubs or flowers, some spring bulbs, so the building didn't look so plain. She moved in time with the music. Keeping time helped erase the feeling that it was cheap and gaudy. Her hands warmed and the jittery feeling subsided. She wished the service would end.

Once the prayer meeting started, she would absorb the faith of the other women. Her brain would stop analyzing and worrying and remembering.

ELISE WAS THE first to enter the room. She wore emerald green pants and a white silk blouse, sleeveless, despite the cool spring air. Her arms were lightly tanned. Blonde hair, almost too golden to be natural, but it was, flowed over her shoulders. She'd come out of a raucous worship service, and yet her hair looked like she'd just finished giving it the traditional one hundred strokes. Her skin was smooth. Her lipstick was pale and her eyelids dusted with pinkish brown shadow.

"We missed you at the service," she said.

Melody pressed her spine against the window frame. "I wanted some time alone with the Lord." Standing only a few feet from Elise, Melody felt like she was back in high school, awkward and unable to control her movements, needy and uncertain. Her feet, even in the delicate ballet slipper shoes, were large and bony compared to Elise's feet, sleek in black leather pumps.

"The message was amazing. Pastor Tom really dug into Abraham's sacrifice of Isaac. You could almost see the knife blade when he raised it up, ready to kill his only son, if that's what was required."

Melody smiled but it felt more like a grimace. Was this meeting a mistake? Exposing her doubts, her failure, to these

supremely confident women? Admitting that she either lacked
faith or that God Himself had rejected her and had no
intention of giving her the gift of tongues? She closed her
eyes. This had to be done. Eventually they would have
noticed, during a service, or a prayer meeting, that no
heavenly sounds ever came from her lips.

Of course there were plenty of churches that believed the
gifts were more distributed — healing, discernment,
hospitality. But who wanted the gift of hospitality? All
women were expected to demonstrate at least a minimum
level of hospitality. Of course, some career-minded women,
clawing their way up to the executive ranks, might not have
those traditional expectations laid across their backs like a
shawl. Still, she could never understand why it was tossed into
that list with the interesting gifts, like healing. That would
really be something, to rid people of cancer or other diseases
eating away at their nerves, their muscles, their minds. The
gift of discernment could be interesting too, knowing when
someone was controlled by Satan, recognizing when slick
behavior was false, no matter how cloaked in beautiful
language.

For some reason, she wasn't drawn to those gifts. Maybe it
was selfish. She wanted something all her own, not something
that obligated her to others. Those gifts could be a little
frightening. You would be put on display. The expectations
could crush you. What if you placed your hands on a woman
to rid of her cancer and you failed? What if she stopped

getting treatment, or her pain increased and the uncontrollable cells raced across her body, making a liar out of you?

Besides, like her former churches, Triumphant Life Tabernacle taught that the gift of tongues was given to all true believers, a personalized language for prayer that transcended rational thought. It put believers in a state of ecstasy where they could more easily understand what God was saying back to them.

"I'm sorry I missed the lesson, but being alone seemed like the right thing to do."

Elise nodded. "You're scared. Like Abraham was."

"I'm not scared."

"Your hands are shaking."

"I'm excited."

"Sarah and Jennifer will be here in a minute." Elise ran her fingers through her hair, pulling it away from her neck. Her pink nails protruded between the strands of hair, looking like small fish swimming in a stream of golden water.

The door opened. Jennifer and Sara entered the room. Jennifer was close to Melody's age — thirty-three — with brown hair woven into an elaborate braid, a face empty of make-up, yet stunningly beautiful. She wore a yellow dress with a tiny matching jacket and yellow sandals. Beside her, Sarah was a withered shadow — brown hair streaked with gray, falling in tangled waves to her shoulders, fine lines in her skin. Her eyes were a rich hazel and she looked like she might wink at any minute, telling all of them this gathering wasn't necessary because she'd had a vision that Melody already had the gift of tongues, she just didn't recognize it.

Melody smiled. She folded her arms across her ribs. Suddenly, she knew. God wasn't going to deliver the gift of speaking in tongues at their command, as if she'd plopped herself on Santa's lap and asked for a wrapped package that he'd miraculously pull from the sack near his feet, the very object she longed for.

Sarah gestured at the thinly carpeted floor. "Go ahead and lie down so we can get started."

"I thought we would talk first, or pray or . . . something," Melody said. Her voice was a fragile whisper.

"Why would we do that?" Sara slipped her arms out of her sweater.

"It's so sudden."

The women stared at her. She tried to enhance her smile.

"Are you letting doubts take root in your heart?" Sarah's voice was stern, not the friendly, sympathetic tone, the soft murmuring that she'd offered when she first heard about Melody's problem.

Melody felt like a disobedient child.

"Are you?" Sara said.

"I told you what happened . . . before. I told you I'm doing everything I can to believe, but it's hard."

Elise moved closer. She put her hand on Melody's arm. Her fingers were warm and too tight. The fabric of Melody's shirt twisted across her skin. "You can't *try* to believe, you can't *want* to believe. You just have to *do* it. Get down." She tugged Melody's arm.

Melody stumbled. She lowered herself to her knees.

"All the way," Sarah said. "You must prostrate yourself before His Throne. That's how He'll know you're serious this time."

Why wasn't Sarah more sensitive to what she'd gone through? It was so easy for everyone else. They opened their mouths and the words tumbled out — glossolalia — beautiful, throaty sounds, trilling. No harsh guttural noises, stopping and starting, not knowing what to say next. Melody shivered. She wanted to cry, but not in front of them — all so supremely sure of what God wanted.

Melody put her palms on the carpet. Once her face was pressed against the stiff nubs there would be red streaks and indentations and the chance of a rash sprouting on her nose and chin. Or maybe she'd turn her head to one side, torturing one ear and one cheek. She was thinking too much. She should just flop down, but this wasn't what she'd expected. She'd assumed they would stand, or possibly kneel, maybe she'd sit on the couch and they'd gather around her.

She lowered herself to the floor. Her hipbones ached, her breasts were squashed flat, her neck strained. She turned her head to the side. Sarah's brown leather sandals and thick toes were the only feet within her line of sight. A piece of dead skin clung to the big toe of Sarah's right foot. Melody closed her eyes. "Should we lock the door?"

"Why would we lock the door," Sarah said. "Are you ashamed of what you're doing?"

"No," she whispered. "I thought it would be better if we weren't interrupted."

"The Lord knows life is full of interruptions."

Melody nodded. The carpet scraped her cheek.

Fabric rustled and someone's knee joint popped as the women settled themselves around her. She opened her eyes slightly. Sarah sat cross-legged facing her head. Jennifer was at her right, sitting on her heels. That meant Elise was on the other side. Now that Elise was this close, Melody hoped the perfectly groomed music minister's wife wasn't peering too intently at her hair, noticing that funny bump, a fleshy growth of some kind on the back of her skull, sometimes visible when her hair fell forward. She had an urgent need to touch it, as she often did, to stroke it and wonder at its inappropriate presence on her scalp. She tucked her hand under her belly.

"Close your eyes." Sarah's voice was firm. "Tell the Lord why you want to receive the gift of tongues. Tell Him you're a completely empty vessel, that going forward, you won't insist on your own desires."

Melody's heart clenched. Hadn't she done that? So many times? So many times she couldn't count them. Already doubts were taking shape, as if a slender caterpillar were spinning a cocoon inside her skull. "Well, I . . ."

"Don't hesitate," Elise said. "Be bold, declare your intentions."

Tears rushed to Melody's sinuses. It wasn't fair that this was so hard. No one else had special interventions. What was *wrong* with her? "I love the Lord so much, more than anything. I want to be completely filled with Him and ..."

"Don't tell us," Sarah said. "Tell *Him*."

"I want to praise You with my whole heart. I belong to You completely. There's no one else, nothing else." She took a deep breath. It was difficult to fill her lungs, lying with her face on the floor, the mobility of her jaw restricted, her ribcage compressed. A piece of hair fell across her cheek and stuck to her lip. She poked out her tongue to push it away, but the hair remained stubbornly planted in the crease between her upper and lower lips.

"Is that all?" Jennifer's voice was kinder than Sarah's, but there was still the suggestion of a command. It might be that her voice was only kinder because it was softer.

"I think so."

"That may be an issue," Elise said. "You're tongue-tied, you keep things inside, you're letting fear freeze your lips."

"I don't think I am," Melody said.

"Let the words flow."

"I do, when I'm alone with Him."

"It shouldn't be any different now. The gift of tongues isn't for someone who restrains her feelings, who's concerned about what others are thinking."

Melody took a deep breath. "You know I belong to You. I want to sing Your praises in a language that's beyond what human words can express, to feel Your power, to be filled with Your Spirit every minute."

For ten minutes, maybe longer, she continued to outline everything she hoped to receive, everything she was willing to give. The others seemed satisfied, because when she paused for breath, she felt six hands touch her shoulder blades, upper spine, and head, as if they'd planned it with a signal passed between them over her back. Their hands were warm, their fingertips gentle. A sense of comfort she hadn't felt earlier washed over her. For a moment, she felt loved and utterly at peace. She didn't have to worry or fret or strain. If she could simply let go, like unclasping her fingers from the string of a balloon, everything would be okay.

Then, as quickly as it arose, the feeling was gone.

She wondered if she'd drifted to sleep because she was now aware of all three women murmuring. Unintelligible sounds flowed from their lips. Phrases that could be Hebrew, maybe some Arabic words that Melody would never be able to identify.

It sounded so beautiful, the same burbling she heard all around her on Sunday mornings, while some sang in English and others slipped in and out of using their prayer languages.

"Speak, Melody. Open your mouth and let your heavenly language pour off your tongue like oil."

She parted her lips. She made a sound. It emerged as a

clearing of her throat, a small cough.

"That's right," Sarah said.

"Don't hold back," Elise said.

"Loosen your tongue."

"Ogla . . ."

"Yes," the women said in a single voice.

"Speak the language of the angels, Melody," Jennifer said.

"Sing His praises."

"Hallelujah!"

Their hands pressed more firmly into her back, she felt they were pinning her to the floor. She moved her other arm under her body to ease the pressure on her pelvic bones. They pressed harder. As she tried to inch away from Sarah, her chin dragged on the carpet.

"You're resisting."

She couldn't tell who spoke, they all sounded the same now, shrill commands. Impatient. They were judging her, doubting she was a true believer. "I'm not."

"Let go," Sarah said.

"I can't." A sob heaved out of her throat.

As quickly as they'd descended, all of their hands lifted off her back. She felt exposed. "Wait. Don't stop. I want it, I do."

"Sit up, Melody." Sarah's hand smoothed the back of her hair, fingertips passing over the bump without pausing to explore the anomaly.

Melody rolled onto her side and raised herself to her hip, sitting with her legs angled toward Jennifer.

Sarah and the others stood. Melody was nearly four or five inches taller than all of them, but in her half-reclining position, the other woman towered above her. "The reason you haven't received the gift of tongues is because you won't let yourself go. You're unwilling to be a fool for the Lord."

Jennifer nodded. Her braid slid over her shoulder.

They were wrong. She was nothing if not a fool, feeling them condemning her for failing to achieve the simplest thing. Trying to force words that were nothing but made-up nonsense out of her mouth made her feel terribly foolish. She shouldn't have to try. The words should just be there, without the sense she was fabricating them herself. God didn't love her. He'd turned His back on her.

"There's something blocking you," Sarah said.

"Sarah knows — she has the gift of discernment," Elise said.

Sarah went on, "You feel shame toward the Lord, perhaps shame in speaking the truth to unbelievers, or shame about something in your life. Until you can be free of it, you'll have trouble with the child-like attitude that's required for the gift of tongues."

Elise walked around to stand near Sarah, as if they were forming a wall. The three women walked to the door.

"Think about it," Sarah said.

"Don't be discouraged. He'll show you the way," Jennifer said.

"God showed Abraham what was required, He'll do the

same for you."

They went out, closing the door behind them.

Elise's words echoed in the empty room. She'd made it sound like a threat, as if God required the sacrifice of someone's life. This wasn't a pagan god who enjoyed seeing the innards torn out of human beings, who wanted to hear screams, and see crazed people feasting on chalices filled with blood.

Melody collapsed on the floor. She brushed her hair back and covered her face with her hands, smelling her skin, taking deep, gasping breaths through the spaces between her fingers. Did they expect her to remain alone in the room all day until God delivered a message, a command, an ultimatum?

Three

HER FATHER STOOD on the curb smoking. Again. Sometimes Ashley wondered if he only did it to piss off her mother.

She stepped away from the window. She pushed her feet into rubber flip-flops and went down the hall to the stairs. The flip-flops slapped each step, echoing against the wood. It puzzled her that she loved that sound so much, unless she liked making her presence known, or maybe it was reassuring to hear that her bones and skin, her psyche, had an impact on the world.

She pushed open the screen door and stepped onto the front porch. The air was warm for March. Summer was coming fast and soon she would be a year out of college and still living with her parents, still fending off Jack's insistence that they move in together, get engaged, still waiting for her career to materialize. Any day now. That's what told herself every morning. It was true. You didn't get straight A's in high school, a scholarship to Northwestern University, and kudos at an internship for the Chicago Tribune, and then languish in a part-time job as a receptionist forever. The economy was down, the media was changing every minute, continuing to adapt to the digital age and competition from amateurs. She'd find her place. Soon.

She walked down the front steps and along the path to the hedge. An unpruned branch snaked out, straining to touch her face. She ducked under it.

"Mom won't like it that you're smoking."

Her father turned. He lifted the cigarette to his lips and took a puff. "It's only one a week."

"You had two."

"Are you spying on me?"

"I was doing yoga. I can't help looking out my window."

He nodded, dropped the cigarette on the concrete, and pressed the toe of his boot on it.

"Do you want breakfast? I can make French toast."

"It's almost lunch time," he said.

"Is that a no?"

He kicked the cigarette butt to the curb.

"You're littering."

"The street sweeper will get it."

"It's still gross."

"French toast sounds good," he said.

"You didn't eat breakfast, did you."

"Nope."

"It's not healthy."

"Okay, mom."

"Daddy!" She poked his arm with her elbow.

He grabbed her ponytail and gave it a quick tug. She felt a rush of anger mixed with something else. In the space of three minutes he could make her feel like a shrew, a four-year-old, and a stranger. Mostly she felt like a stranger, never quite sure what he thought of her or if he even knew her at all, or if she knew him. Growing up she felt they were close, shooting baskets together when she was a kid. He pushed her hard in high school, and made her feel like she could do anything. Anything. She didn't have to settle for an average job or an average life. He never said it in so many words, but it was there, asking her what she wanted instead of telling her what to do. Since she'd moved home, it wasn't the same.

When she'd stood on the front steps of her dorm at the start of freshman year, and watched her parents' rental car turn out of the driveway, she'd felt she was an adult. Now, four years of hard work, parties, and answering to no one seemed like a dream. She lived in limbo-land, sleeping in her twin bed, sitting with one parent at each end of the table during meals, reporting what time she'd be home from work every day and providing itineraries for her weekend plans.

She needed to do something to shake things up. There had to be a creative way to leap over the resume slush pile. She'd thought the name of her university, her internship, and her grades would get her a string of interviews.

She followed her father up the front path and onto the porch. His boots thumped on the wood, her flip-flops slapped it, and the spot near the doormat creaked when they passed over it. No matter how she tried to avoid it, that one board always protested. Her mother said it was friendly, reminding them this was home, and showing the character of a house built in the 1930s. Ashley thought it sounded unstable and wished they'd fix it.

Once the eggs were cracked and yolks swimming freely in their clear liquid, she slid two slices of butter into a frying pan and turned up the gas. While the butter softened and quickly turned to bubbling liquid, she whisked the eggs with a splash of milk, and pressed a piece of bread into the bowl. Once again, she felt like her four-year-old self, transfixed by egg soaking into bread, first reluctant, than making its way through the resistant grain, turning it yellow and sloppy wet. She stabbed the bread with a fork and dropped it into the pan.

Her father worked at the opposite counter, dumping coffee grounds into the trash, emptying the pot from his early morning coffee, and refilling it with fresh water and dry grounds.

Her mother appeared in the doorway. "Smells good."

Even on a Sunday morning, her mother's straight, light brown hair was blown dry, a bit of gel in her bangs to force them up over her narrow forehead. She wore jeans and a pink sweatshirt, which meant she was prepped for working in the yard, yet her hair was perfectly styled. Ashley could count on one hand the days her mother went without shampooing, conditioning, and blow-drying her hair. Ditto for the foundation, eye shadow, and a quick flick with the mascara brush.

From the corner of her eye, she watched her mother go into the breakfast room, pull out a chair, sit at the table, and adjust the placemat so the bottom corners were an equal distance from the curve of the oval table.

Her father walked around the table and kissed the top of her mother's head. There was no mention of the smoking, but maybe her mother really didn't smell it, between the aroma of coffee, sizzling butter, and frying bread.

They sat in the same positions at the table as they had for twenty-three years. Or she assumed it was twenty-three years, she obviously couldn't remember when she was a baby, but knowing how their other patterns remained the same, she imagined her high chair had also faced toward the kitchen so her mother could see her while she cooked. Her father's chair faced the window looking out on the front yard, and her mother's chair faced through the archway into the dining room.

"One of those holy rollers almost ran over me again this morning," Bob said.

Ashley laughed. "That's funny."

"It was not funny."

"Don't you get it . . . a holy roller, rolling over you?"

He smirked. "Every single time. She comes tearing around the corner and slams her front tire into the curb. The car almost jumped onto the sidewalk today."

"I'm sure she didn't run up onto the sidewalk."

"You weren't there, Dana."

Ashley had hoped her lame joke would shift the conversation. It sounded like they were planning to repeat the exchange they had nearly every Sunday, sharpening their nails, preparing to defend their positions. It seemed as though they liked fighting about the tacky church across the street. She more or less sided with her father, that the members were all a little nutty, shouting and spilling into the aisles while they danced to religious rock 'n roll.

Next, her father would start raving about the stupidity of people who thought god was a vending machine and her mother would try to steer him to a politically correct position where all points of view had at least some validity. Maybe she should rat out her father for smoking again.

"You look at everything they do through a negative lens," Dana said.

"I don't need a very strong lens to see that they're delusional and arrogant."

Ashley squirted syrup onto her French toast. A large puddle formed, spreading quickly, running over the edges. If she coated the whole piece of toast and filled her plate, would either parent tell her to stop? She could drink the syrup from the bottle and they might not notice right now.

"If you didn't stand out there smoking every Sunday, you wouldn't even notice them."

Touché. Score one for her mother.

"Don't forget Wednesday nights. And the teenagers on Fridays. They're probably worried god won't know who they are if they don't show up every other day."

"They've found something that satisfies them. How does that hurt you?"

"Stupid people hurt the whole world."

"Believing in God doesn't make someone stupid."

"It does when they act like there's a cosmic vending machine. They think someone up there is so concerned about their football team, he's going to engineer a win? A trip to the Super Bowl? That some god cares that they get the last parking space? What about the other twenty guys who need parking spaces? Why did god pick that guy? And why doesn't he concern himself with more important things like children with bloated stomachs and skin sticking to their bones?"

Every time, it was the same. They used different words, different examples to make their points, sometimes the disagreement turned one direction or another. She wished she could understand why they kept talking about it. Was there something wrong with them? Or was it a characteristic of a multi-decade marriage, that you had no choice but to repeat certain things? Maybe the conversations dulled over so many years, and arguing was the only way to provide a spark. Maybe they used it as some prelude to sex, getting themselves all lathered up and then making up later, when Ashley was out with Jack or her friends, or watching a movie in her room. She shuddered. The last thing she wanted to think about was her parents' foreplay, but she couldn't help it. All she was trying to do was understand why they had the same boring conversation over and over again. There must be something else behind it.

It wasn't going to be that way for her. Maybe her parents weren't soul mates. If you were soul mates, it was different. Not this existence where two people turned into the walking dead. It was painful to watch. She wished more than ever she lived in her own place, or that she was back at school when every day was exciting and offered something unexpected.

She cut a large piece of French toast and stabbed it with her fork. Syrup dripped off the end as she lifted it from the plate. She popped it into her mouth.

"It makes you sound bitter." Dana put a piece of toast in her mouth. She chewed slowly and swallowed. "Don't take it out on them because you've given up your faith."

Her father sipped his coffee. His eyes looked tired, vaguely questioning.

This was new. Ashley dragged another piece of French toast through the syrup. She lifted the fork and licked at the toast like she was consuming an ice cream cone. She didn't know her father had lost his faith. Growing up, religion had been nebulous. Her mother believed in a God who was nice and kind and required only that people be polite and open-minded and generous with one another. A God who was happy to be noticed on Christmas, given a wave at weddings, who provided a heavenly welcome after a funeral. Her father never said much about religion when Ashley was small, at least not that she could remember. Her mother took her to Sunday school, and a summer vacation Bible school once, but the Sunday school stopped when she was about seven or eight. They'd never explained why.

Bob put down his coffee cup. "I haven't lost anything. But I'd like to knock some sense into their thick skulls."

"It's not your job. Everyone has a right to believe what they choose."

"They don't think I have that right."

Score for her father. Her mother's silence told her she recognized that this was correct. That brand of church was always handing out booklets, the members wanting to talk to you about heaven and hell and sin and salvation.

"You should have heard that woman this morning," Bob said. "She told me I needed to be forgiven. For what? I've lived an exemplary life. She told me I should attend their services." He laughed and drank more coffee.

"Inviting you to a service doesn't mean they're trying to change your beliefs."

"Like hell it doesn't. Don't play that goodness of their hearts game. You know what they want. And they won't be happy until the whole planet believes the same shit they do."

"They're just happy and feel like they have answers in life

and want to share it, that's all."

Bob drew his knife across the stacked slices of French toast as if he were cutting a heart in two. The bread squashed down in the center as the knife made its way across, dragging through bread and syrup, too dull to form a clean cut. "They have no right to act as if they own the secret to life and if I don't buy it, there's something wrong with me."

"Why do you care?"

"Methinks he doth protest too much," Ashley said.

Her father placed his knife across the edge of the plate. "I'd like to see them get what they deserve."

"What are you saying?" Dana said.

Her father looked directly at Ashley. "What do you think, Ash?"

"Don't put her in the middle," Dana said.

"In the middle of what? She's a college-educated woman now, I'm interested in what she thinks."

"About what?" Ashley said.

"Can society function in the twenty-first century, a global community, with hordes of people who think they can get what they want by asking their god to give it to them? Refusing to help the rest of the planet because god will take care of it?"

"A lot of people think that, Daddy. A *lot* of people."

"And they're all on a mission to get us to think the same way. Why isn't there a mission to get them to face reality?"

She shrugged. Her mother was right, she didn't want to get

dragged into this thing between them, this game, or this battle, this . . . thing.

"I'd at least like to get them to admit that god let them down. Instead of rationalizing everything they don't get as god's will, and leaping around with glee when they do get what they want because god answered their prayers. I'd like to hear just one of them say, *I don't get it, god let me down.* That's all. They don't even have to say *screw him*, just admit he didn't deliver on his promises."

This seemed to be going further than it had before. Ashley shivered. He was so angry about it. Her mother was right, why did he care so much? How was it hurting him? "We should talk about something else," she said.

"Why?"

"It's not a battle," Dana said. She pushed back her chair. "Are you finished?" Without waiting for a response, she picked up Ashley's plate. The syrup swam close to the edge as she lifted it, receding when she stacked it carefully on top of her own plate. She went to the doorway, then turned. "I think it would be healthy if you stopped sneaking a cigarette every Sunday, and even healthier if you stopped watching them and plotting whatever it is that goes through your head."

"I'm not plotting anything."

"Whatever it is you think about when you're out there."

"I'm not thinking anything. I'm fascinated, if you want to know the truth."

"Fascinated with what?"

"It's like people who are hooked on reality TV. There's something addictive about watching people behave stupidly. I'm intrigued by their plastic smiles and their phony voices, like crows shrieking because they found road kill."

"That's gross," Ashley said.

"That's what it reminds me of."

"I think it would be healthier . . ." Dana said.

"I know what you think. And maybe I don't want to be healthy."

Dana heaved a deep, dramatic sigh. She went into the kitchen. She returned with the coffee pot. With the other hand she picked up Bob's plate. "More coffee?"

He shook his head.

"No thanks," Ashley said.

Her mother stood in the doorway, the white plate in one hand, the pot filled with dark brown coffee in the other. She looked like Lady Justice, holding unbalanced dishes on each side. "I don't know what you want anymore."

"Maybe he doesn't either." Ashley had no idea why she'd said that. She didn't normally, hadn't ever, spoken about her father that way, as if he were a child, or a peer. Maybe it was payback for him yanking her ponytail. But why did that bother her? He'd always done it, and he was just showing affection in one of the few ways left to him, now that she was an adult.

Why was he so angry with people who were passionate about God? Maybe because he wasn't passionate about anything. Or maybe some other reason she could never hope to figure out.

Four

THE HARDWARE STORE was a home away from home. At least that's how Bob described it to Dana, to which she smiled like she had a secret. He wished he knew what that smile meant. After twenty-six years, should she still have secrets? Of course, he did, so why wouldn't she?

The thought that she might keep secrets from him had never occurred to him until this very minute. It could have been that woman — Melody — hitting the curb. He'd felt a jolt when the car slammed against concrete. Not the actual impact of course, but the adrenaline-laced fear that results from a vehicle slightly out of control — the mass and weight and potential deadliness of it. With it, his brain had shifted just a bit inside its bony shell and everything looked a hair off.

Dana might have all kinds of secrets. She was so optimistic and kind, she doted on him, but who knew what she was really thinking? When she argued about religion, tried to force-feed him with nice feelings for those nut cases, a different side of her appeared. A more dogmatic and opinionated side.

They rarely argued, and when they did, their words, and the feelings behind them, were mild — was the temperature really going to drop enough tonight to warrant covering the plants to prevent frost damage? Had she reminded him to pick up detergent at the store or just thought it? Should they buy a new car or something used for Ashley?

Some couples they knew could turn topics like those into battlegrounds peppered with land mines. Even when they argued about his *obsession* with the church across the street, they never shouted, never said cruel or hurtful things. He wasn't even sure what they were really arguing about. Maybe that's why the arguments lacked intensity. Maybe their whole marriage lacked intensity.

He walked inside the warehouse and grabbed an oversized shopping cart. He pushed it to the far right aisle. Since he had no idea what section he needed, he might as well work his way along every aisle, looking for plastic orange cones or a similar traffic control device. A house three blocks from his had yellow plastic figures of a child holding a sign that read — *slow down, children playing.* The house was on a corner and the woman put a sign on both streets when her children were in the front yard. There must be something similar that he could use to restrain the holy rollers. He laughed. Ashley really had turned into a witty young woman. He should have laughed harder to let her know he appreciated it.

Shelves of cleaning implements and supplies filled the first aisle. He walked quickly and rounded the corner. Next came doors — interior and exterior, screen doors, and rolls of screening material for repairs. He walked through lumber, hand tools, electric tools, nuts, bolts, and nails. What he wanted wouldn't be in any of those sections, but it was satisfying to walk past all the well-organized supplies, all the things that made homes stable and secure, the things required to keep life in good repair. When he reached the plumbing section he began to lose hope.

It probably wasn't technically legal to block the curb. Maybe traffic cones weren't available for sale. The woman's plastic figures with their warning signs were slightly different. Still . . . he circled past the home remodeling area and headed toward storage bins and shelving at the back of the store. Maybe his neighbor had purchased her figures online.

A man in a blue apron stood on a rolling staircase at the end of the aisle. Bob increased his pace and hurried to the staircase. "Hey."

The man, shorter than Bob, but looming above him, three steps up, had thick gray hair long enough to require constant tucking behind his ears. A plastic tag stated his name was Terry. "What can I help you with?"

"Do you carry traffic cones?"

"No. What do you need them for? Maybe something else will do the job."

"We have a traffic problem on our street."

"You should call public safety."

"I doubt they'd do anything."

The man took two steps down so his eyes were level with Bob's. "I know what you mean. We have dogs that make a mess in our yard all the time, and no matter how many times we call, they brush it off. Even if you tell them you know who the dog owners are."

"Yup. Unless someone robs you at gunpoint, they don't seem to want to get involved."

"What's the traffic problem?"

"We have a church across the street. Not a real church, one of those offbeat ones."

Terry nodded. "I know what you mean."

"They park all over the street, don't care if they block driveways. A few of them can't drive."

Terry nodded more vigorously. His hair flopped forward but he didn't place it back behind his ears. "So you want to keep them in their place."

"Good way to put it."

"Well, like I said, we don't carry plastic cones, but you could probably find them online."

"Okay. Thanks."

"Good luck. Hope the cops don't come by and remove your cones. It could end up backfiring. The guy whose rights are infringed ends up being the bad guy. They don't like you taking the law into your own hands."

"No, I guess not. But we'll see. I can't just stand there and let them run over my life."

"I know what you mean," Terry said. He climbed back up the steps.

Bob returned to the front of the store, left the cart with the others, and walked outside. It was always disappointing to leave the hardware store empty-handed, but he was optimistic — he should have checked the Internet first.

The tricky part would be the arrival of the package. Dana wasn't going to like his increased lack of tolerance, and he knew that's how she'd view it. Funny that she applauded his lack of tolerance when he reported his boss for cutting corners on required quality control a few years ago and was rewarded with a very nice bonus. For some reason, she wanted him to tolerate those church people. She saw that his rage was misdirected. Maybe that was the secret in her smile — she knew more about him than he realized. Maybe her secret was that she knew all his secrets.

AT HOME, ASHLEY had disappeared up to her room. Dana was in the backyard, kneeling at the far corner like a woman in prayer, her shoulders slightly rounded, her head bent so her hair fell forward and the tender back of her neck was exposed. A plastic sack of potting soil sat next to her, torn open, filled with fresh, moist dirt.

Bob backed away from the family room window and went into the single bedroom on the first floor, which they used as an office. Neither of them had a job that required a home office, but that's what they called it. As if being a family was a business in itself, requiring office space. And maybe it was — with taxes and insurance and estate planning and tracking the household budget on the computer.

Occasionally he worked from home in the evenings, when the company was in the frenzy of bringing a new product to market, but the rest of the time he preferred to go into the office. He couldn't comprehend people who spent their lives like trolls, working out of spare bedrooms, never stimulated by the interaction in the hallways and cafeteria that helped you stay connected to the pulse of the company, kept you abreast of the politics, the gossip, and the micro-shifts in the business that happened daily. Kept you human and social.

Dana certainly didn't require an office — she was a preschool teacher at Fresh Sprouts. He sometimes wondered if that's why she'd adopted an unquestioning, simplified view of religion, centered around angels and a Disney version of stories about whales and women hunting for lost coins, with no thought of the central, often unspoken theme — eternal hellfire. The question of unanswered prayer didn't trouble her. It was as if she didn't even notice the disconnect.

He pulled the wooden swivel chair out from the desk, sat down, and wheeled it forward. A comfortable chair would be nice, but Dana liked the old fashioned look. Maybe it was better because the lack of cushioning kept them from spending too many hours in front of the computer, drifting into numbness, their brains mildly stimulated with changing images, and a constant stream of new, usually unimportant, information.

The screen came to life and he typed *traffic cones* into the search box.

Three sponsored sites popped up. He could choose from an entire rainbow of colors. It was best to stick with orange. People were conditioned to know what that meant.

The Internet was an amazing thing. The access to everything you wanted to know, the ability to purchase whatever you wanted, was astounding. Ashley and her friends had no idea what they possessed, how things used to be. It wasn't as if he was that old, only forty-nine. There had truly been a revolution during his lifetime — email and social networks, shopping and government bureaucracy moved to cyberspace. A man's world had exploded to encompass the whole planet — knowing in an instant what was happening in Asia or the farthest parts of Europe, reading the thoughts of total strangers, the famous and the nameless alike, on Twitter and in comments on news sites and forums — the universe condensed to a screen in front of a single person, no need for physical contact at all, no need to leave your house, your home office, your bed with a tablet computer propped up, for that matter. Everything came to you — movies, music, pseudo friends with precisely the same interests, images of exotic places that didn't require effort to reach. Heck, you could travel through the pyramids and probably get a better virtual view because you didn't have to contend with thousands of hot, sweaty, pushy, loud-mouthed actual human beings. Occasionally he worried that the scenario from Star Trek and Sci-Fi films of people existing as nothing but disembodied brains would soon be reality.

Sometimes he imagined entering prayer requests in the blank box and watching answers returned. Not prayer requests exactly, that never worked no matter what you did, but questions of the universe — *How do national leaders allow people to go hungry and sick? Why are women so difficult to comprehend? Why don't children turn out more like their parents?* Of course, on one level, he knew the answers to all those questions.

He ordered six cones to be delivered in five to seven business days. As soon as the email confirmation arrived, he shut the tab with his order receipt and went back to the family room window. Dana was in the same spot. He walked to the hallway that ran from the front door to the back and went outside. The air was cool on the porch, but the minute he stepped out of the shade, it was warm.

"I'm home."

Dana sat back on her heels. "Did you get what you needed?"

"Yes."

"Good."

Was it really that easy to think you were communicating? He waited for her to ask what he needed, what he wanted, but she didn't.

She dropped her trowel on the grass and stood. She wiped her hands across her knees, but they were wet from pressing into the damp earth below the grass, so her effort was useless in removing the dirt stains that streaked her jeans. "Are you going to help me get the vegetable garden ready?"

"Don't I always?"

"I wasn't sure if you were still sulking."

"I don't sulk."

She laughed. Even though he was annoyed, and it wasn't the kind of laughter he enjoyed — the kind that proved he'd gotten past her defenses, succeeded in entertaining her, surprising her — he still liked hearing her laugh. Despite the slightly mocking tone, her laugh sounded like glasses chiming together in a toast, her lips parted, smiling, revealing her perfectly straight teeth. When she laughed, her whole face changed, she looked right at him and all other thoughts seemed to fly out of her head.

"I don't sulk. That's what teenagers do."

"And men."

Her breasts looked soft inside her sweatshirt. It was hiked up to her waist. Her slim hips, her figure nearly unchanged since the day they were married, so inviting he wanted to grab her and press himself against her, but she stood just a foot or so beyond his reach.

"I wasn't sulking," he said. "Those people are obnoxious. And that woman can't control her car. It's dangerous."

"You can't correct others' behavior."

"Someone has to."

She folded her arms across her ribs, which pushed her breasts up. He could touch them and change the course of the conversation.

"You're obsessed," she said. "You know this isn't about bad driving."

"I loathe stupidity."

"Why can't you focus on something positive, like remodeling the bathroom?"

"It's on my list."

Her voice was suddenly quieter. "It's been on your list for six years." She looked down. She spread her fingers and studied the backs of her hands. The bones stood out like the thin branches of a tree, the skin stretched, but not as tight as it used to be.

He stepped close to her, touching the toes of her trainers with the toes of his boots. He rested his wrists on her shoulders. "It's expensive. Our kid just finished college. Be patient, it'll happen."

"It's not like we absolutely can't afford it. You just don't think it's a priority."

"Why is it to important to you?"

"I've told you. I'm not telling you again," she said.

"How does an expensive bathroom make you feel sexy?"

"I'm not young anymore."

"Neither am I."

"A nice tub where I can soak with bath oil, bubbles, soft

lighting. I know it's silly."

The muscles in her shoulders tightened under his wrists. He pressed harder, as if he were pounding her body into the ground like an iron stake for support ropes to hold up a sapling.

"It would be something for us. Yes, mostly for me, but something for our house, for the next phase of our lives, when Ashley's gone for good."

"It doesn't look like that will happen any time soon."

"It will be sudden. She'll be around every day, then in the blink of an eye she'll be gone, and this time, she won't be coming back."

"Well let's get the student loan paid down a bit first."

"It would be nice to see you doing something life-affirming instead of trying to attack someone's faith with petty fights." She shrugged out from under his arms.

He let her go. "No matter how loud they shout and how much they wave their arms and fling themselves around and babble gibberish, god isn't going to listen to them. Everything is random."

"Why do you think about it so much? You get so angry."

"It does make me angry. It's lying. It's trying to make the world something it's not, and they're brainwashing children with that BS."

"So *what?*! It has nothing to do with us or our life. People have a right to believe whatever they choose. You need to get your mind on something else." She turned and walked across the yard. She picked up her trowel. Without turning, she called back, "I want to get the garden ready for planting vegetables. Today."

It was her attempt to re-program his obsession, as she called it. She was kind of cute, really, the way she thought he could be diverted, like a child in her classroom, handed a different set of blocks to stop his crying over a truck he wanted. She did it every time they argued.

She was wrong about one thing. It had everything to do with their life. As long as people like that went around preaching their phony happiness, naive children and teenagers like he'd been would be manipulated into years of despair. Life was harsh and unfair, and it was better to know that sooner rather than later.

Five

MELODY SPENT Sunday afternoon at the park. She'd brought a turquoise and pink plaid blanket, a thermos of iced tea, a bag of homemade chocolate chip cookies, and her Bible. She'd planned to read the entire New Testament, starting with the book of Romans, as far as she could go before the sun went behind the redwood trees that stood between the acres of grass and the adjacent housing development. Instead, she'd fallen asleep.

She was ashamed of her lack of vigilance. It was true that her body was exhausted from the effort of the morning — the kneeling, the intense pressure of hands on her shoulders and head and back. When she'd first given her life to God, the warmth of the minister's hands on her head, touching her hair, made her feel special. This morning hadn't been like that at all. She never should have asked for their help. If God really loved her, He'd give her what she was asking for, He'd loosen her tongue to speak a new language, filling her up with thrilling, ecstatic waves that caused her to fall in love with the world.

How could Sara and Elise and Jennifer know she was holding back? Was there a tightness in her muscles, a sludge moving through her veins that seeped out into the palms of their hands so they understood all her secrets? She felt as if they'd seen her naked and reacted with disgust to the lack of flesh on her breasts and hips, the extraordinarily large mole on her left hip.

They had everything — husbands whose devotion to them bordered on worship. They had homes and children. Elise had a glamorous job with a PR company that heaped praise on her for her skill at luring the media into telling stories the way she wanted. All three women behaved as if the gift of tongues was proof of the fact you were chosen by God. It implied He didn't care much for Melody. Is that what they saw in her? Was she not even a believer, was she faking it? She didn't think she was, but she really had no idea what else she could do. If God didn't want her, how sad and pathetic was that?

She couldn't lie on her back in a now-deserted park, staring at the colorless sky, feeling the chill of the earth creep up through the blanket, cutting through her clothes, and digging into her bones. She stood and folded the blanket into a messy square. The cookies were gone. She crumpled the plastic bag and stuffed it in her pocket. She carried her things to the car and put them in the trunk.

Tonight, like every Sunday, was dedicated to serving dinner to the homeless. Most times, twenty or thirty people showed up carrying duffel bags and backpacks. The members of Triumphant Life cooked the meal then sat with their guests so that churchgoers and street-dwellers ate side by side.

Melody had been the driving force to start the program. All three of her former churches had similar programs, but Triumphant Life was so small, they hadn't done much to reach out to the people who lived nearby with children's programs or any effort to help the less fortunate. The program had only been up and running for three weeks, but so far, it was doing well. There hadn't been any problems with outbursts of anger or other hints of madness, no complaints from the neighbors, and no lack of people willing to help provide and cook food and clean up after. She hoped it stayed that way. It made her feel as if she had a center of gravity, that she belonged with the others, that she'd helped make the church more valuable to their community.

Running a program like this was a perfect fit for her. She had a chance to use the skills she'd learned at work, managing a branch office for an insurance company. She was brilliant at scheduling and creating structure so that everyone knew their responsibilities — no room for confusion or stepping on others' toes.

The CD player started up when she turned the key. Soft guitar music without accompanying percussion flowed out of the speakers at a volume that felt as if her brain was being physically stroked by the sounds. She liked her music loud. The louder it was, the more the music entered her body rather than simply existing on the outside. This song was too mellow, though. She pressed the button to advance to the next track. Much better. Snare drums beat rapidly and the base thumped in time with her pulse. She tapped her left foot and rapped her fingers on the steering wheel, enjoying the sense of coordination, the challenge of keeping time with parts of her body while still controlling the pressure of her right foot on the gas pedal and brake as she backed out of her parking spot.

She turned and drove to the exit. She slowed the car and closed her eyes briefly, singing along — she knew all of the words. While she sang, she pleaded silently for the gift. For a sign that she wasn't alone.

When she opened her eyes, three teenaged boys were slouching along the sidewalk. They blocked her way out of the parking lot as they moved at the pace of an elderly person leaning on a walker. Two of them turned to stare at her. The third was holding a smart phone, studying the screen, seemingly oblivious to her presence.

They wore baggy denim shorts that hung to the middle of their calves, oversized tennis shoes, and dark blue hooded sweatshirts that sagged off their shoulders, revealing white, sleeveless undershirts. One of them, the shortest of the three, a boy with a shaved head and a thin beard, raised his middle finger at her.

She gasped. She'd done nothing to deserve that. Nothing.

The sun, hovering just above the tree line, poured through her windshield. She squinted and her eyes watered. The boy kept his finger upright, shook his hand at her, and laughed. The second boy joined in. The third boy looked up from his phone, but not at her. He didn't seem to recognize what they found so funny, but he laughed anyway. Harder than the other two.

The one with the shaved head — it baffled her why he would do that, such a young boy, eighteen or nineteen at most, surely in possession of the same luxurious hair that covered the heads of his friends — moved closer to her car.

She held her breath.

The boy put his foot on her bumper and tried to jiggle the car.

The LeSabre was a solid car, a tank, the used car salesman had said, she'd always be safe in a car like this. She glanced at the door to be sure it was locked.

The boy, very astute for someone so young, so sullen, noticed her sideward glance. He stomped his foot harder and the car yielded to the pressure, bouncing up and down. For some reason, she felt silly, like a child who was too large for the plastic animals mounted on thick springs that dotted the playground area behind her, swaying wildly because the toy wasn't designed to support her weight.

Tears filled her eyes. Her hands shook on the steering wheel as she waited to see what they would do next. Starling

Park was in a nice neighborhood, surrounded by two-story homes built in the seventies — homes with balconies and two car garages and six-foot high backyard fences. They had mature shrubs and trees and weed-free lawns, but on a Sunday, at this time of year, the air cooling quickly as the shadows grew long and thick, the yards and streets were deserted. The park was no longer friendly, a safe place for a nap. It was a vast, empty space, ripe for teenagers dodging adult supervision, if they ever had that to begin with. The boys could rip the metal off the car and remove the wheels while she sat helplessly inside. They could do anything — smash the windows, even drag her out and strip off her clothes as efficiently as they dismantled the car. They could kill her and who would see? Things like that didn't happen in the suburbs, did they? She never heard about it. This was an area with hardly any crime except for petty activities like attempted forgery at a small business or windows smashed and laptops stolen out of back seats, bikes removed from garages with their doors left open, everyone too trusting.

They were just trying to frighten her. They wouldn't actually *do* anything.

The third boy slipped the smart phone into his pocket and approached the car. He put his foot on the bumper and they increased the rocking. She hadn't realized her car was so unstable.

Lord, help me. Save me. Please. I don't know what to do. She didn't move her lips, but let the words run through her mind. She should take her foot of the brake and step on the gas, move forward and let them drop off to the side, like fallen leaves blew off the car when she drove to work. But what if she hurt them? Would she be blamed? Surely not, they were the ones in the wrong. But there were three of them. They'd gang up on her, intimidate her, just like Sarah and Jennifer and Elise had. It wasn't their plan, maybe, but the result was the same, she was alone and the others were a group. All her life it had been like that, others ganging up on her. Was there some signal she gave off to attract this kind of treatment, some animal weakness that brought out equally animalistic aggression in others?

She was starting to feel nauseous from the wild bouncing of the car. In a minute, they'd get bored. They weren't really criminals, just vandals, getting a temporary thrill by scaring her. Once they realized there was nothing else to do, that they didn't have the courage to cross the line into a real crime, they'd leave her alone. She just had to close her eyes and trust the Lord.

The car swayed and bounced but the CD held steady, songs of praise pouring out of the speakers. She forced her mind to follow the lyrics, to think the words even if she was too ashamed to actually sing. That would surely make them laugh, and rile them up to do more, whatever *more* might be. She couldn't think about that, had to force herself to trust, not just trust, but *know* that she was being taken care of.

Her head bobbed back and forth. Trying to steady it was a

mistake because it made her neck ache. Her breasts bounced in time with the movement of the car, only her foot remained steady, pressed hard against the brake. The car was still in drive and moving her foot, releasing the pressure of her leg even slightly, would send it rocketing forward, knocking them over, possibly driving over one of them.

The rocking was less rhythmic now. She opened her eyes. For a moment, only the boy with the phone and the other one with the thick, wavy dark hair were visible. She felt more than saw the one with the shaved head standing at her side, his face close to the window, staring at her. She was sure her nose was red from the tears straining to get out, but she held them back as firmly as she kept her foot pressed on the brake. Tomorrow, in a few hours, all of this would be a memory, a story she'd tell of how the Lord had protected her. She should imagine a shield around her body, fierce angels with swords standing at the four corners of the car.

The boy slammed his fist against the glass. She screamed.

He rapped his fingers across the glass, thrumming a beat to a song she didn't know. The thud of his fingers reminded her of the moths her brother and his friend captured and shoved inside the opening of Melody's guitar. The poor things beat their wings frantically and bumped around the dark interior as they tried to find their way out. She'd been terrified they would die inside the guitar and she'd be required to remove their corpses. But neither could she bring herself to touch the furry bodies and wings, to feel them tremble inside her cupped hand. After a while, the moths stopped trying so hard, they sat near the side, their wings softly brushing against wood, waiting.

She held her breath.

Once again, he slammed the side of his fist on the driver's window.

She cringed and put her hands over her face.

The CD paused between songs and his laugh was loud and rough in her ear. At the front of the car, the others seemed to be growing bored, or tired. They definitely weren't athletic boys, maybe the exertion of using a single leg to move the car had worn them out.

The curly-haired boy stepped away, and then, because the continued movement required more effort now that he was alone, the other one stopped. He pulled his phone out of his pocket and checked the screen.

It didn't seem as if the boys had felt the presence of angels, but they drifted back to the sidewalk nonetheless. They didn't bother to look at her as they continued along the edge of the park. A brief game. If she hadn't been exiting the parking lot at that precise spot, they would have found something else. A trashcan to turn over, or perhaps gone into the small cinderblock buildings housing the restrooms and strewn paper around or written obscene words on the mirrors.

Now the tears spilled out of her eyes. The next song had started, a quieter one again — exactly what she needed. She pulled out of the parking lot, blinking to clear her eyes, determined not to slow or stop for anything. Had God protected her? Had He intervened on her behalf? She drove to the end of the street and turned onto Cascade Drive. The car felt too big, too much for her to control with its V6 engine and full-sized back seat and trunk. A single woman didn't need half this much metal and power and space.

She'd wanted a new car — a Mini Cooper, but when she saw the price, she hesitated. Too extravagant. Still, she noticed every Mini that passed her on the road or waited for its owner in a parking lot. There weren't many of them — they were expensive for what you got. The women in her support group at her former church had assured her of that. She should be practical. And God preferred that his followers not go in for flashy cars and clothes and homes and jewelry. Yes, some churches overlooked things like that, considered them blessings. But churches like Triumphant Life followed a more literal interpretation of the Bible. They didn't delude themselves into thinking it was harmless to get sucked up in earthly wealth and pleasures. Those things ate at your soul.

Still, she loved those little cars. She'd test-driven one and it was as easy to manage as it looked. The salesman, finally reading something in her eyes that she wasn't going to make a commitment, pointed out that the car was a bit small for her five-foot eleven-inch frame. It was better suited to a smaller woman. He didn't acknowledge that lots of men drove them too, that men had all kinds of small cars — men over six feet tall drove Porsches and other sports cars.

The Buick was a reasonable price, a car that had room to carry the Lord's people and the Lord's supplies. Not a selfish car to show off, to feel cute in, to look at with pleasure, but something functional. It was solid and would defend her very well in an accident. It hadn't protected her just now, but maybe it had made her feel safer than she would have if a smaller car had been surrounded by three strong, healthy males. A more attractive car might have aroused their jealousy and resulted in more harassment. So what if they laughed at the large, dull car, at least it hadn't made them want to steal it right out from under her.

ELISE'S AUDI WAS the only car in the parking lot when Melody arrived at the church.

She left an empty space between her car and the Audi so she wouldn't ding the door as she struggled out of her car. That was a strong possibility on any day as she often found it difficult to extract her legs when the car door was opened at a 45-degree angle. With her hands and knees shaking as they still were, despite a stop at the grocery store, she was certain she'd gouge the door.

She opened the trunk and lifted out the first box of food. It was filled with packages of pasta and jars of spaghetti sauce. She set it on the ground, pulled out the bags with ground beef, and put them on top of the other supplies. She piled on bags of lettuce, tomatoes, carrots, and cucumbers. The box was heavy and the pile precarious, forcing her to lean back slightly as she lifted it and carried it through the open kitchen door.

The horrendous shriek of metal table legs scraping the floor came from the main hall as Elise worked to drag the eight-foot tables into place. Melody shivered. She rubbed her arms, sliding her palms over bumpy flesh that grew harder as she rubbed, as if her body was reacting to the assault by those boys as well as the shrieking metal. She hurried out to the car for the last bag filled with oil, vinegar, seasoning packets for making Italian dressing, and four baguettes.

When she returned, Elise stood in the doorway leading to the main hall. She wore designer jeans and a black t-shirt with the sleeves rolled up, revealing muscular arms. Her blonde hair was swept up into a ponytail that looked like it belonged to a cheerleader rather than a woman dedicated to serving food to people who lived in the hidden crevices of suburbia.

"You scared me," Elise said.

"It's almost six. Weren't you expecting me?"

"You shouldn't sneak up on people."

"Sorry."

Elise turned and went down the short hall back to the main room.

Melody wasn't sure why she'd apologized. How much longer was she going to let people push her around, make her feel inadequate?

Because that's what they'd done during their prayer circle that morning. It wasn't sisterly love at all. It was their judgment making her feel as if she wasn't lovable, even to God.

That wasn't the way it was supposed to be. Maybe men could withhold love, reject you when you disappointed them, or you didn't fit some precise blend of submissive and spicy, thin yet shapely female, but God was supposed to love everyone! He loved the whole world, and if you turned your life over to Him, He was supposed to love you back. In fact, He loved you first and was just waiting for you to respond, a lover standing at the altar, watching a bride step slowly down the aisle to become His forever.

It wasn't possible that He'd also tossed her aside for being unlovable. There must be some other reason He was withholding the gift. *Give me a sign*, she whispered. *You have to give me a sign. You know I'd do anything, I have done everything.* All she heard was silence. Just like when she was a little girl and came home from school, calling her mother's name. Sometimes it took four or five tries before her mother responded and made her presence known. Those minutes had been terrifying. Every single time she'd thought that, this time, her mother wouldn't be there. When Melody told her it was frightening, her mother said, *Get a grip.*

She opened her eyes. Elise was standing in the doorway, watching.

After a few seconds of silence, Elise said, "How are you feeling?"

"Good. I'm doing good."

"You don't look like it."

"I was just praying."

Elise tossed her ponytail over her shoulder. "Your hands are shaking."

"Are they?" Melody held out both hands, parallel with the counter top. The tremor in the two smallest fingers of her left hand was barely noticeable. "Too much sugar." She reached into the box and removed two jars of spaghetti sauce. "Will you start the pasta."

Elise walked around the opposite side of the center island. She opened the cabinet near the stove and pulled out an eighteen-inch deep pot. "I'll need your help carrying this when it's full."

They moved around the kitchen silently. Melody chopped onions, tore lettuce into bits, and sliced tomatoes and carrots and cucumber.

"What I meant a minute ago," Elise said, "was how are you feeing after this morning?"

"I'm fine."

"You don't have to be ashamed."

"I'm not."

"I hope you aren't upset."

"Everything's fine."

"But it's not. You weren't speaking in tongues. Unless you received the gift later? After we left?"

"No, I didn't." Melody turned down the heat under the frying pan. She dropped ground beef into the hot oil. It sizzled and steamed and she shoved it around with a wooden spoon.

"It's so strange. I wonder what's wrong." Elise snapped a fistful of pasta in half and dumped it into the boiling water.

She was standing too close. The stove was tiny, and her hip brushed against Melody's as she hovered beside the steaming pot. Elise stirred the pasta and turned the heat down. "It's pretty clear you're afraid to let go. Have you always felt like you had to hold back?"

Melody shrugged. She wasn't going to answer that. Of course she felt self-conscious. That was normal. No one wanted to make an utter fool of herself.

"The gift of tongues is a strange phenomenon. Sometimes you have to just start talking and let the Lord provide the form to the words."

She'd heard that before, too many times. "What does that mean?"

"Open your mouth and just start saying the words."

"Isn't that faking it?"

"It's a matter of letting yourself go. You didn't answer my question — have you always felt inhibited? I can see that about you. There's something wounded, or scared in your eyes, and being so tall. Were you ostracized as a child? Or is there more to it than that? You just don't seem comfortable with yourself.

"Why are you saying these things? Are you trying to upset me?"

"Oh, of course not." Elise put her hand on Melody's forearm.

Melody pulled her arm away and walked to the counter.

"This is what I mean," Elise said. "You seem so unsure of yourself. Are you afraid to be touched? I don't think you've fully given yourself to Him."

"You know nothing about me. You have no idea what I've given to God." Melody felt her voice was louder than it should have been, sharper than what was required to make herself heard over the bubbling water and sizzling meat.

"I've never seen someone who was filled with the Spirit but couldn't speak in tongues. Something's wrong."

Melody whimpered as if the grease from the beef had sprayed across her face, stinging her lips and eyelids, biting at her cheeks and the tender skin of her neck. She scraped the wooden spoon across the pan, lifting up a thin layer of seared meat, pushing bits of translucent onion to the side. She turned over the chunks of meat, trying to get the raw pieces closer to the heat. Cooking three pounds at once had been a mistake; she should have split it into smaller portions.

The raw meat looked pulpy. She tried not to think about what it really was — the flesh of an animal, torn off the bones, ground into fine shreds, stored in freezers until someone thawed it and cooked it and ate it. The whole human race, all the breathing inhabitants of the earth were nothing but cannibals, devouring other creatures, feeding themselves, preserving their own lives by destroying another.

Her chest convulsed.

"Did the grease hit you?" Elise said.

She shook her head once.

"You're a hard person to get to know," Elise said. "Help me lift this pot." Elise turned off the gas and handed a potholder to Melody. They each took hold of a handle and carried it to the sink. They tipped it forward, pouring water and pasta into the colander Elise had centered over the drain. Steam rushed up and clung to their faces. "You've been at Triumphant Life for how long? Two months?"

Melody nodded.

"And you're almost a stranger."

"Our lives are different."

"But we're sisters in the Lord. We should know each other inside and out."

"I suppose."

"Like your love life. I know nothing about that part of you. Why you decided never to get married, or are you still waiting? It's not too late. Thirty-five? Thirty-six?"

"Thirty-three."

Elise nodded. "Have you ever been in love?"

Melody turned on the cold water. She adjusted the faucet, aiming it over the colander. Water coursed through the pasta, turning it slick.

"It's rinsed long enough." Elise reached past Melody and turned off the water. "You must have been in love. Everyone at least has a crush or two. Who was your first crush?"

Melody didn't understand the grilling. They'd cooked dinner for the homeless and worked side by side on other projects. What was Elise's sudden interest?

She didn't want Elise knowing her inside and out. Elise seemed like the kind of person who was determined to hurt you. The kind of person who had to be superior in everything, have more, be more. It seemed as if Elise wanted to humiliate her, commenting on her physical flaws, demanding to know what was wrong with her that she hadn't been given the gift of tongues. Did Elise need to see someone squirm before she could feel good about herself? But with her good looks, her adoring husband, her job, her kids, why on earth would she need to damage another woman to feel good about herself? Melody had never understood what drove people to humiliate others. It seemed so pointless. Humiliation had been her lot in life for as long as she could remember. She would never tell Elise about her first love. Never.

His name was Aaron. He had blonde, wavy hair streaked with brown, long and falling over brown eyes, a piece that curled around his ear. The back of his hair, when he was bent over a video game, playing with her brother, demanded to be stroked. His fingernails were well trimmed and perfectly shaped. For some reason, his hands made her feel as if her stomach was melting.

He was so sweet, and so cruel. Somehow, the boys had guessed how desperately she loved Aaron.

She wasn't sure exactly what started it, but once it happened, it went on for nearly a year, until her mother took her shopping for her first bra. A bra she still didn't technically need, but her mother conceded that the other girls all had them, and it was important for Melody to feel like a woman, even if her body wasn't quite there yet.

But before that . . .

She'd stood in the hallway, watching them through Brian's partially opened bedroom door. They whispered and laughed, throwing back their heads. Aaron's grin showed his perfect teeth, except for the one on the bottom that slightly overlapped, highlighting the straightness of the others.

"Why are you spying on us, Mel?" her brother said.

"I'm not spying." Her voice caught in her throat, then slipped out in a strangled whisper.

"Don't be scared," Aaron said.

"If you're in love with Aaron, why don't you show it?" Brian slid off the bed and sauntered to the doorway. "Come in." He pushed the door open wider. "Aaron wants to get to know you better."

She stepped closer to his room. Brian grabbed her shirt and pulled her inside. He closed the door then picked up the controller for his game. "I'm bored already."

Aaron grinned at her.

She pressed her back against the door, aching to turn the knob, to run out of the room, but unable to stop looking at him. The pure joy of being so close to him, having him notice her, staring at her like that.

"What do you want?" Aaron said.

"I . . ."

Her brother dropped the game controller. He moved up close to her and tugged her hair, hard, like he always did, so that tears filled her eyes. She knew she should leave, knew they were going to hurt her, but she couldn't stop looking at Aaron, couldn't let go of the pleasure of his curious, somewhat aggressive gaze focused solely on her.

Brian grabbed her wrists and pinched them together between his hands. He spun her around so she was facing the door and briefly let go of her wrists, only to yank her arms behind her, gripping harder this time. He turned her around. Her scalp stung. Tears spilled out of her eyes.

"You're such a baby," he said. "Too young to have a boyfriend."

He dragged her to the bed and pushed her down on her back. Only her toes touched the floor. He sat next to her and kept her hands pinned near her side. "You don't even have titties. How can a girl that's so big still look like a little kid?"

Aaron grabbed her shirt and pulled it up. "A little girl. What's wrong with you? Maybe you'll never have them."

Tears swam across her eyes as if someone had poured a glass of water on them. Their faces blurred, making their grins more terrifying. Her shirt was bunched under her armpits. She felt them staring at her.

"Maybe she'll get them soon," Aaron said.

"I don't think so," Brian said.

"Oh ye of little faith. We'll keep a close watch."

"Good idea," Brian said.

"Every day. Doesn't that sound good, Mel? We'll check every day. And maybe if you grow any, then I can be your boyfriend."

Tears spilled across her face. Her nose filled with mucous that began to trickle out.

"Don't be a crybaby," Brian said. "You better not go rat on us to mom and dad."

When he'd said that, heat flooded her body, the thought of telling her father. Of course she wouldn't, she'd never tell him, she'd never tell anyone. And she never had.

Was that the kind of first crush story Elise wanted to hear? Maybe other people had first crushes, first loves that worked out well.

Elise seemed to know the mind of God. Was it possible He did want more from her than she'd already given? It wasn't enough that she viewed every decision of her life in light of what was required of her? Now He wanted more? What was left?

Six

ASHLEY SLIPPED HER key into the lock and turned it carefully until the deadbolt clicked. Although her parents' room was on the second floor, her mother's hearing was as refined as a bat's echolocation.

Ashley shouldn't have to sneak into the house and creep upstairs before her mother woke and met her in the hallway to sniff out alcohol on her breath. She was an adult. But here she was, slowly turning the knob, pushing open the door, prying off her sandals, and stepping barefoot into the entryway. She closed the door and turned out the porch light.

A giggle bubbled up in her throat. She hated that about alcohol, the way it made her laugh at nothing, or maybe she was laughing at her stealthy moves, her bare feet, the loopy feeling in her head that transformed every object she touched into something filled with significance, strange yet familiar.

She walked down the hallway on the balls of her feet, which wasn't necessary without her shoes, making her want to laugh again. She should stop in the kitchen for a glass of water, but she really needed to pee. That was it — she'd use the downstairs bathroom, get the water, and then climb the stairs, the part of the journey most likely to wake her mother. Sometimes she wondered if her mother didn't ever actually sleep. It seemed as if a neighbor's sneeze, or a cat jumping onto the porch rail woke her.

All through Ashley's high school years, Dana had existed in a state of half-sleep, waiting for Ashley to come home from parties or dates. Worrying. She never admitted it, but Ashley knew that's what it was, worrying she'd gotten drunk, that she'd tried pot, that she was having sex with Jack.

The funny thing was, she'd never tried any of those things in high school. She and Jack hadn't done it until the summer before she left for college. And those other things were stumbling blocks on the way to her goal — the top of her class, the best journalism school she could get accepted into, playing tennis. Partying meant letting down her teammates. She'd saved all that crazy stuff for college. She wondered if her mother had sat up all night, every night, when she was in Illinois, worrying about what Ashley was doing.

This time, she wasn't able to suppress the giggle. She slapped her hand over her mouth and a snorting sound came out of her nose. She hurried down the hall to the bathroom and closed the door, taking care to turn the knob rather than just letting the latch snap into place. There was no way to muffle the sound of urine hitting the water, especially the amount of urine produced by four margaritas.

She crossed her fingers and squeezed them tight. It was a silly, childish habit, but it always worked. She'd done it since before she could remember. It worked when she manipulated circumstances to get Jack's attention focused on her, and it worked when she turned in three papers written by someone else for her AP English class during junior year. She wasn't great at Math and had to focus if she was going to pull off all those A's. She'd already known she could construct excellent essays, and buying the papers had allowed her to be all about Algebra and Trig all the time.

Those three papers each nailed an A, helping finalize her position as one of five valedictorians. She would have preferred to be the sole holder of that title. Her father said that was rare now that high school classes were dummed down. Even so-called AP classes weren't as tough as his regular classes had been. At least, he admitted, despite the easy classes, her generation was smarter than his in other ways. They didn't rush to get married or have kids too soon. They didn't tie themselves down with a single company for a lifetime.

Right now, she'd be happy to sign up with one employer for a lifetime. Instead, she was stuck spitting out resumes and posting online for jobs, getting lost in a black hole of keywords and tens of thousands of applicants.

The toilet flushed with a roar. There was a good chance she wasn't going to make it to her room without getting caught.

From ten feet away her mother would be hit with the vapor of alcohol seeping out of her pores. She should have gone to Maggie's house for the night, called home and babbled about a spontaneous sleepover.

She stepped out of the bathroom and crept along the hallway to the stairs. When she reached the top, her parents' bedroom door opened. Her mother wore a white gown with a smocked inset around her collarbone. The gown hung to the floor, covering all but her toes, the nails painted pale pink. Ashley couldn't see the color in the dark, but her mother's toenails were always pale pink, they'd been that way for at least ten years. Her hair was only slightly mussed.

"It's late."

"I know. Sorry I woke you."

"You've been drinking."

"Just a few margaritas." She felt that persistent, irritating, uncontrollable giggle at the back of her throat. She swallowed hard, which probably gave the impression she was nervous — lying.

"How many?"

"Come on, Mom. Go back to sleep. I'm tired." She turned slightly and started toward her bedroom.

"I bet you are." Dana stepped into the hallway, her feet as soundless as Ashley's. "It's dangerous to drink and get in the car."

"I didn't have that much."

"You sound goofy."

"Probably because I'm tired. G'night." She turned and walked quickly to her room.

Her mother was right behind her.

"Please, Mom." She didn't turn, hoping that would weaken Dana's drive to have a mother-daughter chat at two-fifteen in the morning. She didn't need a lecture on drinking. She knew what was wrong with it. She didn't do it all the time. She never got wasted — falling-down-puking-passing-out drunk. She pushed open her bedroom door, stepped inside, and turned to face her mother. She leaned on the knob and edged the door partially closed.

Her mother put her palm on the door and held it open. "I'm disappointed."

"Come on, Mom. I'm an adult. You know I drink sometimes. You and Dad drink wine all the time."

"Not like this. You're drunk."

The giggle erupted, as if her body was taking her mother's side.

"See? You can't fool me."

"I'm not trying to fool you. I just want to go to bed." This was only the fifth or sixth time she'd really partied since she'd come home from school. Mostly she spent her time with Jack, reconnecting after four years of separation, as he called it. Trying to avoid planning their future as a couple. Tonight had been an escape from all that, a night with the girls — all of them as driven as she was. And most of them, like her, underemployed and back home with their parents, watching their aspirations simmer on the back burner while they tried to figure out how to access the careers they'd spent years planning for. So she drank too much every so often. Big deal.

"Why are you doing this?"

"It's one night, Mom! My friends and I went out for Mexican food. We had margaritas. It doesn't mean I'm an alcoholic."

"We didn't send you to a good school so you could come home and act like a slacker."

"Can we talk about this later? Tomorrow?"

"If this happens again, you won't be allowed to drive."

"*Allowed?* I'm twenty-three!"

"You're putting yourself and innocent people in danger."

"I'm going to sleep. I'll talk to you tomorrow." Ashley pushed hard on the door. Fortunately, her mother yielded and took a few steps back. Ashley shut the door.

She didn't want to talk about it tomorrow. She didn't want to talk about it ever. She wanted to get out of this house, on her own, but she didn't want to do it by moving in with Jack.

Despite the effort she'd expended to snag him all those years ago, despite staying sort-of a couple through four years of only seeing each other at winter break and a month or two each summer, despite both of them periodically hooking up with others and surviving that, she was no longer sure he was the one for her. Moving in would make breaking up way too complicated. She wasn't ready. She wasn't sure he was her soul mate. And just like she refused to accept a ho-hum job instead of the platinum career path she'd studied for, she refused to accept a marriage that resulted from habit, or indecision. She wanted a soul mate. She wanted everything, and she would have it.

SUNDAY MORNING THE sky was Easter egg blue without a single cloud. The sun was already high and bright. The air coming through the partially open bedroom window smelled clean and sweet. She heard the thumping of music across the street and knew her father would be out there — smoking. Watching. *Brooding*, as her mother said.

Although she'd tried to remember him smoking and watching them before she'd left for college, she couldn't. But she'd been oblivious back then, so maybe his obsession had been going on for years. Maybe her parents had argued about it all the time and she was too young, too unaware of adult nuances to notice. Or maybe they'd hid it from her. That was more likely. Since she'd been home, she noticed they were more outspoken with each other, no longer trying to protect their child from the burrs and gouges in a marriage of twenty-something years. Exactly the kind of marriage she did not want. She would die if she had to live with a mate she scarcely noticed, going hours without speaking, eating the same meals every week, going out to the same three or four restaurants, doing the same things with their friends, year after year after tedious year.

She pushed off the sheet and sat up. So far so good. No

headache, no wave of nausea. She'd been careful to drink two large glasses of water before she left the restaurant and the third glass when she got home, hoping it would stave off a hangover, and it seemed to have worked. It wasn't that her body was in perfect condition, her head and mouth were fuzzy as if a soft growth of mold spread across her brain and her tongue in the same way it crept over the skin of an orange left pressed against another piece of fruit.

She stood. It looked like she would be okay. Another glass of water and two or three large mugs of coffee should do the trick.

She opened the slatted door of her narrow closet and grabbed a black tank top off the hanger. She pulled on shorts and stuffed her arms into the sleeves of a hoodie, just in case it was cooler than it looked.

With the same stealthy care she'd used a few hours earlier, she crept down the stairs. Hopefully her mother was working in the garden or out at the grocery store and she could avoid the promised chat for now.

Someone was watching out for her — the kitchen was empty and silent. The coffee had been turned off. She dumped out the cold coffee and grounds and made a fresh pot. While it brewed, she tiptoed into the dining room, which gave a clear view of the family room. Her mother wasn't reading a magazine. She went to the back window. The yard was empty and there were no shovels or bags of potting soil to indicate she was in the garage getting another tool. She must have gone to the store.

When the coffee was finished, she filled a mug and carried it to the front door. She stepped out onto the porch. Her father wasn't visible beyond the hedge, but the smell of smoke was strong in the soft air. She took a sip of coffee, then blew on the surface. She took another sip and walked down the steps.

Her father stood near the edge of the driveway. Judging by the butts scattered on the sidewalk around him, he'd abandoned his limit of a single cigarette.

"Hi," she said.

He blew out a stream of smoke but didn't turn.

Hopefully her mother hadn't filled him in on her supposed lapse the night before.

"Where's Mom?"

"Went to the store."

"Anything interesting going on across the street?"

"It's always interesting."

She gulped down some coffee and stepped closer. "Do you mind sharing a cigarette with me?"

Without a word, no mention of starting a deadly habit, no complaints about her heading downhill, he pulled the pack out of his pocket, removed a cigarette, and handed it to her.

She put it in her mouth. He flicked his lighter, held it to the tip, and snapped it closed when the cigarette caught fire. He didn't ask how or when she'd learned to smoke.

She smiled to herself. It could be she was regressing, acting the part of the rebellious teenager, smoking in front of the house, knowing how her mother despised it. But she didn't think that was the case. She truly hoped her mother would not come home until she and her father were finished. Instead of the rebellious child, she felt like an adult. Doing as she pleased, an equal with her father as they lost themselves in their own thoughts, no compulsion to make conversation, but not caught in an awkward silence either, combing her mind for a topic to relieve imagined tension. At least she hoped that's how it was, that he felt the same lack of pressure to speak.

Smoking made her feel like an adult and she'd never understood why. Driving a car had made her feel the same way when she first learned, but why not other things? Why not paying bills or buying groceries? Was it because those were chores? Possibly it was the forbidden aspect, that children were prohibited from smoking and driving. Although children never paid bills. So maybe it was symbolic of something else.

She'd smoked occasionally in college — when she studied for exams, during parties, when she and her friends and classmates sat gazing at the blend of modern buildings alongside structures built in the nineteenth and early twentieth centuries, feeling very intellectual, discussing politics or philosophy, drinking coffee and smoking cigarettes. She didn't think she'd become a permanent smoker, it really was deadly. And it made your clothes and hair, and most of all your breath, stink. But right now, it felt good.

She hoped her father wasn't killing himself. Surely a few cigarettes a week weren't going to give him cancer. Of course, maybe he snuck in more smoking breaks than he let on. Maybe this was the only one her mother knew about. Ashley's master plan for a well-designed life didn't include the premature death of her father. She took a puff and tapped her finger on the cigarette to knock off the ash.

"Why do you watch them?" she said.

"I'm fascinated by their cluelessness. They never give up, marching in there every fucking week. Sorry."

"It's okay, Dad. I've heard the word."

"I'd love to find a way to get them to realize god isn't going to deliver what they want all wrapped up in Christmas paper with a pretty bow."

She laughed. She hoped he didn't think her dreams and plans were equally hopeless. "Why do you want to do *that*?"

He sucked in smoke and blew it out slowly. "It would make me feel like I won."

"Do you believe in God?" she said.

He took another puff, more slowly this time. "There might be a creative force in the universe, but there sure as hell is not some fatherly guy up there taking care of us. I don't know how anyone can look at the state of the world and think that's the case. If there is someone up there, he's a heartless bastard. Look at all the children being abused, disease, war, poverty. And these people come bouncing out those doors every Sunday, wiggling their fingers in the air, grinning like idiots, and praising the lord this that and the other, gushing how Jesus cured their runny nose or provided a hamburger at just the right time."

She wasn't sure what to say. She wanted her parents to treat her like an adult, but this was more than she'd asked for. He sounded so angry.

"Sorry to shock you, Ash. It's just the way it is. When you make this journalist thing pay off, you'll see that. Isn't it all about exposing injustice? And this country, the whole world, is nothing, if not unjust."

That's what she loved about her father. He didn't say *if* she settled into the career she'd dreamt of, he said *when*. And he didn't fuss around about it as if he was trying to build her confidence. It just slipped out, showing it was part of his usual thoughts. He believed in her. He knew she'd be successful. All her life, he'd acted as if she could do anything she wanted, that she could be someone remarkable. He acted as if she had potential and she didn't have to settle for just any job.

"I'm not upset. I like hearing what you think."

In some ways, she felt he'd forgotten she was his daughter. Quietly smoking together, talking to her like he'd talk to any other person. Trusting her not to nag or get upset by the things he said.

"I guess that's why people like religion. It makes them feel better about all that stuff."

"It shouldn't. It should piss them off. It's delusional." He dropped his cigarette on the sidewalk, pressed his toe on it, and pulled out another. He lit it and held out the box to her. She pulled one out but didn't put it up for him to light. She still had a few more puffs on the one she had tucked between her lips.

"Why do you want to disrupt their faith? What difference does it make?"

"Wouldn't it be a great feeling to win? To beat god at his own game by turning some of his soldiers to the other side?"

Ashley shivered. She pulled the sides of her hoodie together and clutched the two halves of the zipper in her fist.

A man dressed in jeans that were black with grime, a thick winter coat with a fur-trimmed hood, and a baseball cap, lurched around the corner. He leaned against the post holding the street sign and stared at the church as if he were trying to place the building in his memory. "Hallelujah!" he shouted.

Her father snorted.

Ashley puffed quickly on her cigarette. She hoped the man didn't look at them, or come over and try to talk, ask for a cigarette. She wasn't sure what her father would do. Homeless people walked down their street sometimes, pushing shopping carts full of stuff. Other times, people who might or might not be homeless, carrying beer cans or liquor bottles wrapped in brown paper bags staggered past their house. It was the downside of living in a historic neighborhood, odd zoning laws before more modern suburbs cordoned themselves off even further, meant nearby thrift stores, run down long-stay hotels, and even the church across the street. She sometimes wondered where they'd come from, where they were going. She'd never heard of a shelter anywhere in their neighborhood, she never saw them sleeping in parks or in the quaint downtown. It was as if they fell out of the sky during the day, then evaporated at night.

She knew they were harmless, but it scared her, seeing how easy it was to lose your mind. It would be the worst thing in the world, watching people steer a wide path around you, looking at you with pity, walking away because your conversation made no sense.

"Hallelujah!" the man shouted. He shook the pole.

"This problem has gotten worse since they started serving food over there. You need to be more careful when you're coming and going at night. Probably even during the day."

She shivered again, remembering how she'd stumbled from her car the night before, thinking of nothing but getting inside quietly and into the bathroom before she peed in her pants.

"I don't mean to scare you. Just be careful."

"It's the economy, I guess. More people out of work."

"Yup. That's one thing to their credit over there. At least they put their money where their mouths are. But I hope they don't fill people's heads with that bullshit about god rescuing them — *come have dinner but after pie and ice cream you have to convert. God will fix everything nice and neat, cure your addiction, find you a job, and return you to society."*

She dropped her cigarette on the ground. She felt bad littering, but her father would sweep the sidewalk when they were finished. She didn't want a second one. She was lightheaded from smoking so fast. She sipped her coffee. It was cold now. She never understood why cold coffee tasted so nasty, but coffee poured over ice cubes was delicious. She drank the rest anyway.

The homeless man let go of the pole and staggered back around the corner.

Her shoulders relaxed. She bent her head to the left, then right, feeling the muscles loosen. Watching the man, obviously disoriented, probably drunk, stirred up a tickle of confusion inside her chest. What did it take to go from drinking margaritas with your friends, getting drunk and letting loose once in a while, to ending up like that? It was scarier than thinking of the man assaulting her, trying to grab her purse, pushing her to the ground. She was nothing like that, was she? Her parents had consumed alcohol for as long as she could remember, although she'd never seen them drunk, as her mother pointed out. Supposedly it was a disease; some people just couldn't handle it. But how did you know? How did you know if you were one of the unlucky ones who had the genes that determined the disease?

She handed the unlit cigarette to her father. "I don't think I'll have another."

He tucked it back in the pack.

She turned toward the front path. "I'm going to grab a shower." She glanced past him. A large, red sedan was parked with the front end a few inches past their driveway entrance. "I hope mom doesn't hit that car when she comes home."

"She won't. I'm planning to do something to take care of that problem."

AFTER A SHOWER and a vigorous brushing of her teeth to get rid of the tobacco taste, Ashley decided to confront her mother head on. She'd heard Dana's compact SUV scrape into the driveway when she was getting a clean pair of navy blue shorts and a cropped shirt out of her drawer. Skulking around, worrying about when her mother would decide to continue the barrage of parental concerns was leeching the pleasure out of her weekend.

She'd offer to make BLTs for lunch, that would smooth the way, let her mother see she was a contributing adult. When she moved home, she'd thought they'd become closer, adult friends. She'd thought she would be able to bounce ideas and plans off her mother, get her perspective. At least have a friendly ear where she could expose her fears without the risk of looking weak. Instead, her mother only seemed to want to lecture her about her lack of direction, fret about Jack, and push her to stop waiting for an earth-shattering opportunity. *You have to start at the bottom. That's how it is for everyone.*

Ashley had shot back, *there is no mailroom to start in any more. This isn't a movie from the sixties. There's hardly any mail at all now.*

She pulled a head of lettuce and two tomatoes out of the crisper. She picked up the package of bacon and peeled loose twelve strips. The limp strips of fat streaked with meat clung to her fingers. She placed them on the microwave tray with grooves designed to catch the grease. She was glad for the darkened microwave door that hid the bacon as it shriveled and curled like something still alive. She washed her hands with hot water and two squirts of dish soap. While the bacon cooked she sliced the tomatoes and pulled off a few pieces of iceberg lettuce.

Her mother appeared in the doorway. "What are you doing?"

"Making BLTs."

"Those tomatoes were for the salad tonight."

"Oh. Sorry. I'll run out and buy more."

Dana walked into the kitchen. She opened the refrigerator and peered inside. "I suppose we could have cherry tomatoes."

"Okay."

"Is this penance for getting drunk?"

Ashley rinsed the knife she'd used for the tomatoes and dropped the first two slices of bread into the toaster. She pressed down the lever and the bread disappeared. "I just had a few extra drinks with my friends.

"You could have killed someone."

"You already told me." She glanced at her mother. "But I guess I should have slept over at Maggie's."

"That wouldn't do any good. You were still driving. I hope it doesn't happen again."

"It won't."

"You're an adult, you should be more responsible."

"O-*kay*." The toast popped up. She set the pieces on a plate and dropped two more slices of bread into the toaster. "It seems like you only pay attention to me when I do something wrong. I thought you and I could have some girl time. I wanted to talk to you about stuff — an idea I had for how to get more interviews. I though I could make a YouTube video that . . ."

"The bacon's done."

"I know. Why are you so cold?"

"I'm not, but you want too much from me, you want me to make you the center of my world and I can't do that."

"No I don't."

"I can't make my whole life about you because what will I have when you're not living here anymore?"

"Why do you have to hedge your bets for when I'm gone? I'm here now."

"And we're eating dinner together and breakfast together. I'm cooking for you. We aren't asking you to pay rent."

"That's all you care about? Whether I pay rent?"

"No. That didn't come out right."

"Then what is it? I don't expect to be the center of attention."

"You always have."

"Wow. Just wow, Mom. That is so cold."

"It's the truth. I thought journalists were all about the truth."

"Why do you hate me?"

"Don't be dramatic. I love you more than anything. I'm trying to transition our relationship into two adults. It's hard. You'll see if you have kids. They want to be the center of everything. Now that you've been on your own, you need to be more self-sufficient. I'm not your one-woman fan club."

"Well you should be! Daddy is."

"Really?"

"Yes."

"You're not twelve. You shouldn't need mommy and daddy to make your decisions."

"I'm not asking you to make my decisions."

"You're stagnating. How long are you planning to stay here?"

"I don't know."

"You can't always have exactly what you want when you want it. You need to figure out how to support yourself. Maybe you'll need to share an apartment with three or four girls. Find a job that's not just part time."

"It's hard to find a job right now."

"Yes, but especially if you're only willing to take one that's designed exactly to your liking."

"I studied for a certain field. I'm not going to go work in sales or something else completely unrelated."

"When you're an adult, and you have to put food on the table, you take the job you can get."

Ashley spread mayonnaise on the toast and piled up bacon, tomato slices, and laid the lettuce on top like tiny blankets over the food.

Dana left and returned with Bob.

Ashley put their plates on the table in the breakfast room and looked up. Her father was staring at the sandwich as if he felt obligated to eat it.

Ashley broke off a piece of bacon sticking out of her sandwich. She put it in her mouth and sucked on the salty flavor for a moment before she chewed it. Maybe something wasn't right between her parents. Was that why her mother was so eager for her to move out? If so, they were on the same page there. She wanted to get out on her own, but finding the perfect job would be a lot harder if she were working full time, paying rent, exhausted, with no time to plan her next move.

Seven

BOB'S TRAFFIC CONES arrived on Tuesday. He couldn't
have planned it better because on Wednesday, the night of
the weekly prayer meeting at Triumphant Life Tabernacle,
Dana went out to dinner with her tennis friends. She hadn't
asked about the contents of the box. Maybe she just didn't
care.

He put the box on his workbench and lifted out the plastic
cones. They were more flexible than he'd expected. He
flattened the box and put it in the recycling bin. He carried
the stack of cones to the curb. Not as many people attended
the Wednesday night event. There was plenty of room in the
lot to make parking on the street unnecessary.

He placed three cones in front of the neighbor's house to
the left of his, leaving three or four feet between each cone.
He should have ordered more. They weren't that expensive,
and he worried he wouldn't be able to block off enough
space directly in front of his house. The truck was in the

garage. He didn't want to have to keep parking it in the street to stake out his territory. After tonight, it would be clear whether or not that was still necessary. He put the other three cones in front of his house, leaving about five feet between each one — not quite enough space for a stubborn driver to insert her car.

The homeless guy was there again, hanging on the street sign. The poor guy must really be confused about when the weekly meal was served. Did he enter into their Wednesday night prayers? If he did, their requests weren't being acknowledged. The back of his filthy jacket was torn, a tear so sharp it looked as though it had been slashed with a knife.

It was three minutes to seven when the Buick rounded the corner. The tires didn't squeal, but the car still leaned heavily to the right as she tried to navigate the turn with a last minute attempt at control. She slammed on the brakes but not soon enough. The bumper hit the cone furthest from Bob's driveway. It toppled over and disappeared under the car.

Bob put his hands in his pockets and waited.

She backed up and stopped. The car's idle had a rough spot, like an old man with a persistent cough.

She backed up further and swung around so the nose of the car was in front of the apron to his driveway. She put the car in park, opened her door, and stuck one leg out. She half stood. "Will you move the cones?"

"No."

"There's not enough room for my car."

"That's the point."

"Where am I supposed to park?"

He pointed at the lot beside the church.

"I like to park on the street."

"You can't."

"It's a public street, you can't block it for no reason."

"There's a reason."

She ducked back in the car and turned off the engine. She got out and slammed the door. "I'm going to be late to prayer meeting."

"There's plenty of room in the parking lot."

"Why are the cones there?"

"To prevent people from parking in front of my house and blocking my driveway, taking the spot my daughter needs for her car."

"You're now allowed to do that."

"Pretend it's a car parked there."

"Why are you being so difficult?"

"Maybe Jesus will find you a better space."

She opened her mouth. The muscles around her lips tightened and her nostrils flared slightly.

"If god wants you to go to the prayer meeting, he'll find you a parking spot, isn't that right?"

She stared at him for several seconds. Her eyelids were opened too wide, gleaming with a touch of madness.

"I feel very sad for you," she said.

"No need."

"Are you going to let me park here?"

"No."

"What if I call the police?"

"I don't think they're interested in parking problems. Especially when there's a half-empty parking lot."

A crow swooped down. It strutted toward one of the cones, paused, and tipped its head to one side. The woman flapped her arms and lunged toward the crow. It took off into the darkening sky.

"I was so excited for tonight's meeting and now I've probably missed the praise time. A woman in our church has a forty-year-old son who got the flu. His fever shot up to a hundred and five. They took him to the hospital and found out his immune system was shutting down and they didn't know what was wrong. They had to give him a blood transfusion. They thought he was going to die. He has five kids and . . ."

"Why are you telling me this?"

"Just listen." Her voice was suddenly louder, almost squawking, as if the crow had given her additional authority. "We prayed for him last week. On Monday she sent us email that the fever was completely gone and he was being released. It was a total miracle! Praise the Lord." She looked up at the tops of the trees.

He laughed. "Do you ever listen to yourself?"

She looked back at him and folded her arms. "What do you mean?"

"One guy dodges the grave and it's god coming to the rescue. What about all the guys who don't recover? All the fathers who drop dead of heart attacks when they're fifty-two?" He tried to breathe, to force his tone into an even cadence, but it was as if his nervous system and vocal cords had run away without him. "What about all the sons who were killed in Iraq? Where was god then?"

"Stop shouting. Why are you attacking me?"

"Because your little story makes no sense."

"You have to have faith. This woman has tremendous faith." She backed toward her car.

"That's not an answer. Lots of people have faith. And their prayers never get answered."

She opened the door. "Faith means believing when you don't see the answer. And never giving up."

"God did not heal that guy. He was lucky."

"You don't even know him. You haven't seen the power of prayer in action. If you want to be a jerk, go for it."

She flopped into the seat and slammed the door. She started the car and put it in gear. The car shot across the street, stopping a few inches from the opposite curb.

He shouted at the closed windows. "What about all the *sons* who aren't healed? What about all the sons who are never born?"

She drove down the street and parked on the opposite side. Several minutes passed before he saw her walking along the sidewalk, her head deliberately turned toward the houses on her right. She cut across the parking lot and entered the church through the side door.

He walked over and righted the cone she'd knocked over. There was a hollow feeling inside his rib cage. All sense of purpose for the evening had drained out. Maybe there was a basketball game on. The running, thudding ball, the shouting crowds, usually made him feel as if he had something to cheer for. He walked up the driveway and cut across the lawn to the porch steps. He'd have to remember to pick up the cones in another hour or so, before Dana came home.

Eight

THE PRAYER MEETING was a blur. Melody couldn't get her mind to settle down after being shouted at and listening to those venomous words of doubt. She'd never encountered such rage. The man across the street looked like he had a nice enough wife, a daughter who had it all together, and a charming house. It was upsetting and confusing — his desire to prevent her from simply parking her car, his sudden explosion. He acted as if it were her fault that people died. He definitely thought it was God's fault, but he seemed to think she was somehow complicit.

Her hands shook, even when she folded them together. She unfolded them and lifted them out in front of her, palms up, like everyone else did. It made her uncomfortable that she knew they did this. Prayer was supposed to be private. She should not be looking at the others, pulled into an uneven circle of folding chairs. But she knew. Someone had to be the last to close her eyes.

With her hands stretched out on her lap, the tremors slid up her arms as if they planned to consume her body. She turned her hands over and gripped her thighs. Her fingers continued to shake. The mind could have one intention, but the body took over, betraying you, letting others know your true thoughts. Just like it had when Brian and Aaron pushed her shirt up into her armpits and stared at her, laughing at nothing. They pinched her nipples until her flesh became hard, red buttons, then laughed more. Goose bumps ran down her sides and across her ribs, a strange mixture of pain and cold air and wanting Aaron to like her in that way, despite what they were doing. She wasn't even sure what she'd been ashamed of. She still didn't know. And she hated that it continued to torment her. Who thought about such things for twenty years? There must be something inherently wrong with her.

Her hands ached from gripping her thighs. She relaxed them and interlaced her fingers again, squeezing as hard as she could. She had no idea what they were praying for. She couldn't even remember who else was here tonight. Since she'd come in late, she slipped into the chair, dropped her bag on the floor, and closed her eyes in one fluid movement, hardly glancing at the others, whispering, *Sorry I'm late. Sorry.*

She uncrossed her ankles and pressed the soles of her feet hard against the floor. She straightened her spine and let her head drop lower to feel the stretching in the back of her neck.

They prayed until she lost track of the time. Their voices flowed over each other, occasionally woven into long silences where no one spoke. From time to time a female voice and then a male voice let praises flow out across the group like a gurgling creek, words that were intelligible only to God. They prayed in English for the sick, the hungry, for children struggling in school, teenagers using drugs, new opportunities for employment, financial help, and unfaithful spouses.

As the gaps of silence between pleading and praising lengthened, someone began to hum softly. She thought it was Elise. Usually Elise was the one to signal they were finished by humming, then moving into a song that the others joined. Occasionally her husband led the way with his professional-quality voice, but Elise seemed more impatient, more uncomfortable with the silence, always ready to wrap things up.

The prayer time was ending, and Melody had experienced nothing but torturous bodily sensations, proving again she was nothing but a lump of flesh, not deserving of rapturous visions or the gift of tongues. Tears gathered at the backs of her eyes. Silently, she prayed the group wouldn't break into full song for another minute or so. Once that happened, all eyes would open. They'd see her red nose and liquid pooling in her lashes. She squeezed her eyelids, pressing the tears back. She swallowed. Salty moisture coated her throat.

The humming turned to words — *Joy is the flag flown high from the castle of my heart, the castle of my heart. Joy is the flag . . .*

She took a deep breath. Singing would help, it would focus her mind on something outside of herself, overpower the thoughts racing around her head. The louder the better. She let her voice join the others and the tears subsided, her sinuses cleared. Her voice grew stronger. Hopefully she wasn't too loud, drifting off key. There were so many things to think about, it was exhausting. She opened her eyes.

Twelve other people sat in the circle of chairs. Surrounded by empty space, they looked like they were gathered on a tiny raft in the middle of the sea. The ceiling rose twenty feet above them and the stage at the front looked like a distant cliff. She never understood why the prayer meeting was in the main hall and not the smaller room designated for prayer. There were never more than ten or fifteen people.

At the side of the hall was a long table that held a plate of brownies and bottles of flavored sparkling water and soda pop. People stood and drifted toward the brownies as if the food was an oasis, drawing them, promising to replenish the sugar in their veins after expending so much emotion on all the pain throbbing across the planet.

Melody took a brownie and opened a can of coke. She ate the brownie in four bites. She slid her tongue around her teeth, dragging sodden bits of chocolate out of the crevices around her gums. Sarah and Elise stood a few feet away. They turned.

"How are you?" Sarah said. She took a gulp of berry-flavored water. She coughed. She held a brownie on a napkin, but there were no bites in it yet.

"I'm okay."

"It's too bad you were so late."

"It was only five minutes."

"More like ten, I think. We were going to lay hands on you again. Everyone was in agreement that was how we were supposed to begin tonight. Rooting out your attachment to the things of the world." She smiled gently.

Melody sidled toward the table. She grabbed another brownie and took a bite, willing Sarah to yield to the temptation of the brownie perched on the palm of her hand.

Sarah moved closer and looked into Melody's eyes, not blinking, waiting.

"I'm not attached to worldly things at all," Melody said. "Look at my hideous car." She laughed and sipped her coke. She hadn't realized until this moment that she thought her car was hideous. Sarah's accusations were correct after all because, secretly, she longed for a Mini Cooper. She hadn't given up that desire. Buying the ugly car hadn't changed her feelings at all. Under their scrutiny, she realized she hated her car. It made her feel like she was too large for a normal car, made her feel middle-aged, even elderly. She was young, she should be able to enjoy life. Elise didn't seem to have any spiritual conflict over her Audi.

Melody tried to give up all the demands of her flesh while Elise glided through the world doing whatever she pleased, no sacrifices required. Why was it so unbalanced?

Compared to others in Melody's small part of the world her life appeared impoverished, but if you traveled just a few miles east, people lived in apartments that were a few steps above a slum. And look further, into rural areas where migrant workers put up with grueling labor living hand to mouth, and outside the western world and the horrors were sometimes beyond her ability to even think about.

That man's bitter view of the world had infiltrated her thoughts. She took a big bite of her brownie and chewed. She didn't care if they noticed brownie in her teeth and stuck at the corners of her lips, didn't care if she looked piggish chewing such a large bite, washing it down with coke. He'd said all those things about God, implying He didn't care about the human race at all, making her question His infinite wisdom. She swallowed more coke.

The other women seemed to be waiting for something. Neither one commented on her car. Maybe they agreed it was hideous. Or were they waiting for her to confess the truth? Did they know she really wanted a nicer car, that she was lying to them, to herself, even to God? She wanted so many things. The car was only the most obvious. She had no idea what God expected from her, yet they seemed to have a very clear idea.

"Are you angry at the Lord?" Elise said.

"No."

"We're trying to help," Sarah said. "You asked for our help and now you're pushing us away."

Besides the three of them, only Gordon, Sarah's husband, and an elderly woman remained in the building. The other two stood near the front of the hall, leaning against the edge of the stage, talking. Right there, yet far away. Melody had no idea what she was supposed to say, or do. She'd had her chance on Sunday and nothing had come of it. To ask for a dedicated prayer session again would be utter humiliation. A thought flitted across her brain and she tried to shove it aside before it took root — she could lie. She could tell them she had the gift. Would she be able to mimic their sounds when they were in a group? But what if they could tell? What if she was the only one who thought the babbled phrases sounded more or less the same? Perhaps if you actually had the gift, you could distinguish between different varieties, and they would know, the whole church would know she was faking it. *What* did God *want* from her?

"I'm going to be honest," Elise said. "You haven't thrown your pride on the fire, you haven't cast yourself on the ground and given everything. *Everything.* I can feel your anger and your holding back and your concern with what others think about you."

How did she know? Was she guessing?

Elise and Sarah stepped closer. Elise's shoulder touched Melody's arm. Sarah's breath was cool on her neck and face, smelling slightly of stale coffee instead of her berry drink. The brownie was still in her hand.

Melody took a step back, but they moved with her as if

they were engaged in a strange, slow dance. She half-expected their arms, like aggressive wild vines, to wrap around her, pulling her elbows and hands tightly to her sides, winding around her ankles until she was unable to move.

Sarah put her hand on Melody's forearm.

"The Lord is trying to tell you something," Elise said. "Are you listening?"

"All of your desires need to be yielded. Don't hold on to anything. Be willing to go where He calls, speak what he asks, risk your pride, your comfort, even your life," Sarah said.

Their words felt like weights placed on her chest. It was difficult to breathe, and impossible to think. Her head was filled with a rushing sound. The edges of her vision were darkening. Finally she whispered, her voice pinched. "I need to sit down."

They remained where they were, as if they hadn't heard her. Or were they waiting for her to faint, thinking it was a test, that her total collapse would be a sign of her giving in? She'd tried to yield her feelings of shame, her anxiety, she'd asked God to remove them and He hadn't. She had no control over all of that. They were just . . . there. How could she yield any more?

The rushing sound grew louder. "I think I'm going to faint."

"No you're not."

"I think I am."

"The flesh is weak. Your spirit must be stronger."

"I don't know what God wants from me." Tears ran down her face. She had no idea how long they'd been standing there, it seemed like hours.

"There's something holding your tongue."

"Listen to the Spirit. What is He saying to you?"

"Where does he want you to go?"

"What does he want you to say?"

Sarah began to speak in tongues. Elise joined her.

Melody wanted to run, to escape their voices, their eyes, the cold, empty building. It was obvious God wanted nothing to do with her. No one else had to suffer this assault, this prying into her life, as if they wanted to creep inside her head and inspect every errant thought, looking with disgust on each one that didn't measure up.

"You need to speak out for him."

"You need to preach the gospel."

"Is there someone who needs salvation that you've been afraid to reach out to?"

"The man across the street?" she whispered.

"Yes!"

"He's so mean. I think he hates God."

"And he's leading his family astray," Elise said.

"The whole city is in need of salvation!" Sarah's voice was loud, sharp, tinged at the edges with either a scream or a near-hysterical laugh.

The women backed away from her. The dizzy feeling faded.

"It's connected, you know," Elise said. "Being afraid to tell others they need to turn to God and not receiving the gift of tongues. You need to unbind your tongue."

"Yes." Melody nodded. "I can see that."

"You can't be afraid of appearing foolish."

"Say it," Elise said.

"Say what?"

"Tell the Lord now, that you'll do whatever is required to bring that man to his knees."

"I will."

"Say the words," Sarah said.

"I'll bring him to God."

"All of it."

"I'll do whatever is required to bring that man to his knees."

"Yes!" Elise and Sarah wrapped their arms around her, squeezing her so that her breasts hurt and her arms were completely immobilized. She worried Sarah's brownie was smashed against the back of her shirt.

Nine

THE DAY HAD been summer-like, the temperature climbing to seventy-eight degrees. Ashley felt light and carefree in her swirly green and pink skirt with a pink camisole top and gladiator sandals. The evening was cooling fast, but she didn't want to change her outfit.

She was spending the night at Jack's and tomorrow they'd go to the beach, maybe hang out at the boardwalk and ride the roller coaster, walk around for a while. Then they'd drive to a beach further north, less crowded, and with better waves for body surfing.

She stuffed her black bikini into her overnight bag and zipped the clear plastic case containing her make-up and other stuff.

Downstairs, her mother was pouring marinade over two chicken breasts. The flesh was pink and slightly translucent. Bits of garlic clung to the meat as the liquid ran down the sides and pooled in the baking dish. Pale skin, ripped off the meat, lay on the counter. She backed away so she didn't have to look at it — the chicken dish her mother prepared once a week.

"I'm leaving."

Dana tore off a piece of plastic wrap and covered the pan. She pulled the plastic tight and put the dish in the refrigerator. "I wish you could see your life is going nowhere."

"I see that, Mom. More than you know."

"Then why aren't you doing anything?"

"I'm trying!"

"Why do you go spend the night with him? Why don't you either get engaged or break it off? You're not interviewing, you're not trying to find a full-time job at all."

"It's a fantastic day. Why are you trying to pick a fight?"

"I'm not picking a fight." Dana brushed the backs of her wrists across her cheekbones to push her hair off the sides of her face. "I just don't understand you."

"Because you won't sit down and listen to me. You just make these drive-by attacks."

"Sorry. But this is the best time of your life, you should be making the most of it."

"I'm trying! I'm staying over with my boyfriend, who I'm not ready to move in with or get engaged to or any of that stuff until I know for sure he's the one. We're going out to dinner. We're going to the beach. We're having *fun*. And if you'd let me talk to you, I'd explain my idea for getting my career going. But all you want me to do is lock myself into a boring, robot job."

"There's nothing wrong with a so-called robot job. Working for any company can be satisfying if you do your work well, make friends, build a good reputation. Like your father has."

"I'm trying to keep a positive attitude about the career I went to school for. I think it helps to stay positive, not just give up."

"You need to do more than be positive."

"Okay. I told Jack I'd be there at five-thirty. And it's five twenty-five. So . . . can I tell you about it later? It's a really good idea."

"Have a good weekend."

"I'll be home tomorrow night."

Dana nodded.

Ashley walked across the kitchen and squeezed her mother's shoulders with her free arm. Her purse swung around and slapped Dana's thigh. "See you."

When she went out to the front porch, the street was quiet. The whole neighborhood looked vacant. People were either still at work or locked inside their homes. Not even a squirrel or a crow wandered past.

JACK LIVED IN a massive apartment complex with hundreds of residents, built in the eighties and showing its age. Although it was kept freshly painted and the grounds well maintained, it looked tired — a middle-aged woman covering spongy skin and discoloration with liquid foundation, blush, and eye shadow.

It was a nice enough place, easily affordable on his salary working for his uncle's construction company. Despite a college degree in business, he'd defaulted to the work that left him tanned and muscled every summer while he was in college. He thought his work was noble, and he liked being outdoors. Ashley wondered if he could have tried harder to think of something important, but there was still time for him to realize his mistake.

Ashley grabbed her bag and her pillow out of the back of the Prius, set the alarm, and walked past the man-made creek that wound through small trees and out to a grassy area. Daffodils filled a small strip of dirt than ran along the building where Jack's apartment was located.

The sense of a deserted world that she'd had at home lingered as she walked through the empty complex. It could have been the end of time, all the occupants snatched up to heaven, like the people at Triumphant Life Tabernacle expected to happen any day. She knew this because kids at school that attended miracle-believing churches talked about it a lot, trying to persuade Ashley and her friends to be afraid of what waited for them after death.

But the possibility of dying was too far away, almost impossible to believe.

She knocked on the door, wondering, as she did every time,

why she didn't have a key. Yet when he invited her inside, she knew she wouldn't ask for one. He never seemed to think about it. She knocked again.

Jack opened the door and grabbed her around the waist. With his bare feet pressing on her toes, he pulled her through the living room furnished with a couch, an armchair, and an old, bulky TV. Two coffee mugs and what looked like the dishes and utensils from his last three meals sat on the bar that separated the living room from the kitchen.

When they reached his bedroom, he took the bag out of her hand, tossed the pillow on the foot of the bed, and pulled down the comforter. He moved back to where she stood and wrapped his arms around her shoulders, pressing his face into her hair. "Do you want me as much as I want you?"

She nodded.

"Say it."

"I want you."

"But I *need* you." He lifted off her top and unhooked her bra. "Do you need me?"

"Yes."

He sucked on her left breast. She tipped her head back. Thoughts about the end of the world and her mother grew fuzzy and vague. After a few minutes, he moved to her right breast, always careful to give them equal attention. "You look great." He ran his hands down her sides and slid them up under her skirt. "You're perfect."

She smiled at the top of his head. She was proud of her

body, and her long, straight hair. It was difficult not to be in love with his admiration. It was one of the things that worried her, made her doubt whether he was really the guy she was meant to be with. When he praised her and stroked her skin, she felt proud and excited by his attraction to her. She wasn't sure it should be like that. But how did you know? It wasn't as if she could ask one of her friends. Or her parents.

Finally, she closed her eyes and let herself dissolve into the cool breeze coming through the open window, the pressure and hunger of his mouth, and the desire spreading through her blood, making it warm and thick.

They sank onto the bed and made love until every thought and sensation that wasn't Jack slipped off her skin as the world shrank to their small space.

She drifted to sleep for a few minutes. When she woke, it was still light outside. Immediately the pleasure faded and her thoughts began to gnaw along the same route they always took. They swam right back to the worries she'd had right before she yielded her brain to the sensations in her body. At dinner, he would ask again about moving in together. It was becoming as predictable as their habit of making love before they went out. He needed her too much. Without any plans beyond showing up at whatever construction site he was assigned to, he tried to pull her into his orbit, reducing the obligation to think about his own future. They'd have a shared task — setting up house. He was satisfied with so much less. He thought average was something valuable, a worthwhile aspiration. If he went to the same job every day, working with the crew he'd known since high school, remodeling homes, and came home to Ashley, ate dinner at a casual restaurant, took vacations in Las Vegas or Lake Tahoe, he'd be content. Forever. She was rarely content. She didn't want to be content. Not like that.

Every morning, she woke up thinking about how she could connect with the right opportunity, a position worthy of her education and her talent and the promise she'd shown as an intern. Jack seemed to wake up and think about what he was going to eat, or what he wanted to do on the weekend. Shouldn't they be equally ambitious if they were meant to be together? She'd done such a terrible thing to get him. When they'd separated during college, she'd started to question why she'd fallen for him. Being back at home caused the doubts to spread throughout her mind. She was slipping into a life that should be in the past.

She sat up and pushed off the sheet. Her muscles were jittery, as if she hadn't made love at all. Her eyes itched and her mouth was sticky and dry.

"What's wrong?" Jack's eyes were still closed, his voice clogged and dull.

"I'm hungry."

"Already?" He rolled on his side and pushed his face against her hip. "Come down here with me."

"Aren't you ready for dinner?"

"I'd rather have you."

"Later." She stood and went to the foot of the bed where her clothes were scattered across the beige carpet like stones in a Zen garden. "Where should we go for dinner?"

He groaned. "I want you back in bed."

"Let's go eat. We need our strength." She tossed his jeans onto the bed.

He sat up. "I forgot. I have something to show you first."

"What's that?"

He sat on the edge of the bed and shoved his legs into his jeans. "Be patient. You'll see."

They dressed and he led her to the second bedroom. Except for a small pressed wood desk with a computer, the room was empty. He slid open the closet door. One half was filled with built-in shelves and the other stacked with boxes. He squatted slightly and reached to the back of the shelf near his knees. He pulled his arm back out and stood. "Never mind. Maybe later. After dinner."

"What?"

"I'll show you later."

She rubbed her arm. The jittery sensation was still there and she wasn't sure if it was hunger, dehydration, or now, irritation at his teasing. "What did you want to show me?"

"Lift up your top and let me see your gorgeous tits and then I'll show you."

She folded her arms around her waist. "Come on, Jack. I said I was hungry and you wanted to show me something.

Why are you doing this?"

"I don't know if you really want to see it. You have to prove it."

"I don't even know what it is."

"You know it's something huge," he said.

"How would I know that?"

"Because I haven't showed you yet."

"You're being a pain in the ass."

"You're no fun." He grabbed her wrist and pulled her toward him.

"I'm hungry. And thirsty." She ran her fingers through her hair. She twisted out of his arms and scratched both knees.

"Why are you so jumpy? You should be all blissful after the way I made you feel."

"I don't know. I told you, I'm hungry. Are you going to show me or not?"

"I don't want you to freak out."

She backed away from him. "I'm tired of this. Either show me or don't."

"Okay. Hold on." He reached to the back of the shelf and pulled out a dark blue towel wrapped around something the size of a beer bottle. "Let's go in the other room."

She turned and went into the living room. She flopped on the couch and crossed her legs.

He sat next to her and put the towel on his lap. He unfolded it. Lying in the center was a handgun. It was brushed gold with a wood-grain plate decorating the grip.

"Isn't it awesome?" He picked it up and inserted his finger through the loop that circled the trigger. He lifted the gun and pointed it at the TV.

She wriggled away from him.

"Don't be scared. It's locked."

"It's loaded?"

"Of course. What would be the point of an unloaded gun?"

"Why do you have a gun?"

"My dad gave it to me."

"Why? I don't like guns."

"What's not to like?"

"They kill people."

"Not if you're careful. Not if you know what you're doing."

"That's not what I've heard. More people are killed accidentally with their own guns than anyone who stops a crime with one."

"Well you heard wrong."

"Why did he give it to you?"

"Haven't you heard the police force is shrinking?"

"I guess."

"Getting their benefits cut, lower pay compared to other cities. And so much gang stuff around here, cops are quitting and they have a hard time hiring more. When was the last time you drove south on 101?"

She shrugged.

"There's graffiti all over the overpasses once you get past the airport."

"Why does graffiti miles away mean you need a gun?"

"My dad's worried about me. This apartment's about as solid as a cardboard box. You know how many cars have been broken into."

"What good is a gun going to do if someone breaks into your car?"

"He just thought it was a good idea. To be safe."

She stood and adjusted her skirt. She smoothed it over her hips, feeling her bones, and the muscles of her upper thighs. The thought of a bullet plunging into her body made her legs rubbery, her belly collapsed in on itself. "I don't think you should have it."

"Why not?" He turned it sideways and ran his hand down the barrel.

"Because you might have an accident."

"Are you afraid I'll shoot you by mistake?" He grinned.

"That's not funny. Why would you say that?" She looked behind her. Where had she left her purse? "Put it away. I think you should give it back to him."

"I like it."

"I feel like I don't know you. I had no idea you were into guns."

"I'm not *into* guns. I like this gun. I like having it. There are a lot of crazy people out there. Do you know if you call the cops for a break-in now, they tell you flat out they probably won't show up unless it's in progress, if your life is in danger?"

The room was getting dark quickly. They hadn't turned on any lights and it was past seven-thirty. The only object that was clearly visible was the gun, the metal glistening in his hands, shimmering like it was pulsing with energy, useless until it was fired — wanting to be fired. "I'm really hungry. Can you please put it away so we can go eat."

He placed it on his lap and folded the towel over it. He put both hands on top of the towel and stared at them.

"What are you doing?" she said.

"Nothing. I thought . . ."

She waited. Outside, a dog yelped. "You thought what?"

"I thought you'd think it was cool."

"Well it's not cool. Not at all."

THEY WENT TO a Sushi place tucked between a dental office and an antique store. The exterior was designed to mimic a Japanese home with a curved, pointed roof and dark, decorative trim. One wall of the main room was lined with secluded booths, each bench backed by a rice paper screen.

The server, dressed in a blue and green kimono that glistened like water when she moved, brought a plate of warm edamame followed quickly by two bowls of miso soup. Ashley ordered California rolls, the chef's twelve-piece selection of sashimi, a spicy tuna roll, and a bottle of sake.

Jack pried apart his wood chopsticks. He poked around in

the broth and lifted out a strip of seaweed and set it inside the domed cover of his soup bowl. He fished around for more seaweed and bits of tofu. When he'd cleaned out all the non-liquid contents, he pushed the cover toward Ashley.

"Thanks." She scooped the unwanted food into her own bowl. She never understood why he ordered the soup if he didn't like half the contents. The broth was good, he'd said. What was so offensive about a few small cubes of tofu and delicate strips of seaweed? It didn't even have a definite taste.

"Are you still being all PC on me?" he said.

She poured sake into their tiny glass cups.

He raised his, waiting for her to touch her cup to his. She took a quick sip and put it down.

He swallowed the entire glass full.

"You don't need it."

"We live in dangerous times." He refilled his glass. He picked up a piece of edamame and sucked out the soybeans.

It was a perfect example of him not thinking. The tofu was made of soy and he hated it, yet he loved the whole beans. He'd explained the texture of tofu was creepy. In reality, he was addicted to salt — the salty broth, the salt-soaked edamame pods. He'd never met a snack food he didn't like. He even liked European black licorice that was sprinkled with salt.

"I feel nervous being in your house when there's a gun lying around."

"It's got a safety lock."

"That doesn't matter."

"Why?"

She picked up her bowl and sipped the broth, letting two silky cubes of tofu slide across her tongue, and down her throat. "You don't need a gun."

"Does this mean you won't move in with me?"

She put down her bowl. She picked up a piece of edamame and sucked on it but didn't extract any of the beans. "I told you a hundred times, I'm not ready."

"And the gun makes you less ready?"

"No. But I'd never move in with a gun there."

"So it's me or the gun?"

"Please don't mix up two different issues. This is hard enough."

"What's hard enough? Are you breaking up with me?" His face twisted into an expression that tried hard not to show fear or hurt.

She took a sip of sake and a swallow of water. She didn't mean to torture him. There was too much she loved about him. But she wasn't sure if she loved him with her whole being. Was she lying when she said *I love you*? She'd met him when she was sixteen. That was too young to find a soul mate. "I'm not breaking up with you. Why would you think that?"

"You took a long time to answer. You won't move in with me. Now you're making a big deal out of something my dad gave me because he's worried about me."

"If you think your place is unsafe, why do you want me to live there?"

"I don't think that, my dad does."

"There you are."

"There I am what?"

"You don't need a gun."

He took another shot of sake.

"You're not supposed to drink it like vodka shots."

"I know. But you're making my head hurt. I don't know if we're talking about guns or moving in together."

"Right now, I'm talking about *not* moving in together. And we've already talked about it, and I told you I don't want to think about it right now. I need to focus on my career."

"Why can't you do that when you're living with me?"

"Because I'll get distracted."

"Then why don't we break up, if I'm so distracting?"

"Don't. You know this is important to me. I'm kind of depressed. I told you, I thought my degree plus all the amazing feedback from my internship would open lots of doors. But it's still not happening. I need to figure out a new plan."

"You don't have to be the star of CNN right now."

"That's not what I'm talking about. But I have to get started."

The server approached the table. She set a rectangular white plate in the center. The pink and red and pale orange flesh of fish glistened like large gems, surrounded by greenery, small curls of ginger, and a pasty cone of wasabi. The rice-encrusted California rolls were dotted with orange fish eggs, clear and shimmery.

Ashley put a piece of tuna on her plate. She stirred up a small dish of soy sauce and wasabi and dunked the tuna in, swirled it around, and took a bite. Delicious. She took another bite and a sip of sake.

Jack bit a piece of tuna. As he chewed, a drop of soy sauce dribbled from the corner of his mouth.

She reached across and touched her finger to it, wiping it away. She licked her finger.

"You make me crazy when you do that."

She smiled.

"I don't know what you want," he said.

"I want an awesome career. We don't need to change things right now. Everything is fine the way it is."

"Well if you're not moving in, I have no reason to get rid of the gun. Or does that mean you're not coming over at all any more?"

"I don't know."

"Can I stay over at your house?" He grinned.

He knew the answer. She popped a California roll in her mouth. The fish eggs burst against her teeth.

"So you aren't coming over any more?"

"I guess if you keep it locked. And wrapped up in that closet. I don't ever want to see it."

"You don't think it's even a little cool?"

She shook her head, but it was a lie. There was something powerful and alluring about the gun. Something frightening that made her want to try it out. Maybe that's why she hated it.

Ten

ON SUNDAY MORNING Bob got up at six. He crept to the bathroom and put on jeans, thick socks, and a t-shirt, taking care not to bump his elbows on the towel rack when he turned. This was part of the reason Dana kept pleading for a re-modeled bathroom, and it made sense. What he couldn't process, despite her explanations, was the desire for luxury — the oval, elevated tub, the picture window so she could look out at the trees, the richness of a beautifully tiled floor and a long counter with two sinks. When were they ever in the bathroom at the same time? They didn't need two sinks.

The floor creaked as he walked across the bedroom. Dana's breath remained steady and soft. It was funny how she heard a floorboard shift all the way from the first floor when Ashley came home, but he could walk back and forth across their room, three feet from her head, and she heard nothing. Maternal instinct trumped everything else.

Downstairs, he sat on a chair in the breakfast room and put on his work boots.

It had rained the night before, with a gusty wind, and the front porch was soaked. There were a few small pools of standing water. He went down the steps and around the side of the house to the garage. The sun was peeking over the foothills and the sky was clear.

He opened one of the cabinet doors near his workbench and pulled out the traffic cones. He carried them to the front yard and placed them along the curb on either side of the driveway.

He knew he was being a jerk, knew it was unlikely he'd get away with it for long, but he couldn't stop himself. All his animosity toward religion had shrunk to a spot of light, the red dot of a laser pointer in the center of Melody's forehead. The absurdity of his behavior pleased him — they were so damn sure god would supply everything from medical care to parking spaces to eternal life, it made him laugh to think about removing one or two parking spaces with six well-placed plastic cones.

It also amused him that the church members were so law abiding that the cones were able to fulfill their purpose. She would never consider getting out of her car and tossing the cones to the curb. She asked him to make room, and then huffed when he refused. On the other hand, she was not concerned with basic traffic laws and general safe driving. She was always late, always in a hurry, always had her mind in the clouds. It terrified him to think how many people there might be on the roads who were not paying attention, who had tenuous control of enormous vehicles.

It was too early for churchgoers to start arriving, but he wanted to get ahead of the game. He'd make a pot of coffee and eat some toast, read part of the paper, and then it would be time for a smoke while he watched the lemmings march into their tacky building. For all he knew, there were mysterious, obscene rituals taking place inside those flimsy walls —maybe animal sacrifices. There wouldn't be a crucifix or any statues of saints, that was for the Catholics. There was a plain white cross at the front peak of the roof, but it was smallish. There were no stained glass windows. Potted poinsettias were clustered around the glass front doors in the winter, lilies in the spring, and ferns in the summer and fall.

He imagined the floors covered in the cheapest grade carpet, stained with spilled coffee and grease from shoes and food. He imagined stark rooms for prayer, lined with folding chairs, cast-off furniture, and artificial potted plants, giving off the same hopeless aura as the grief rooms at a funeral home.

When he was a child, his parents dragged him and his brother and sister to church every Sunday. Maybe dragging wasn't really the right word. There were classes for kids and he seemed to remember them being okay, not overly boring. He'd gone to confession nearly every week. They'd celebrated all the holidays in the typical American hybrid fashion of

Crèche and Santa, stockings and hymns, cookies and candlelight mass. The same went for Easter — rabbits and crosses, dying eggs a sickening half-red and blue and pink and orange and green after Good Friday mass.

Ashley had been baptized as an infant, and they'd taken her to services at least once a month without ever discussing it, knowing it was something you did, and half-thinking a kindly heavenly father was watching over them, blessing them, always semi-available, waiting for them behind golden, pearly-studded gates when it was all over.

His dismissal of god had taken years. Unanswered prayer after unanswered prayer tore at his soul like nails pounded through flesh into a wooden cross. There was no justice, no fairness in the world. There were no answers, not really, and the sooner humanity got that through their thick skulls, the better off they would all be.

The house was silent. Often on Sundays the three of them had a large breakfast. When Ashley was a kid, he shot baskets with her while Dana cooked. He loved watching her jump and dart around him, dribbling the ball. She was so fast, just like he'd been as a kid, before he stopped short at five-eleven, and the other guys, who had a chance at being ball players, sprouted up over six feet. Once Ashley moved on to tennis, he hadn't shot baskets again, even by himself.

He was too worked up for a big breakfast today. He filled the coffee maker with fresh grounds and water enough for two mugs. He'd make a second pot when Dana and Ashley woke up. He stuck two halves of an English muffin in the toaster.

With the muffin buttered and the coffee sugared and creamed, he sat in the breakfast room and looked out the front window at the hedge. It concealed his house from the street, or the street from the house, whichever way he preferred to look at it on any given day. The hedge needed trimming — he'd work on that later, after he was done with his newfound game. And he knew it was a game. He was behaving like a pre-teen boy, determined to have the final word, needing to taunt a girl until she cried — some incomprehensible male urge to evoke an emotional reaction. It didn't matter. If he could derail just one idiotically grinning, praise-the-lord-babbling, bad-driving nut case, it would be a pleasant conclusion to the weekend.

For a while, he lost himself in the newspaper and forgot about his coffee. When he took a sip, it was cold. He swallowed it in two gulps, refilled the mug, and turned off the pot. He got his cigarettes out of the drawer in the office and went outside.

The front walk was even wetter than earlier. The rain hadn't fully dried and the sprinklers had come on while he was reading the paper. Water was pooled near the front corner of the lawn where the ground wasn't quite level. He should try to fix whatever was causing the problem. It looked like a simple task — fill the area with dirt and re-seed the lawn. Or was it really that easy? He worried the dirt would sink down to the depressed area and the water would continue to collect and flow onto the path and into the dirt around the hedge.

At quarter to eight, the street was still empty. He had come out too early. The service didn't start until nine-thirty. By then, Dana would be up, looking for him. If she saw the cones, she wouldn't understand. She'd shift to that quiet tone of voice, the one that insisted she wasn't nagging, and then she'd nag him about getting a hobby more substantial than watching basketball. She'd ask whether something was wrong at work, if he was feeling his age. She would ask questions until his whole life had been distilled into a few vapory puffs that made him feel he didn't exist, made him wonder why he'd been born and why he was going through the motions of dressing and eating and paying bills and going to the office very day.

He'd have one cigarette then go back inside and finish reading the paper until she came downstairs. He'd be able to divert her with his plans for trimming the hedge and fixing the leaking sprinkler, and let her know he wasn't in the mood for waffles or pancakes.

IT TURNED OUT he'd over-estimated Dana's interest in him. Her shoulders relaxed when he said he was satisfied with his English muffin. She wanted to read the newspaper and drink her coffee on the back porch.

"I'm going to take a look at that spot where the water's collecting around the sprinkler."

She nodded.

He slipped out the front door, walked down the path, and through the narrow opening between the two sides of the hedge. He pulled out a cigarette, put it in his mouth, and snapped the lighter. The flame shot up but he'd miscalculated the position of his hand and had to jut his head forward to touch the tip of the cigarette to the fire. As the flame burned a moment longer than usual, it made him think of those little tongues of fire you saw standing over the heads of saints in religious paintings. He moved his thumb and let it die. He shoved the lighter in his pocket.

Smoke wove into his lungs and out through his nostrils. It hung in the air, thick and hazy. There was no breeze to temper the slowly spreading warmth of the sun. Even the birds were quiet, finished with the songs and trills and squawks of pleasure that had filled the cool, early-morning air.

Sometimes he wondered why he even pretended to limit himself to a single cigarette a week. Since he'd started taunting Melody, he'd been smoking two or three. Maybe the habit would slowly expand throughout the other parts of his life, creeping first into Saturday afternoons, then the rest of the weekend, finally, invading his workdays. He'd be forced to join the few pariahs at Argatech who spent thirty or forty minutes a day standing the required distance from the building, enduring looks of disgust, surrounded by a cloud of smoke.

He was on his third cigarette when the parking lot across the street began to fill with mini vans and compacts. By twenty past nine, the lot was full. Drivers began parking along the curb in front of the church, the line of cars creeping along the street like a relentlessly spreading rash.

The red Buick roared down the street three minutes before the service was due to start, this time coming from the opposite direction. She'd obviously anticipated the cones. The curb in front of the church was occupied and she didn't appear to realize, until she was directly across from his house, that she'd have to turn around and park further away.

As she passed the spot where he stood, pop rock religious music billowed out of the partially open window. Layered with the music from her CD player, her voice was a fraction off the timing of the words, but pleasant, carrying the tune and blending with the recorded voices.

She drove to the corner and began a u-turn. She miscalculated the required space, stopped, backed up, then turned sharply. The car lurched toward the house to Bob's left. She slammed on the brakes and moved forward, driving past the first and second cones. She bumped the nose of her car against the third, shoving it against the curb. The car door flew open and she climbed out. She wore a magenta and yellow flowered top with a black skirt and Birkenstock sandals. He stared at her feet for a moment. He couldn't imagine driving a car with those thick shoes slipping around on his feet. Although Dana and Ashley both drove in flip-flops and open-back sandals with tiny heels, so maybe women had a special knack.

"You pushed the cone out of place," he said.

"I know. If you'd move them, my car fits perfectly." She smiled as if he owed her a favor.

"The cones are there for a reason. You need to park somewhere else."

"It's a public street."

"We already had this conversation." He sucked in smoke and blew it out in a thin stream. "Put the cone back and move your car."

"I'm late."

He shrugged.

She reached into the car, dragged out her purse and Bible, and slammed the door closed.

"Hey!" He dropped his cigarette. "I told you to move your fucking car!"

She gasped. A dark red spot formed on her forehead and her eyes bulged as she stepped toward him. "Don't talk to me like that."

He hadn't meant to shout at her, hadn't meant to use that word, but it was rewarding watching her cringe as if he'd thrown sewage on her skirt.

She used her free hand to push her hair away from the side of her face. "You need to apologize," she said. She took a few steps closer to where he stood. She smiled gently, even though the red spot continued to glare from the center of her forehead. "I'm sorry I got angry. The Lord told me that you feel left out, that you wish you could be part of our family, but you're not sure what to do."

He laughed.

She smiled with tight lips. A shadow of confusion passed over her eyes.

He laughed harder. "The lord told you wrong. There's no way in hell I want to associate with a bunch of crackpots who think an invisible guy in the clouds is talking to them."

She stepped onto the curb, crossed the grass strip, and stopped a foot or so away from him. "Why are you playing this silly game? Acting like the whole street belongs to you?"

"It surely doesn't belong to you." He reached into his pocket and pulled out the pack of cigarettes. How did she know it was a game? He supposed his childishness was just as obvious to her as it was to him.

"Why don't you give it a try? You seem like an intelligent man. Don't you wonder what it's all about?"

"I know exactly what it's about."

"Are you angry at God?"

He lit his cigarette. He took a deep drag and felt the smoke catch in his throat. He coughed slightly, then took another drag and blew the smoke past the side of her head. She moved to his left.

"Are you?"

"There is no god." His voice lacked conviction, but she didn't seem to notice.

"You wouldn't be so angry if you really believed that. You wouldn't care."

Something inside him curled up like a leaf that was ready to drop off a tree, turning under at the edges, shrinking and tightening. He took another drag and turned his head slightly to blow the smoke away from her.

"Thank you."

"Move your car."

"I don't have to. I'm in the right. If I called the police, they'd agree with me."

"If you called the police, I'd point out that you speed, that you gun your engine and crash into the curb."

"They wouldn't care if I crash into the curb. Everyone does that."

"Everyone does not do that. My daughter is a better driver than you are, and she's only twenty-three."

"I don't understand why you're so angry. What did I ever do to you?"

"It's none of your business."

She backed to the curb. "So you are angry. At God? Or me?"

"Move the damn car." Once again he dropped his half-smoked cigarette on the ground. This time he stepped on it to make sure it was out. If Dana saw the mess, she'd be disappointed and annoyed. More annoyed than disappointed. He'd clean it up later, when he put the cones away.

He turned and walked up the front path. Somehow, he felt

he'd lost. It had been foolish to buy the cones, to make such a big issue out of it. She wasn't going to abandon her beliefs because some middle-aged guy mocked her and prevented her from parking where she wanted. Like she said, why did he care? If people wanted to believe god was on their side, let them. They'd find out soon enough it wasn't true. And maybe for some of them it was true, because they always got what they wanted. Maybe some of them never had to face up to the knowledge that god didn't give a shit about what would make them happy, what they longed for. There was no way to argue with her and show her how wrong she was without telling her how god had stuck it to him. And that was none of her business.

HE FOUND DANA in the backyard. She wore a straw hat, jeans, and a thin blue t-shirt. She knelt in the center of the lawn that extended from the back porch to the covered patio near the fence, which housed the picnic table and gas grill. She shoved a metal probe into the lawn, wiggled it around, and plucked out the offending dandelion.

"I wish you wouldn't mow right over these," she said.

"I don't always see them."

"That's because you're not looking."

He walked to where she knelt and squatted beside her. "I can help you with that."

"I'm almost done." She nodded her head toward a pile of limp dandelions, the yellow flowers already appearing semi-melted in the sun. "But thanks."

The timbre of her voice hinted that she was smiling, but with the brim of the hat shading her face, he wasn't sure.

"Did you figure out how to stop the water from collecting?"

He'd forgotten all about his white lie. There was no way to stop it. To eliminate the problem, he'd have to dig up the lawn, jackhammer part of the front path, rip out part of the hedge, and re-build the ground with soil and rock. He'd probably have to move the sprinkler pipes. There was no way to fix anything in life without completely dismantling it. "No."

She nodded. "I guess we just have to live with it."

"I don't like being forced to live with things that aren't right."

She laughed. "I know."

He stood and went to the pile of weeds. He scooped them up and carried them to the waste bin. He flipped open the lid. The aroma of rotting grass and weeds mixed with fallen, moldy lemons spilled out. He dropped the dandelions inside and let the lid crash closed. When he turned, Dana was standing. He remained by the waste bin and watched her adjust her bra, then her t-shirt, then hoist up the waist of her jeans. Why did he feel so far away from her?

He started back across the yard. She shoved the weeding tool in her pocket and tugged the hat lower on her forehead.

"Now what?" he said.

"Why are you so listless? You wander around like you're not quite sure where you are, or you numb your brain with the TV. Why can't you be interested in anything?"

"I am," he said.

"Such as?"

"What brought this up?"

"I feel like you've lost your forward momentum."

He hadn't lost momentum all. He just had a different focus. Despite conceding their most recent skirmish, Melody was still a fascinating project. Strangely, he was certain she viewed him the same way — someone to scoop up in her fishnet.

"What are you thinking about?" Dana moved closer and lifted the brim of her hat, staring at him as if she could peel back the skin of his forehead, chip a small hole in his skull, and peer inside his brain.

"Nothing."

"You've been this way since Ashley moved home."

That's where she was wrong. He'd been this way a hell of a lot longer than that. In fact, he did have momentum now that there was a focal point. During business hours he managed to switch his brain to the work at hand, but the minute he walked out of the building, felt the heavy glass door fall away from his fingertips and slam shut, his thoughts turned to the woman who personified the swarms of crazy people inside that church.

"You're not going to talk to me, are you?"

"I don't know what you think is wrong. I'm fine."

"I'm going to have a coke. Want some?"

She walked to the back porch. The brim of her hat bounced and swayed. Her hips moved in quick, sharp ticks to the right and left. Her jeans were tight and there was no sign in her hips or thighs that she'd ever given birth. He wondered if her girlish shape proved her body was unwelcoming to children. He knew she was pleased with her slim hips, but sometimes the form of her body was a knife in his heart.

The yard was in full sun now. His t-shirt stuck between his shoulder blades. He yanked it away from his skin. He couldn't stop watching the tick-tick of Dana's hips, imagining himself jogging across the lawn, pushing her onto the soft grass, climbing on top of her, sliding her jeans down her legs. Twenty years ago, he would have done that. But he could see the worry in her eyes — Ashley, the neighbors, though their yard was surrounded by a six-foot fence topped by lattice with vines wound through the holes. God, looking down from heaven, might notice and deliver some form of punishment.

When Ashley was an infant, Dana had no concerns about anyone seeing her body. She pulled out her breasts, one after the other, and let Ashley suck away with her eyes closed. Thin, soft lips pulled in what she wanted. She sometimes drifted to sleep, still refusing to loosen her grip. Dana fed the baby in restaurants and in friends' homes and in the car while Bob ran into the grocery store. She even fed her in church, insisting anyone who was bothered was a pervert — *what better place to nurse a human life?*

He peeled off his shirt just as Dana reached the top step of the porch.

She turned. "What are you doing?"

"It's hot."

"It's not that hot."

He balled the shirt in his hand and walked to the porch. He climbed the steps and dropped the shirt on the wooden swing that faced the yard. He stepped toward her, but she moved out of reach, pulled off her hat and placed it on top of his shirt. She turned and opened the door and went inside. He followed her to the kitchen.

"Are you going to put on a shirt? And make sure the other one gets in the laundry basket."

He left the room without saying anything.

When he returned, wearing the same shirt, she was seated in the breakfast room. Two glasses of coke filled with ice sat on the table. A small bowl of pretzels was between them — arranged like he and Dana, with Ashley in the middle. Lying open on the table in front of her was a binder. That binder.

It contained the collection of magazine clippings showing the exotic bathrooms she admired, as well as brochures from tile shops, paint stores, and a few places that specialized in bathroom fixtures. She didn't exactly nag about the remodel, more like a laborious, steady hammering, as if she marked it on her calendar every ten weeks that it was time to whip out the binder and remind him that the only thing missing from her life was the dream bathroom. She envisioned the room expanding into the space occupied by the oversized linen closet next to it, outfitted with a tile floor and textured walls.

Sure, a modernized bathroom would be nice. The current master bath had linoleum that curled slightly near the combo shower and tub, bubbling up from minor water leaks over the years. The toilet and tub and sink were streaked with pale gold hard water stains. The counter was made of small, glossy tiles, the grout lines like toothpaste. The space was cramped and old. But he didn't understand this need for a palace.

"You should be spending your weekends working on the bathroom," she said.

"I don't see why we need a Taj Mahal bathroom."

"It makes me feel like you don't care about what I want. That you don't want to be closer."

"Exactly how would a new bathroom bring us closer?"

She slammed the cover closed. "Because it would. I could pamper myself."

"I thought the manicures and pedicures and massages were your pampering."

"Quit making it sound like something's wrong with me. Like I want too much. I could have a decent bath without having to bend my knees to fit in the tub. We can afford it, and there's something about a nice bathroom that makes you feel exotic."

"You're already sexy." He leaned toward her but she pushed the binder at him. The corner poked his rib.

"I don't know why you want me to beg for it. You said you'd do it. Six years ago. Six *years!*" She stood and picked up her coke. She took a long swallow and put the glass on the table. "If you don't want to do it ever, then just tell me. And toss the binder because all it does is upset me." She walked out of the room. A moment later he heard her climbing the stairs.

He pushed the binder back to the space in front of her chair. He shoved six pretzel sticks in his mouth and chewed. He wasn't sure why he didn't want to remodel the bathroom. It just seemed like a lot of money and trouble and mess for nothing.

Eleven

WHEN MELODY RETURNED to church that evening with two boxes of food for the homeless supper, the traffic cones were gone. The Prius that had been parked there in the morning was also gone.

She didn't understand why he was being so difficult. Rage oozed out of him, blending with his cigarette smoke, fluttering in his eyelids, forming the rigid muscles around his mouth. After he'd cursed at her, she'd noticed something else behind the rage. Maybe she'd been given the gift of discernment after all, because she felt as if she'd entered his body, that his emotions had become her own. There was a deep ache, an indescribable sense of loneliness and loss. Or were those her own feelings? The sense that God had abandoned her?

One tire went up on the curb and the bottom of the car scraped the concrete as she turned into the empty parking lot. She hated it when that happened. This was the trouble with such an enormous vehicle. She could never get the sense of the length and breadth of it, always felt as if she were misjudging turns and parking spaces. It was too big, and it didn't fit anywhere. The oversized vehicle reflected her body — feet too large to fit into the cutest shoes, long fingers, and gangling arms and legs.

She put the car in park but left the engine running. She closed her eyes and hummed along with the song on the CD. She loved this song. It did something inside her that made her feel as if her heart was expanding until it was able to truly love the whole world, like God asked her to. It seemed as if His love was pumping through her body. She smiled without effort and everything seemed right after all. Even her too-big car.

The next song came on. It had a languid, quiet tune and the female singer's voice, clear and seductive, exhorted her to say *Yes* to the Spirit of God. *There is more required*, the voice reminded her. The song echoed Sarah and the others, many others, insisting she had to yield.

That word was troubling. It made her think of a traffic sign. It implied letting someone else go first, not pushing ahead, but she also wondered if it meant she was supposed to snuff out her personality. Did God want an army of people who were duplicates and triplicates of others? No opinions, no will, no dreams or hopes for their own lives, only numb acceptance? *Yielding?*

She opened her eyes and gripped the steering wheel. This

was the exact opposite of what she should be thinking. She was rebelling. Again. Other people got what they wanted and were still confident they were loved by God, while her life was being peeled away, one thin, semi-transparent layer at a time, and soon, there would be nothing left. She had nothing. No home, unless you counted the condo, but that was simply air space in a building owned by someone else. She had no land. She didn't have a husband or children or a satisfying career. She didn't even have a pet.

She wiped her fingers across her cheeks and turned off the car, abruptly stopping the song just as the woman reached the chorus, about to remind Melody to say *Yes*.

She grabbed her purse and climbed out of the car. She slung the purse over her shoulder, slammed the door, walked to the rear of the car, and opened the trunk. As she leaned in, her purse fell forward and slapped the bumper. The metal clasp clanged against the car. She pushed the purse toward the back of her hip and lifted out the first box of food.

She went to the side door and set the box on the ground. She dug around for her key, and unlocked the door. She held it partially open with her foot and lifted the box, taking care not to strain her back.

When she returned to the open trunk for the second box, she glanced across the street. That morning, he'd seemed on the verge of telling her something important. There was a reason he was so angry with God, a reason he was trying to prevent her from attending church by blocking her parking space. The bright orange plastic was almost like the flames of hell.

That was it! Flames of hell, lining the street, preventing any access to the house of the Lord! Or maybe they were the tongues of fire that appeared on the heads of the Lord's apostles when they were given the gift of speaking in strange languages. She wasn't sure. The first explanation was more likely, and more interesting. It felt right. What was He trying to tell her?

She lugged the second box into the kitchen and set it on the counter. She went outside and looked at the house. Had he been watching her? It seemed that he knew she only needed to park on the street on Sunday mornings and Wednesday evenings, so he hadn't bothered lining his territory with fire to keep her out this evening. Did he block the way when the teenagers met on Friday nights? It might be worth stopping by to find out. If not, this was directed solely at her. So did that mean . . . she wasn't sure what it meant. What she did know was that he was being used by Satan. It was clear she hadn't begun to do battle for his soul. She'd given up too easily.

There was something wounded inside him, something dead. And it was her job to eradicate the evil inside him and lead him to eternal life.

She locked the kitchen door and jogged to the edge of the parking lot and darted across the street. Her sandals thunked the pavement, the buckles rattled, and her skirt flapped up so she had to push it back against her legs as she ran.

The hedge surrounding his front yard was cut with an electric trimmer into the shape of a thick wall with little resemblance to living greenery. She walked through the narrow opening and up the front path. Five wide steps led to the porch. There were two iron chairs set to one side. A thin layer of dirt covered the arms and seats. The welcome mat was rubber on the back with tightly woven carpet glued into the center, announcing she was welcome.

In contrast to the grimy chairs, the porch floor was swept clean. The wood railings and posts and the rest of the house looked recently painted. It was a beautiful old house, a place she'd love to own. There was something comforting about it, the porch and the windows, the one to the left partially open, the drapes hanging still in the warm, early evening air.

She rang the bell.

The deadbolt turned and the door opened. The man stared at her. He wore a pale blue t-shirt with a large basketball logo in the center, surrounded by the words — Golden State Warriors.

"What the hell are you doing here?"

"Our conversation ended badly this morning." She smiled, hoping she looked sympathetic, and not like a threatening younger woman, in case his wife came to the door.

"I don't want you coming to my house."

"The Lord showed me you need . . ."

"I don't need anything, so you should check whether you're

hearing voices, or confusing your own thoughts with thinking there's some kind of god talking to you."

"I can feel your rage. It's frightening."

"Won't god protect you?"

"Yes, but that doesn't mean He doesn't want to deliver you."

He laughed. "Do you know how crazy you sound?"

"I know you want something more or you would have shut the door in my face. But some deeper part of you, your soul, is crying out for help. To be set free."

"Oh, for god's sake."

"See! Look how you call on Him when you're not thinking about it." She felt giddy, excited to see this crack in his protective shell.

He started to close the door. She stuck out her foot and pushed on the door.

"Get your foot out of my house."

"Please listen to me. Just for a minute."

She saw a woman appear behind him in the hallway. She was slim with dark blonde hair and wore a loose navy blue jumper. "Bob? Who are you talking to?" she said.

He pushed harder on the door, narrowing the opening. "Just someone selling something no one wants."

The woman laughed. She turned and walked down the hallway and disappeared from sight.

"Why did you lie to your wife, Bob?" Speaking it for the first time, his name sounded foreign.

"I didn't."

"You said I was a salesperson."

"No, I said you were selling something."

"I'd like to invite you to a worship service. I think you'd be surprised what you'll find."

"I know everything there is to know. I think you'll be surprised what you'll find out, when you're a bit older. When you see that if there is a god, he isn't interested in your puny life. He isn't going to answer your prayers or help you out. And he absolutely isn't talking to you, suggesting you make a nuisance of yourself with a complete stranger."

She stepped forward so she was almost inside the doorframe. If she could touch him, maybe it would soothe the wound in his soul. She wished she could know what had caused that wound. If she took slow, soft breaths, if she stayed open and calm, the Lord would reveal it to her. At least she thought He would. "We're not strangers," she said softly.

He stared at her for a moment. He squinted. "Have we met?"

"No."

"You do look familiar. I've thought that before."

"That's because your soul is reaching out. It sees the Spirit of God in me and it looks familiar, it feels comforting, like home." She spread her arms in case he was ready right now to turn his life over. She would enfold him in a warm hug, feel his muscles relax, his whole body melt as the pain washed out of him, replaced by the fire of God. Her breasts felt heavy, the nipples hardening. Blood rushed to her face and her skin burned. She wasn't feeling attracted to him? Was she? That heaviness, the thick feeling of lead where there should be flesh was the love of God, not something warped and unhealthy. She wanted to move away from the door, but she couldn't. She had to be ready, had to trust. Wasn't that what Sarah and Elise were talking about? Not being ashamed, no matter what happened?

He lunged at her, shoving his hands into her ribs.

She gasped as the air exploded out of her lungs. She fell back. The doormat buckled and her sandal caught on the fold. She fell onto one knee, wincing as her bone slammed into the wood floorboards. "Why are you trying to hurt me?"

"Wake up and recognize how deluded you are."

"Oh, it's so sad." She started to cry. "It hurts me that you reject the Lord so violently."

"Get out of here and don't ever come onto my property again."

"I just wanted to invite you to worship with us, to see how your life could be so much different, so much better."

"My life is fine the way it is. And I wouldn't set foot inside that place if it were the last building on earth."

She stood. She couldn't walk away. Everything depended on bringing him to God. Everything. If she couldn't do this, it proved God had no use for her. There had to be a way to get through to him, but no insight was forthcoming. She couldn't determine the source of his pain and couldn't understand why he was taking it out on her. He'd said she looked familiar. Maybe that was it. She reminded him of someone who'd hurt him. But she didn't know what to do with that information. She felt as if she was scraping the inside of her skull, but no words appeared, nothing that would break through the iron capsule he'd wrapped around his heart. She was pushing too hard. That's what caused his unexpected assault. She needed to be more gentle, befriend him slowly over time. She'd forgotten to listen to what he had to say, to let him think she was considering his doubts and giving them credence.

She moved to the edge of the porch. "I think I've made a mistake. I'm so sorry."

He stepped back into the house. No sunlight came under the roof of the porch and now that he was inside, his face was swallowed by the shadows, causing his voice to sound disembodied.

"Yes, you have."

"We got off on the wrong foot. I'd like to get to know you."

"The feeling is not mutual."

"Can't you give me another chance? I want to understand your beliefs." She took a deep breath. "Maybe there's something to what you say about the world, and how God doesn't really seem to notice what's going on."

He didn't move but she felt a shift in his posture, a weakening of his rage.

"You would realize I'm right," he said.

"Well, I'll see you around."

"As long as you watch your driving. And don't come to my door again."

"Okay."

There was a lightness inside her chest as she walked down the steps. This was the feeling she wanted, of knowing she was filled with God's presence. The absolute joy, the sensation of tiny fireworks exploding inside her — the feeling that was said to accompany the gift of tongues, being completely caught up in something outside your control, a surge of spontaneous pleasure. Not unlike having an orgasm, she'd been told.

She'd yielded to everything, just as they'd suggested. The next time she saw him, she'd listen to everything without arguing, and then she'd be able to lead him to salvation.

Twelve

WHILE ASHLEY WAS driving home from her loser job to her loser bedroom in her parents' house, her smart phone jingled out the generic tone assigned to second-tier friends. She glanced at the phone on the passenger seat — Krista.

That was one person she hadn't really wanted to re-connect with when she'd returned to the Bay Area. They'd seen each other once for coffee. Krista constantly posted notes on her Facebook wall, suggesting movie nights, dinners, *a party for everyone still in the area*, but she never followed up with anything specific. Typical Krista. Refusing to take real initiative. It was one reason Ashley didn't want to resurrect that friendship. She needed people around her who were driven, career-minded, friends who weren't going to settle for average.

There was also the other reason. The guilt. It wasn't only guilt, but honest regret for what she'd done.

It was during junior year. Krista had been going on for months about a new guy that was so hot and not only hot, but really nice. She was in love, she said. If it wasn't love, the potential was definitely there.

During second semester, Ashley had Poli Sci with the hot new guy — Jack Morgan. Immediately she understood Krista's infatuation.

When Ashley and Jack were assigned to team up for their final project, Krista went nuts. She pleaded multiple times a day — during lunch, when they were walking home from school, during phone calls at night — *please find out if he likes me, hint that I like him, set us up. Now that you talk to him every day, there must be something you can do.*

The problem was Ashley really did see how cute he was, and nicer than any guy she knew. Charming. She wanted to go out with Jack herself. And she was pretty sure he might be interested in her, until the day he looked up from the computer they were sharing in the school library, squished up close to each other because the computer stands were arranged to make room for only one person in front of each one. "You're friends with Krista North, aren't you?"

"Uh huh." Ashley opened a new browser window and went to YouTube. She wanted to show him a video, hear his amazing laugh. Playing videos in the library might get them tossed off the computer, but that wouldn't be so bad. They'd be in trouble together.

"Do you think she'd go out with me?"

Ashley brought the mouse to a stop and kept her face turned to the screen while she tried to think. He liked Krista?

How unfair was that? Krista wasn't nearly as cute as Ashley. She was short and her breasts were huge, too big for her body. Of course, guys usually liked that. But in Krista's case, it was kind of extreme. How could he like Krista? He hardly knew her. He'd studied and joked and laughed with Ashley almost every day for three weeks, but he wanted to go out with Krista?

"She thinks she might be gay," Ashley said.

"Really?!"

Ashley nodded, keeping her face turned to the flickering screen. "I mean, I shouldn't have said that. I wasn't thinking. Please don't tell anyone. Please." She turned to face him. "She's not really sure. But she isn't into going out with guys until she figures it out."

"Really? That really surprises me."

"Please don't say anything." She blinked, forcing tears into her lashes. "I feel terrible. It's a secret. Please don't tell anyone."

He put his hand on her leg. "I won't. Don't worry."

But she hadn't been able to stop there. The next time Krista brought it up, Ashley told her she'd tried. "I did talk to Jack about you, like you asked."

"What did he say?"

"I didn't want to tell you."

"Why?"

"I don't want to hurt your feelings."

"So he doesn't like me."

"He doesn't not like you, but he . . ."

"What? What did he say?" Krista's face trembled, her eyes opened so wide she seemed to be missing her eyelids. She stared, her lips parted as if she was an invalid waiting for a sip of water.

"You won't hate me for telling you?"

"I promise. I just want to know. I can handle it."

"He said your boobs are too big. That you look like a cow. I'm really sorry. It's so mean. You can't help how you look."

She shouldn't have believed Krista's vow that she could take it. Krista's face looked like a car going through demolition. Everything crumpled — her lips quivered and her eyes were squeezed in pain, her skin pushed to the center of her face. She started crying. Sobbing. She turned away from Ashley and bent over. Her back heaved as she gasped for air.

For ten or fifteen minutes, Ashley rubbed Krista's back and tried to reassure her. The pain filtered into her own heart and she wished she'd thought of something different. On the other hand, it was sort of true. Krista had an abnormal body shape. And she'd never look at Jack again.

Now, it appeared as though Krista was abandoning her passive-aggressive Facebook friendship and taking the bold step of making an actual phone call.

Ashley drove another block before her phone bleeped to let her know there was a voicemail. Even more interesting — a long message.

Ashley pulled into the driveway. Her parents' cars weren't

there. She grabbed the phone, her purse, and the iced latte she'd bought at Peet's and went up to her room. She clicked on the voicemail.

Krista went on for eighty-three seconds, explaining that she was facing a life-changing moment, that she wanted to reconnect, that she realized she didn't cherish her old friendships enough. Besides that, she was working on a *sort of twelve-step program for psychological healing.* She ended by asking Ashley to meet her A-sap. That's how she said it — *A-sap* — *for wine, or coffee, or whatever.*

Ashley wasn't sure about the twelve-step program. Weren't they a little young for that sort of thing?

The message was too intense. She'd ignore it, Krista would give up.

By the time she finished her latte and changed into jeans and checked Facebook, she was worried. Ignoring Krista might be a bad idea.

She picked up her phone and hit the call back button. They agreed to meet for a glass of wine before Ashley went to Jack's on Friday night. Of course, she didn't mention she was going to Jack's, she mumbled that she had plans. Let Krista connect the dots. There was no reason to rub her face in it. Surely Krista had moved on during the past five years.

KRISTA LOOKED GOOD. Ashley had forgotten about her thick dark hair, long and wavy, and so rich it looked like chocolate. Krista still looked top-heavy, her upper body billowy with the smock-like tops she wore to help divert the jaw-dropping stares she received from men, and often from women.

Ashley slid onto the narrow wicker chair on the sidewalk in front of the wine bar. She wished she'd asked some of her other friends to join them. It was one of those perfect spring evenings, the air like silk, the birds still chirping even though the shadows across the pavement, lengthened every minute.

They each ordered a glass of Pinot Grigio. Krista raised her glass and they clinked the edges.

Without any small talk to catch up, Krista said, "I have news."

"So you said."

"It's scary to say it out loud. I haven't told many people."

"What is it?" Ashley remembered another thing she didn't like about Krista — the drama, the way she forced you to ask her questions.

"I'm having breast-reduction surgery."

"Wow." Ashley put down her glass.

Krista sipped her wine. "I know." She laughed. "I can hardly believe it. My whole life will change."

Agreeing would make it sound as if Krista's life was a mess. Telling her she looked fine would not only sound fake, it would undermine what was probably a huge decision. "Is it dangerous?" Ashley picked up her glass and took two sips of wine. It was sharp and cold. Too sharp.

"No."

"You don't hear about it much."

"It has to be warranted."

"That makes sense."

"Anyway, the reason I was in a hurry to see you is because it's next week."

"Okay. How long do you stay in the hospital?"

"It's out-patient. But they suggested I do some psychological healing to go along with changing my body. It's a huge thing, to change your body like that."

"I guess so."

"And they said I need to deal with the issues first. It will make the surgery come from a positive place instead of something negative — self hatred, or rejecting my body."

Ashley felt like her bra had slipped to one side. The misplaced elastic was making her back itch. She didn't want to adjust it, didn't want to call attention to her own, normal-sized, breasts. She tugged on the side of her dress, hoping that would make everything else shift position. It didn't. She took a sip of wine and glanced around. Everyone was smiling, talking. No one else seemed to be discussing psychological healing and self-hatred. She shivered.

"So I wanted to talk to you about all the stuff that happened in high school."

"All what stuff?"

"You telling me I wasn't sexually desirable."

"I never said that."

"You told me Jack said . . . "

"I told you I was sorry for mentioning it."

"That doesn't matter. It still hurt. They said . . . "

"Who is *they?*"

Krista turned her head. For a moment, they both watched a car try to insert itself into a parallel parking space that was too short. Krista turned back. "Anyway."

"I feel really bad about that."

"Not as bad as I do," Krista said.

"I guess not."

"I know you were only repeating what he said, but you were part of it, so they told me I should talk to you first. You were the vehicle for causing all that pain and self loathing."

"What do you mean?"

"What do I mean about what?"

"That you should talk to me first?"

"Before I talk to Jack."

Ashley took a long sip of wine. She held it in her mouth for a moment and when she swallowed, she coughed at the pinch in her throat. She tugged on her bra, no longer caring if it called attention to her perfectly shaped breasts, her lean body. "You're going to talk to Jack? Why would you do that?"

"To claim my body as my own, so he'll understand that what he thinks about me isn't important any more, that it never was. That I'm beautiful and lovable the way I am, and that I'm taking care of myself . . . for health reasons."

"He probably doesn't even remember."

"That doesn't matter. This is for me."

Ashley wiped her palms on her skirt. The back of her neck was hot and she was suddenly feeling not very sexy at all for her date with Jack. She felt grimy and sweaty and worried she didn't smell all that great. "I don't see why you would expose yourself to that ridicule."

"Because it's empowering."

No matter what Ashley said, Krista was firm. She would call Jack tomorrow. She was going to ask him to meet. She had to see him before her surgery.

Jack hadn't spoken to Krista since high school. Maybe he wouldn't want to bother. Maybe he'd be too busy. If he did talk to Krista . . . there had to be a way to stop this.

She'd arrange activities for the two of them that consumed the entire weekend, make sure he didn't have time to see Krista before Ashley could think of a rock-solid way to keep them from talking. Although now it would be out there, haunting her. Even if she could prevent them talking before the surgery, what about after? What about forever?

JACK'S LIVING ROOM drapes were closed. The TV pulsed with scenes from *Kill Bill*. God, he loved that movie. She didn't see how he could watch it over and over. It made her want to scream. What was the attraction?

She dropped her things on the armchair and walked to the couch. She lowered herself onto his lap and pointed her toes, letting her sandals slide off her feet.

"I love it when you do that." He squeezed her ankle and

ran his hand up her leg, slowing as he reached the hem of her dress, then moving between her thighs, pushing her leg to the side to make room.

She took a long, slow breath.

"You smell like wine," he said. "How'd it go?"

"It was okay."

"What was the occasion?"

She turned her head and kissed him slowly. When they stopped kissing, he shifted her off his lap and hit the remote. "Want to do it? Or are you still boycotting gun owners?" He tugged on the strap of her dress and pulled it off her shoulder.

"Let's go to dinner first. I'm starving."

"Come on, just a quickie."

"I'm really hungry."

"Because of the wine. How many glasses did you have?"

"Just one."

"Why was she so hot to see you?"

She turned her back to him. "Unbutton the back. A quickie sounds fun."

"You can't resist me," he said.

"I can't."

"Gun or not."

"Would you stop talking about the gun and focus?"

He laughed.

After they made love, they dressed as quickly as they'd undressed, and drove to El Gordo's, Jack's favorite. They ordered margaritas, and guacamole to go with the free chips and salsa.

After the server delivered their second round of margaritas, she said, "You know, the gun isn't really a joke." She really didn't have much more to say about the gun, but it seemed to distract him from thinking about Krista. She hoped.

"I know. I was just giving you a hard time."

"More people who have guns die . . ."

"I know."

"I was talking to a guy at work and he said he used to have a gun, but he realized whenever he got angry he thought about the gun. So he decided to get rid of it."

"Just because he thought about it?"

"Because shooting someone never would have crossed his mind, if he didn't have it."

"I got what you meant, but I think it's stupid."

"Do you think you could actually shoot someone?" she said.

"If they came into my house, or attacked you? Sure."

"Really? You could point a gun at some guy and pull the trigger and watch his face explode? Blood and brains spurt out? You wouldn't feel awful or get sick to your stomach? You could stand there while someone died?"

"I never thought about it with so many details."

"You should."

"If someone was attacking me, I would defend myself. I

wouldn't think."

"But what if you got angry? If they weren't attacking you physically, but maybe saying things that pissed you off. Would you shoot them?" She'd never seen him display a temper. He shrugged off things that angered others. But how could she know for sure? Everyone had a point that released uncontrolled anger, didn't they? He might not like being lied to. Even after all these years. People who were manipulative, who didn't own up to their opinions, disgusted him.

"I don't think so," he said.

"But how do you know? Now that you have it?"

"I don't think I would."

"What would make you angry enough to shoot someone?"

"Like I said, if someone was in my house. If someone hurt you, or tried to hurt you."

Did Jack even remember his interest in Krista? Knowing about Krista's huge crush, but wanting Jack for herself, she might have over-estimated his interest. It could have been a casual question. If Krista talked to him, would his perception that she was gay shoot to the top of his mind, like a rubber ball held under water, then released with a slight movement of your fingers? Would he be angry or was he so in love with her now, it wouldn't matter that she'd lied to him? She couldn't predict how he'd react. Strange, since she'd been with him all these years, knew him so well. She had no idea what he'd do. Would he feel so betrayed he'd shoot her? Did people do that? Over something so petty? Cruel, but petty.

The restaurant noises around them grew louder. Drinkers stood shoulder-to-shoulder at the bar, like a group preparing for a line dance, all trying to talk over each other. When Ashley spoke, it was difficult to hear her own words, drowned out by the reverberation of sound inside her head. "I thought it was scary how that guy said he thought about his gun whenever he got upset. I can see how that would happen."

Someone at the bar shouted — a loud, bellow of laughter. No one else joined in, but the general noise ratcheted up another level. She scooted closer to Jack. "Don't you? Don't you see how you might be thinking about it even when you didn't want to?"

"I haven't thought about it at all until you brought it up."

"Nothing made you upset, or got you pissed off, this week?"

"I don't know, probably."

"If you'd gotten really upset, you'd remember."

"People get angry every day."

"I mean really angry, where someone did something to you."

"Like what? I don't know what you're talking about."

"If you felt like someone turned against you. At work. If they gossiped, talked about something you'd asked them not to mention. To your boss."

"My boss knows what I think. There's nothing anyone could say about me. Can we talk about something else?"

"This is interesting. Don't you think it's interesting to

wonder how you'd react in a specific situation?"

"Would you shoot someone that pissed you off?" He shoved a chip into the guacamole and lifted a scoop to his mouth. Crunching and talking, he said, "It sounds like you would."

"I don't know." No one would ever betray her. She'd always had the upper hand and she intended to keep it that way. Like him, she wasn't one of those people who pretended they were one person when the boss was around and became someone entirely different outside the office, or behind a closed door. She didn't gossip. "What if your girlfriend cheated on you? Then would you be upset enough to shoot her?"

"Are you trying to tell me you cheated?"

"No. No, of course not. These are hypothetical questions."

"I'm getting tired of them. I'm not going to shoot anyone."

"You never know what you could be capable of, if your whole world was falling apart."

"Okay. Maybe. If you slept with another guy, if you lied to me. I might think about it. But I would never do it. Thinking and doing are light years apart."

"Not always," she said.

WHEN THEY LEFT the restaurant it was dark, but still warm enough that the night air didn't send goose bumps across her bare shoulders. Her stomach was packed with food and she was pleasantly relaxed without being drunk. She smiled. Okay, maybe a little drunk. Now that she'd eaten all that food, she was glad she'd relented and made love before dinner. Hopefully Jack felt the same way and they could fall asleep without messing around. She felt completely unsexy with beans and tortillas and rice and chicken and grilled vegetables and cheese and salsa and guacamole and chips packed inside like Styrofoam in a shipping crate.

At his apartment, they scrolled through movies and found a comedy that turned out to be lame, as most of them were, yet still had enough funny parts that it wasn't a total loss. Jack poured them each a glass of white wine. It tasted sour after the margaritas and she thought about asking whether he had any tortilla chips, even though she wasn't hungry at all. She sipped her wine slowly and tried not to notice the tartness. If she stopped drinking, her head would clear, and she'd start thinking about Krista.

It was too confusing. She didn't want to move in with Jack, didn't want to think about whether they would wind up together forever, yet she didn't want to lose him. She wanted some kind of sign that he was her soul mate. How did you get that kind of assurance? That proof? She couldn't imagine herself without him, yet his lack of drive to launch a career that had solid upward trajectory made her feel superior and she didn't like to think of herself as a snob.

She wanted a guy she could admire, who wowed her. But why? Didn't that wear off after a while? It might be better to have only one superstar in a relationship. And she definitely planned on being a superstar. No matter what, if he turned out not to be the one, she didn't want Krista destroying what they had with some stupid idea about healing past wounds. Krista should just get over it. It was six years ago. She should have her surgery and focus on the future, not muck around with ancient history.

Before they fell asleep, she put her phone on vibrate and set the timer to go off at two-thirty.

AT FIRST, THE buzzing phone confused her. It rattled against her purse. It seemed as if the vibration was inside her head, her brain buzzing from mixing tequila and what had turned out to be three glasses of wine, not counting the glass with Krista. Finally the neurons connected. She reached down and turned off the alert. She slid out of bed and pulled on Jack's t-shirt. She curled her toes, pressing softly on the carpet as she walked to the doorway. She needed to pee, but the sound and the flushing might wake him. Usually nothing did, but she couldn't risk it.

She went into the spare bedroom, inched the closet door along the track, and knelt down so her shoulders were level with the bottom shelf. She reached to the back and felt the hardness of the gun, still wrapped in the hand towel. She pulled it out and set it on the floor. In the other room, Jack grunted. She sat down and pushed the gun under her legs. It wouldn't do any good. If he woke, if he came into the spare room, he'd see right away what she was doing. The gun pressed against the backs of her thighs. Her legs and feet were cold. She was uncomfortable with her legs straight in front of her, but she waited for several minutes until she was sure he'd settled back into a deep sleep.

When her heartbeat slowed to its normal pace, she twisted to the side and removed the gun. She pulled the towel off. It was such a strange-looking object, so unfamiliar with the iron-hard barrel, perfectly fitted pieces, the ominous opening at the end, and the dark tunnel inside. The wood plate on the handle was smooth and the trigger looked insubstantial for what it was capable of — an irreversible action. A simple press of the finger and the world was changed forever, a human being removed from the planet, no way to bring them back. She felt colder and her eyes watered. She covered the gun, wrapping the towel tightly. She held it close to her stomach, pulled the closet door shut, and crept back to the bedroom. She slid the gun into her purse and moved her wallet and sunglasses so they hid it from view, in case her purse fell open when Jack was nearby.

When she was finally under the covers, she was still cold. She resisted the desire to press herself up against Jack for warmth. He might wake.

It wasn't really clear why she was taking the gun. He'd insisted it would never cross his mind to use it when he was angry. But she didn't fully believe him. He didn't have a very good imagination. He never had. Listening to her co-worker, she'd been terrified. He'd talked about how surprised he'd been by the direction of his thoughts, his voice had been full of awe, shocked and maybe a little disgusted at himself for the darkness the gun exposed in his soul. The only solution was to get it out of Jack's life. Just in case.

Of course, why did she assume Jack would use it if he got pissed off, but until this moment, hadn't considered what possessing it might do to her own state of mind?

Thirteen

BOB FLICKED HIS lighter. The flame shot up and wavered slightly before stabilizing. The only movement in the morning air was the flame, energy pulsing as chemicals were transformed by the tiny spark, so quick it was impossible to see most of the time, but here was the result — a tongue of fire ready to do its work, to start paper and tobacco burning, or the dried leaves scattered on the sidewalk, or his clothing, if he moved it in the wrong direction. He touched it to the tip of the cigarette and inhaled. For a moment, as he closed the cap and extinguished the flame, it looked as if he'd snuffed out its breath, killed a living thing.

The cones were in place. The melancholy image of the flame dissipated as he imagined Melody's arrival.

Whenever he paused to analyze his behavior, he was sickened. He was helpless in the presence of a constant desire to see her squint as she tried to remove tears from her eyes, to see a whisper of desolation across her lips, that moment when she knew there was no god, and that all the things she thought she'd received in answer to prayer were random occurrences.

Nothing was as satisfying as allowing his mind to chew on the perverse pleasure of watching her squirm, waiting for that foolish optimism to slide off her back, revealing a woman who was lost and alone and devoid of fantastical dreams.

Stupidity disgusted him more than any other human trait. He didn't think he was alone in that. How else would you explain the insatiable hunger for reality TV, for the American, and possibly global, fascination with watching people try to eliminate layers of fat, wallow in houses bursting with mountains of garbage and useless possessions, listening to people sing off key and be brought to tears as they were mocked for thinking they had an ounce of talent? No one liked stupidity, and no one liked people who didn't blend in with the herd.

His hatred for her had grown. She refused to listen to him. He could almost hear her gritting her teeth, tightening her facial muscles until she looked like her head would crack wide open. He despised everything about her — that oversized car she was too inept to handle, clothes that made her look as if she'd emerged from a covered wagon, her lank hair, her large frame, and bony hands that looked as if they might have a wider span than his. She had the potential to beat him in a one-on-one game of basketball.

The dulcet tone of her voice was the only pleasing thing

about her, and he found himself wanting that voice to turn raw and ragged as she was faced with the truth that no invisible being was conversing with her, guiding her life, offering kindness, and granting her wishes.

If there was a god, the planet would not be steeped in misery — unbearable physical suffering, black thoughts, emotional pain that some had to tie up and shove to the back of their heart in order to function every day. Watching her crumble might ease some of that pain.

His cigarette was gone and he didn't recall a single inhalation, or a tapping of the stick to release the ashes, yet somehow, they'd fallen on the sidewalk around him. He dropped the butt on the ground and pressed his heel on it, twisting his foot as if he were crushing a large spider, turning it repeatedly, far longer than necessary to complete the job. He pulled out another cigarette. The first drag soothed him and he stopped turning his foot, ripping at the thin paper.

The weeks pivoted around Sundays now. During the workday, he walked and spoke without conscious attention. It was fairly simple. Easily fifty percent of his meetings and discussions at the office were rote, people repeating phrases and buzz words, rehashing mistakes made in the past, predicting different, yet eerily similar mistakes in the future, strategizing over how to work around and within the political machinations that dictated every decision. It was exhausting, and he wondered how he would ever manage to continue on the same course until retirement. If he'd thought about it five or six years ago, he would have considered a career change.

Since his single moment of glory, it had all gone downhill. Somehow, he'd passed by the door, years ago, that might have allowed him to rise in the ranks. If that upward climb didn't begin by your mid thirties, it never happened. The problem was, he hadn't recognized it then. He wondered about the men and women who did. It seemed as if they had a rare, additional gene that allowed them to see the future, to understand early on the way things worked. The rest of the population trudged along and didn't notice the landscape until it was too late to change direction.

He hadn't worn a watch or brought his phone outside, so he had no idea what time it was. Judging by the temperature and the height of the sun, he guessed it was creeping toward nine o'clock.

For a few minutes, his mind softened, taking in nothing but the glossy orange cones, the mad singing of birds as they moved from branch to branch in the magnolia tree next door and out to the curbside trees. Every day of the week, the street buzzed with traffic, but Sundays, except during church hours, it was silent. It made him feel as if he had a large piece of property, located in a more sublime suburb — a neighborhood with wider streets, no cars parked at the curbs, ancient trees and gated driveways, and front yards hidden by brick or stucco walls. That's what moving into executive management got you — a more exclusive neighborhood.

It wasn't that he was bitter. He'd made his choices, he was

satisfied with what he contributed. He was proud of his integrity. The day he'd reported up the chain that his boss had skipped steps and fabricated results in the quality control cycle stood out as the pinnacle of his career. He'd thought a promotion to director might come after that.

His boss was quietly let go. But nothing ever happened for Bob. In some ways he was fine with it. He wasn't sure he wanted the grueling travel and the weekend work of a vice president. Most of those guys, and the occasional woman, worked seven days a week.

He discarded his cigarette butt. He really wanted another, but that would make it three, and he knew he couldn't watch the crazies arrive without the soothing movement of smoke. He needed to exercise self-control. When there were six cars in the lot, then he would start another.

The birds grew louder. The desire for a cigarette increased. What was he trying to prove? No one cared how many cigarettes he had. It was his one indulgence a week. Surely god didn't care. He laughed. He pulled out the pack and lit another. The smoke bit into his lungs and he was glad he hadn't denied himself.

"How many cigarettes have you had?"

He turned.

Dana stood in the opening between the two sides of the hedge. She wore a beige cotton blouse with tiny sleeves and belt-less blue jeans. He liked the way the jeans were loose around her hips, that she didn't look all strapped and buckled into place. Her feet were bare. He smiled.

"What are you grinning at?"

"You look nice."

"Thanks. But don't change the subject."

Her hair was pulled back into a short ponytail, her bangs tucked under a narrow silver hair band. She wasn't wearing any makeup and it made him want to kiss her, but she'd push him away because of tobacco breath. Standing near the hedge, she looked small and fragile. He wanted to pull her close and walk inside the house, shut out the world. But he couldn't. Not right now.

"I'm not changing the subject." He dropped the cigarette on the concrete and stepped on it, keeping his gaze on her face. "You really do look nice. And I've had three or four."

"Why do you have to do that?"

"Smoke on Sundays?"

"Stand there and stare at the church all the time? It's weird." She crossed her arms and tilted her head to look past him. "Where did those cones come from?"

He stepped to the side as if he could block her view, but of course it was too late. "There's that woman who can't drive and . . ."

"Did you put them there? Where did you get traffic cones?"

She walked past him and out to the curb. She stared at the first cone as if she expected it to explain its own existence. He waited for her to bend over and pick up the cone. If she did, her shirt would pull up and he could see her soft, smooth skin.

He walked up behind her and put his hand on her hip. She moved away. "You smell like stale smoke."

"I ordered them. I told you about that woman who blocks the driveway."

"You have both sides blocked."

"To be on the safe side."

"The safe side of what?"

"To make sure she doesn't park here."

"You're crazy." She backed along the curb, keeping her eyes on him. Her lips looked like they were about to part, but they didn't.

"She can't control her car. And she can't park to save her life."

"Who cares? Besides, she can't be going that fast, she wouldn't have time to get to the speed limit between the stop sign and our house, and no one is trying to get out of the driveway. Your truck is in the street."

"It's the principle."

"The principle of what?" She took a step back. Her foot slid off the edge of the curb. She stumbled, coming down hard on her left leg. "Ow."

"Are you okay?" He stepped forward and held out his hand.

She put her hand in his and he helped her onto the curb, even though it wasn't necessary.

"Don't you see how it looks? Standing out here smoking, staring at them every week? Now this." She swept her arm along the street. "You seem unhinged."

"There's nothing wrong with me. The people who go to that church are the crazies. You've seen them. And heard them."

"They're joyful."

"Is that what you think?"

"Yes. Maybe if you trusted God more, you'd be happier."

"I don't believe in god."

She smiled. "Keep telling yourself that."

He didn't want to fight. If he had a cigarette, it would distract him, but it would do nothing to draw them back toward each other. They stood in silence for several minutes. He heard a car approach and pull into the parking lot, followed quickly by another. He didn't look.

"Please move the cones."

"They should have provided adequate parking."

"It's a public street."

He walked along the curb to the house next door and stepped into the street. He picked up the first cone, grabbed the second and shoved it inside the first. At least feeling them fit together so snugly gave a glimmer of satisfaction, the pleasure of well-made objects, but he hoped Melody didn't come flying around the corner and see him giving up. She'd crow about how his heart had been changed and her prayers answered.

Dana picked up the cones on the other side and they met at the center of the driveway apron. She smiled and handed her stack of cones to him. She rubbed his arm. "Do you want some more coffee? And an omelet?"

He held the cones like he was carrying a large child. He walked up the driveway. "That sounds good. In a while. I'm going to have one more smoke."

She sighed. She walked between the sides of the hedge and disappeared from view.

HE'D ONLY TAKEN a single puff on a fresh cigarette when the Buick careened around the corner and flew up to the curb in a skid and a screech of triumph. There was no hesitation, as if she'd known there would be a space for her.

Carefully, he sucked in a bit of smoke, removed the cigarette from between his lips, and exhaled. If he continued the rhythmic motions, it would prevent him from running to the curb and pounding his fist in the center of the hood, already pocked with several small dents. He put the cigarette back between his lips and puffed slowly. He used his thumb and forefinger to remove it again while he blew out another stream of smoke. Inhale. Pause. Release the smoke. Don't think.

The car door flew open and Melody climbed out. She looked at him and smiled. She waved.

Once again he placed the cigarette between his lips.

"Good morning! Thank you for removing the cones."

She hauled bible, purse, and sweater out from the back seat and slammed the door. His left shoulder twitched at the sound of the impact.

She walked to the edge of the driveway. "I could hug you."

He folded one arm across his ribs and rested his opposite elbow on his forearm.

"How are you doing today?" she said.

"Fine."

"You look sad."

"Not at all."

"I don't think that's an honest answer."

"It's the answer."

"God wants to give you so much."

"Did he give you that car?"

"Yes."

"No thanks, then."

"There's a lot more to life than earthly possessions."

"Your earthly possession is blocking part of my driveway."

"Just a little bit."

"Move it or I'll have it towed."

"What can I do to start over with you? I don't like to have enemies." She walked toward him.

"The bible says people are either on god's side or against him — no middle ground," he said. "If you're on his side, you'll have enemies."

"I don't like to think of it as taking sides."

"Good and evil," he said. He blew out a puff of smoke,

but she stood her ground.

"It doesn't have to be that way."

"You're right, it doesn't. But people who preach what you do have made it that way."

"You seem to know the word of God," she said.

"Most educated people do."

"No they don't."

His cigarette was getting dangerously low, but there was no reason he couldn't have another. She was following his lead, getting drawn into an argument she couldn't win. Of course, they never cared if they won. They retreated to senseless statements, performed like Buddhist koans. The problem was, they didn't recognize the koans for the paradoxical riddles they were, acting as if they were coherent arguments. Or maybe she was sucking him into *her* agenda.

"How come you know the word of God so well?" she said.

He dropped his cigarette butt on the ground. He was all smoked out. That omelet sounded good. With a few splashes of Tabasco. Maybe Dana would scramble up some shredded potatoes. His stomach grumbled. He turned toward the house.

"I'm praying for you," she said.

"I'm sure you are."

"You'll come to see how much you need the Lord."

He spit on the sidewalk. "What has he done for you?"

"Given me eternal life."

"Nice. If there's eternal life, shouldn't everyone get it?"

"Not if they reject Him."

"That's kind of small-minded, don't you think?"

"You're saying it all wrong."

"So what else has he given you?"

"That's all I need."

"Then why are you at the church praying all the time, if you have everything you want?"

She glanced across the street. He could see she was struggling to swallow.

"It doesn't mean you can't ask for things. It's amazing the things He's done. Healing people, fixing broken marriages. It makes your heart just . . ."

"That's enough."

"Why won't you listen to me? It makes you seem pig-headed or uneducated that you won't even listen, won't even consider the evidence that God is working in the world, that He wants to help you and be in your life."

He wanted to smack her face with the real evidence — a man could plead with a nameless, faceless being for years and be ignored until he realized what a fool he was, talking to thin air, acting as if someone were listening, waking up one day to see how pathetic he was, on his knees, fingering beads, believing some superior being cared about him. But why would he tell her that? If he did, she'd gain the upper hand.

An urge to attack, hurt, inflict physical damage, pumped through his blood vessels. He stared at her face. It was pale, as if she'd been caught in the rain and all the normal color variations had been sluiced clean — her eyebrows barely visible where she stood in the shadow of the hedge, and her light gray eyes like those cheaply made silver balls his mother used to hang on the Christmas tree. Her lips were like coffee with too much cream and even her hair was drained of color. It made him want to slap her cheeks until they bloomed red, punch her jaw and neck until her skin exploded with purple florets.

He took a step back and shoved his hands in his pockets. It didn't help much. The desire was still there, pounding like something trapped in his chest, demanding to be let out.

She was beyond stupid. The things he'd said to her pinged off her like bullets hitting an iron wall. And she accused him of not listening? He knew he should let it go. It wouldn't do anything for his life to bring her to her knees, force her to abandon the fairy tale. But he couldn't. He couldn't stop looking at her blank, moderately stupid eyes, listening to her delusional words. Mocking her satisfied some deep inadequacy, some unrecognized flaw in himself. He wanted to turn away, but instead, he was a rubber-necker at a gory accident.

"I can see you aren't ready, yet," she said. "I'm going to be late. But I'm enjoying talking to you every week. I hope you know I'm here to listen, that the Lord is listening. And thank you for offering me a parking space.

"I didn't offer you a parking space, you dumb bitch."

She gasped. She closed her eyes and lifted her free hand up

toward the sky. She murmured something, but he couldn't decipher the words. Maybe it was that speaking in tongues thing.

He thought about going into the house, leaving her standing on the sidewalk looking like an escapee from a psych ward, but the minute he started to turn, she dropped her hand and opened her eyes.

Her voice was soft and whispery. "It's not the time. It's not the time." She turned and stepped off the curb. Like she always did, she crossed without looking for oncoming traffic.

He lit another cigarette. The omelet still sounded good, but he was unsettled. *Very* unsettled. He sensed he was losing the battle.

Fourteen

AS MELODY PULLED open the door into the lobby, Mike, a regular guest at the Sunday evening dinners, appeared in her peripheral vision. He shuffled across the strip of grass that ran alongside the church. He stopped before he reached the paved area around the sign and leaned against the side of the building.

"Bitch," he said.

She felt the pinch of tears in her eyes. Twice in less than five minutes a man had directed that degrading, filthy word at her. She knew it wasn't about her. Language like that was all about the person using it. But it burned. It made her feel dirty and unattractive and sub-human. Did men know that when they tossed the word around? Was that the intent, or was it the only word they knew to get your attention in a negative way, something to make them feel superior? When she heard it, she hated every man on the planet. God hadn't made them that way, but so many of them had deteriorated into monsters. She didn't want to call them animals because animals were decent and good.

"Dinner isn't until this evening," she said.

"I know that," Mike said.

"Okay." Her arm ached from the pull of the door, but walking inside and leaving him behind was rude. "Did you need something?"

"Bitchy bitch."

"You've been drinking. You can't eat dinner here unless you get sober. That's the rule."

He grinned. The bulge of his teeth beneath his gums was visible. She hardly noticed his teeth, surrounded like they were by slimy, bright pink gums, as if she was looking at the inside of his body, seeing flesh exposed to the world for the first time.

Sarah and Gordon Wilson came along the sidewalk and turned up the path.

"Good morning," Sarah smiled and gave a half wave.

Melody wasn't sure if the greeting was for her, or Mike. She smiled.

"Did you want to join us for the service?" Sarah paused and looked at Mike. "You know you're welcome."

"I think he's drunk," Melody said.

"Oh." Sarah walked toward the lawn. "Go get some rest. We'll see you at dinner." She turned back and put her hand on Melody's shoulder. "How are you?"

Gordon held the door, relieving Melody of its weight.

"Good," Melody said. Everything about the simple word felt like a lie so huge it threatened to explode her intestines.

Mike turned and walked toward the back of the building, disappearing from view, hopefully able to find a place to sleep where the police wouldn't nudge him to move along.

The three of them went inside. "Do you want to have lunch with us after the service?" Sarah said.

Melody nodded. "Okay. Sure."

Sarah cocked her head and smiled. It looked warm and true and seemed to suggest that Melody's failure to speak in tongues was the furthest thing from Sarah's mind.

SOMEHOW, NEAR THE end of lunch with Sarah and Gordon, the conversation took an abrupt and awkward turn.

"Do you have a boyfriend?" Sarah's voice was kind and casual, genuinely interested. "I've never seen you bring anyone to church."

Gordon sipped his tea and looked past Melody's head, surveying the rest of the strip mall outside the picture window.

"No." Melody scooped up a forkful of fried rice. She hoped Gordon would bring his attention back to his companions, that he'd change the subject. She didn't understand this sudden interest in her dating life. First Elise, now this. Out of nowhere.

"Anyone you're interested in?" Sarah said.

"I don't really think about it." She shoveled in another

forkful of rice.

"Most people need a companion."

"I have friends, at work." Did she? Most of her time was spent at church. Wasn't that how it should be, a life built around a community of people with common views? When she went to dinner or a movie with her co-workers, she felt out of place and slightly uncomfortable, as if she had to keep the majority of her thoughts to herself.

"But not a mate." Sarah smiled, keeping her lips stretched wide until her expression looked frozen. "Still, you're young, there's plenty of time."

Before she could think, Melody said, "I was engaged once." As if her tongue had disconnected itself from her brain, she continued spilling information she'd always kept to herself. "It didn't work out. And after that, I told the Lord I would devote my life to Him."

"You can have both."

"I know. But I'm fine. I'm happy."

"Was it a bad experience? I don't mean to pry. Just say so if you don't want to talk about it."

Suddenly, she did want to talk about it. Sarah's eyes were kind. Gordon continued to stare out the window, giving no indication he was even listening. Melody's chest flooded with warmth. Sarah cared about her, she really wanted to hear about Melody's life. "It turned out he was on the fence about God — my fiancé."

Sarah nodded. Gordon refilled his teacup, then dribbled

golden tea into Sarah's tiny cup. Melody was glad he wasn't speaking, she felt almost as if he wasn't there, as if she could open her heart to Sarah, that maybe Sarah wasn't judging her after all. Maybe. "After we got engaged, he assumed we'd start having sex."

Sarah nodded again. Melody wished Sarah would say something more, help her talk about memories still tinged with pain. Maybe this was another test. She needed to stop being ashamed of her feelings and experiences, she needed to be bold, to speak out. She did need to loosen her tongue. "The minute that diamond slid over my knuckle everything changed!" She laughed. She curved her hand over her teacup. "He acted as if he owned me, as if what I wanted didn't matter. He said it was stupid to think God cared about whether or not people had sex."

"Oh, but He does," Sarah said.

"I know! And Bruce refused to believe that. It started to seem like instead of loving me, he just wanted things from me. He said I was a prude. He broke up with me." Her voice shook. She tried to sip her tea, but couldn't get the liquid to flow toward her lips, fearing it would dribble down her chin. She put the cup down and pushed it away. "It felt like . . . I think he only wanted to use my body. He didn't love me at all."

Sarah moved the teacup back toward Melody's side of the table. When Melody didn't touch it, she nudged it closer. "I really did love him. If I slept with him, maybe he would have taken me back. But I knew I had to choose between him and God."

"The right man will come into your life at the perfect time." Sarah pressed her lips together. Her eyes flicked past Melody's shoulder, unable to hold her gaze, shrinking from the pain that Melody knew was clouding her eyes.

Melody sipped the cold tea. She waited for Sarah to say something, unsure what she wanted to hear. Any words acknowledging that Sarah actually heard and understood what Melody was saying, anything that would let her know she wasn't completely alone, that she'd eventually find true friends at Triumphant Life, that she wouldn't always feel isolated, standing outside the window, looking in. She took another sip of icy tea. She put the cup down and pushed it away again.

"It's admirable that you put the Lord first," Sarah said.

Melody smiled. She wanted to ask why God didn't love her enough to give her the gift of tongues. Was she required to deliver Bob's soul on a platter? Maybe all these people had done something remarkable for God before they were granted special gifts, and she just didn't know about it. She wished Sarah would tell her, but Sarah smiled weakly and pushed the teacup back to Melody's side of the table.

MELODY PULLED INTO the church parking lot. Elise's Audi was there and the door to the kitchen propped open with a wooden wedge. She got out of the car. Across the street, Bob was clipping stray branches from his hedge.

She waved, but he didn't wave back. Maybe he hadn't noticed her. Thin clouds were scattered across the sky. They promised to create a beautiful sunset, but by the time the dinner and cleanup was complete, it would be dark.

Inside the kitchen it smelled of roasting chicken and potatoes. Elise wore pale tight-fitting jeans and a flowered sleeveless top. Her hair was pulled into a ponytail and folded in half. She stood at the counter slicing tomatoes. Her feet were bare. It was unsanitary and possibly dangerous, but Elise wasn't a person you corrected. She did what she wanted and it always seemed to work out for her.

"Smells delicious," Melody said.

"Thanks."

"Did Ken already set up the tables?"

"He didn't come tonight, he's finishing up our taxes."

"Okay. I'll do it."

The sound of another car pulling into the lot came through the open door. Most likely Sarah and Gordon, unless all the men were procrastinators and Gordon also had to finish preparing their tax return. Melody had filed hers in February.

She went into the main hall and angled the first table away from the stack leaning against the wall. It was more of a two-person job, setting the tables on their edges, pulling out the metal legs, snapping them into position, turning them upright, and dragging them into place, although Elise had managed by herself.

One table would hold the food. The other three would be

set perpendicular to it, surrounded by eight or nine chairs each. The conversations usually ranged from depressing, to slightly bizarre and incoherent, to dead silence. The guests never wanted to hear about God, unless they launched into a monologue covering their own views on the subject. Still, she was hopeful that as the members of Triumphant Life persevered over the months and years, their guests' crusty, battered hearts would open up.

She loved cooking and serving food to the homeless. When she ate, she looked around the table and prayed for each soul buried inside thick, scarred skin and faded, cast-off clothing. As she watched them eat, she was aware of God's heart, buried inside hers, beating in a shared rhythm. The muscle of her heart seemed to expand until she ached with love for the entire world. She wasn't sure how, but she knew that at some point, she wanted to find a way to help other churches offer a similar program, until the city was blanketed with love. That's how the world got changed — one person at a time. If nothing else, she would leave the world with less hunger, less pain than she'd found when she entered. Unless those things were multiplying faster than anyone could keep up.

It angered her when she encountered people who enjoyed secure jobs and owned large, comfortable homes, whose most pressing difficulty was being required to provide their own shopping bags at the grocery store, yet complained viciously about homeless human beings soiling their neighborhood. They acted as if a few missteps, a lost job, or an addiction to alcohol meant you didn't deserve to live.

At five-thirty, people began arriving. It was a small group tonight. There were two women who always looked apologetic, both with graying hair — Cora wearing jeans and a red sweatshirt even though it was warm out, and Pam dressed in beige slacks and a white polo shirt with a faded logo. Five men joined them — all regulars.

Mike was the last to arrive. He appeared to have calmed down from the morning, but as he walked across the hall, he jerked his head around every few steps, glancing over his shoulder as if he expected someone else to enter the building behind him. Maybe he was as surprised by the small group as she was.

Once the food was set out, Melody stood behind Mike in the line. He put two pieces of chicken on his plate and stepped to the right. He scooped up three large spoonfuls of potatoes, arranging them carefully next to the chicken to leave space for the rest of the meal. Next was a pot of baked beans, followed by a bowl of corn, and a huge metal bowl of salad.

As he reached for the ladle in the pot of beans, he glanced over his shoulder again. He twitched to the left and glanced over the other shoulder.

"Is everything okay?" Melody said.

He glanced over his right shoulder. His arm trembled and the ladle fell out of his hand.

"Can I serve you some beans?" Melody said.

He reached for the ladle again and looked toward the kitchen. The door to the hallway between the kitchen and the worship hall was closed.

"Are you worried about someone who isn't here?" Melody said.

He smelled of alcohol. It was stale, not as if he'd just taken a drink, but as if it flowed through his veins and seeped out his pores, saturating his hair and clothes. The odor hadn't been noticeable when he arrived, but now she worried they had been too quick to welcome him. Although the guests were told they wouldn't be allowed in if they arrived drunk or high, there wasn't any definite plan for addressing that situation if it happened.

The thick paper plate, soaked with juice from the chicken and a puddle of butter from the potatoes, slipped out of Mike's hand. It hit the edge of the table and fell on the floor with a soft, wet sound. He grunted.

Melody put her plate on the table. "It's okay. I'll throw it away and you can start over."

"Bitch," he said.

"Please don't talk like that. I'll clean this up and you can get another plate." She put down her own plate and knelt on the floor.

"Bitchy bitch."

She started to cry. It didn't mean anything. He was intoxicated, or crazy. It wasn't about her. It was about whatever story was reeling through the calcified pathways in his brain. Still, he wasn't saying it to Elise or Sarah. It seemed that the crazy part in him connected with some wounded part inside of her and the two entities were communicating with each other, one lower nature lashing out at another. "Please don't. I want to help you."

He shoved his hip against the table. The ladle flipped out of the pot of beans and fell to the floor on the opposite side.

He stumbled back and stepped on her fingers. She yelped and looked up just in time to see him lift the pot of beans. She inched to the side to take cover under the table, but his foot was still on her fingertips. He turned the pot upside down and twelve cups of warm, soupy beans poured onto her head.

Sarah cried out. Elise's bare feet smacked the floor as she ran to the kitchen.

"Hey!" Gordon shouted.

The beans and liquid ran across her face and down her neck. They weren't hot enough to burn. They felt strangely warm and comforting, and revolting. She'd never get the mess out of her hair and wiped off her skin without a shower. She didn't want the others to see her.

Mike's foot slid off her fingers and she fell to the side, curled into a ball.

She saw Gordon's feet circle around. He grabbed Mike. Gordon was not a large man but he managed to drag Mike away from her range of vision. The other male guests had moved away from the table and stood watching. Through the beans she saw that Cora and Pam remained in their seats, cutting up chicken.

"Someone. Do something." Elise had returned.

Elise's voice was quiet but not because the room was silent, because the sound was muffled by beans clogging Melody's ears. She remained curled in a ball, half under the table, half expecting another assault.

"Who are you calling?" Elise said. "You can't call 9-1-1 from a cell phone."

Melody heard Sarah's voice. "Can you come to the church? We had an incident. Do you mind?"

"Who's that?" Elise said.

"Gordon's brother. He lives a few blocks away. He's a big guy, he can help."

"Call the cops," Pam shouted.

Melody heard Elise's bare feet behind her. Elise reached down and tugged her out from under the table. "I'm so sorry," she said. She wiped Melody's face with a paper napkin. "Are you okay?"

Melody nodded.

Sarah took one arm, Elise the other, and they pulled her to her feet. "I don't want to call the police," Sarah said. "We can handle this. Let's clean up and then we can pray for Mike."

Melody couldn't help wondering why the Lord hadn't helped Mike before he poured a pot of beans on her head. She whispered His Name to herself, trying to accept what had happened, to erase the feeling of disgust, to stop noticing the smell of baked beans, cringing as a thin layer of gluey liquid hardened on her skin.

"I'll mop up," Sarah said.

While Sarah urged the other men to fill their plates with food before it got cold, Elise led Melody toward the women's restroom.

The paper towels soaked with warm water shredded as Elise dragged them across Melody's face. After the worst of the mess was wiped out of her hair and off her clothes and skin, Elise directed Melody to bend over the sink.

Melody's back stiffened from the awkward position, trying to make herself small enough to get her head under the faucet.

Elise took a small paper cup from the dispenser on the wall and filled it with water. She poured it through Melody's hair and combed the strands with her fingers. The water was warm on the back of Melody's neck, but the small cupfuls didn't penetrate to her scalp.

"I'm not going to be able to get all of it out," Elise said.

"That's okay. But thanks." Her voice echoed off the porcelain.

After fifteen or twenty more cups of water, Elise turned the faucet off. "Stay there for a minute, I forgot to bring a towel."

The bathroom door opened and closed. Melody's knees ached and her muscles quivered from holding the awkward position. She tried not to think about the beans, tried not to drown in self-pitying questions that couldn't be answered. She was in the wrong place at the wrong time. Things like that happened to everyone. God was not singling her out.

A few minutes later Elise returned with a dishtowel. She patted the water out of Melody's hair, then handed her the towel so she could dry her face and neck.

When they returned to the hall, the guests were eating. Sarah had joined them. "Gordon's in the kitchen with his brother and Mike."

"Shoulda called the cops," Pam muttered. "Shoulda called the cops. Shoulda . . ."

Sarah put her hand on the Pam's wrist. "Do you want another piece of chicken? Or should I get the cookies?"

Pam stood and went to the food table. She put another piece of chicken on her plate. Melody and Elise followed, filling their plates. They went to one of the empty tables and sat down.

Melody cut off a piece of chicken breast. She wanted to go home. Her wet, still-goopy hair, and the sugary smell of beans on her clothes had taken away her appetite. She put a piece of potato in her mouth and chewed. No matter how guilty she felt abandoning the others, she was not staying to help clean up. Any person with half a heart would understand.

A few minutes later Gordon and his brother came into the worship hall. No wonder they'd called him — Gordon's brother was easily six feet, five inches tall. He had broad shoulders and reddish-brown hair cut short, gelled so it stood up at the crown of his head in a way that looked good without trying too hard. He wore a black t-shirt, jeans, and work boots. His arms were thick with muscle and lightly tanned. As they approached the cluster of tables, Melody had the disturbing thought that her head would fit inside the palm of his hand.

"This is Tim," Gordon said. "He took Mike outside, gave him a few bottles of water and a piece of chicken, and told him to find some place to calm down."

"I hope he doesn't get hurt," Sarah said.

Gordon and Tim filled their plates. They sat across from Melody and Elise.

"You okay?" Tim looked at Melody.

She thought about the reddish brown slime smeared across her shirt and visible in her hair despite all of Elise's effort with the tiny paper cup. She wasn't sure if she looked ridiculous or pathetic. Tim's dark brown eyes looked directly into hers, almost as if he didn't notice her hair or the coating of bean juice.

"Sure. I'm fine."

They ate in silence for a few minutes.

"You wonder what makes people drink too much," Tim said.

"Numbing the pain," Melody said.

"I wonder if it works."

"It must or they wouldn't do it."

"It makes you feel helpless," he said. "When a person can't control it, can't seem to stop."

She glanced up. He was staring at his plate. He stabbed his fork into a tomato and put it in his mouth, chewing methodically. Or maybe everyone chewed methodically and she'd never noticed. She felt her own jaw moving. There was a rhythm to it. She swallowed.

He told her he was a graphic designer. It was difficult to picture — a man so large, doing detailed work with a computer mouse.

After she was finished eating, she tossed her plate and napkin in the trash. No one looked resentful when she said she was going home. Elise gave her a hug, not seeming to care if she got bean juice on her shirt or her bare arms. Tim shook her hand and she wondered again how such a large man had been drawn to graphic design and whether he required a specially sized computer mouse.

Outside, the air smelled sweet and her clothes and hair felt less disgusting. The beans poured on her head, Mike cursing at her instead of the others, his aggression — they were signs from God, but she had no idea what they meant or how she was supposed to respond.

She got in the car and turned the CD up loud enough to feel the bass in her arms and legs. She sang along all the way home, eager for a long soak in the tub with fruit-scented bubbles.

Fifteen

ASHLEY UNLOCKED THE front door and went into the house. Her mother wasn't in the kitchen. She walked through the empty rooms and glanced out at the backyard. The grass was dark and lush in a thick covering from the steps of the porch to the covered patio at the opposite end, agapanthus growing along the length of the side fence, all the dead leaves from winter plucked clean. Evidence of her mother filled the yard but it looked vacant, waiting for human life.

She climbed the stairs. As she neared the top, she looked down the hallway. Her mother stood in the doorway of Ashley's bedroom. Sunlight poured through the window, casting her mother in a shadow, making it impossible to read her expression.

"Hi," Dana said.

"Why are you in my room?" The gun was inside a shoebox at the bottom of the stack of boxes in her closet, surely her mother wouldn't go digging through shoeboxes.

Ashley was constantly aware of the gun's presence, worried that it somehow posed a danger, although she couldn't say what that would be since no one else knew it was there, and she would never take it out, never even think about firing it. But it pressed on her mind. She found herself thinking about it the minute she woke in the morning. It floated through her thoughts when she was on the computer, or lying in bed texting her friends.

"I opened your window. It's stuffy up here and I wanted the cross-breeze."

"Oh. Okay."

"Why do you sound so anxious? Are you hiding pot in there?" Dana laughed.

"Of course not. I don't sound nervous."

"Yes you do."

"How can you say that? It's not like you can read my mind."

"I know you. I've known you since you were the size of my pinky." Dana held up her little finger and smiled.

"Well I'm not nervous."

Dana moved to the side and Ashley went into her room. She opened the closet and hung her purse on the hook. She glanced at the floor. The shoeboxes were stacked in the same order as always. At least she thought they were. She wasn't definite about which boxes had been at the top of the two stacks. She closed the door and turned. Her mother looked like she wanted to say something but couldn't bring herself to speak the words.

"Why are you staring at me like that?"

"I'm surprised you put your purse in the closet."

"Don't read into every little thing I do."

"You've been distracted or upset the past few days."

Ashley smiled. "I'm not."

"Okay." Dana pushed her hair off her face. "I'm going to start dinner."

"I'll be down in a minute."

"Thanks."

Dana thumped along the hallway. When she reached the stairs, there was no more sound.

In her mind, Ashley saw her mother's toes curling over the edges of the steps, trying to secure her foothold as she walked down the stairs. It was odd that she knew how her mother's toes curled over the edges of the steps in that way. She supposed it was the same as her mother's awareness of Ashley's quirks and gestures and tone of voice, it was knowledge that buried itself in your core after years of living with another person.

She pulled her phone out of her pocket, kicked off her shoes, and flopped on the wrinkled sheets, pushing her comforter toward the foot of the bed. Her mother hadn't complained about the unmade bed, or the clothes from the day before scattered across the carpet, or even the plate with a pizza crust sitting near her computer. Had she been poking around?

She got up and went to the closet. She opened the door and pulled out the glossy black shoebox where she'd put the gun. She removed the lid. Nothing looked different. She unfolded the towel and stared at the gun. The attraction was baffling, the desire to gaze at it and test its weight in her hand. She'd never been to a shooting range and had no idea how loud it was or how hard it was to aim, whether it was scary to know a bullet was rocketing through the air. It was so easy to make a mistake with something like this. She should get rid of it, but how did you get rid of a gun? Besides, it belonged to Jack. Had he noticed it was missing? Surely he would have mentioned it if he had. He claimed he didn't think about it. Maybe he was telling the truth.

Somewhere deep in the frame of the house, wood and plaster creaked. She glanced at the doorway. She flipped the towel over the gun and shoved it in the box. She felt jittery. It wore at her, wondering whether Krista had contacted Jack, wondering if her life was going to dissolve one piece at a time. Since she'd returned home she felt like the parts of herself were falling away, one after the other, her world shrinking. Soon, she'd be transformed back into a child, living in this same room, waiting for her life to start.

She slid the box back into place. She changed into shorts and a tank top and lay back down on the bed. She typed a text message to Jack — *My day was shit. Yours?*

The phone was silent. She placed it next to her.

First, she'd moved home and most of her independence

melted away as if it never existed. She no longer went out when she felt like it, never seemed to do anything spontaneous, always required to report to her parents. It wasn't as if they would prevent her from doing what she wanted, but she hated having to provide the information. Her roommates hadn't cared. Sometimes they'd given explanations, sometimes they hadn't.

Then she started work — sitting at a reception desk in an echoing lobby for six hours a day, the temperature set too low, shivering and unable to leave her post to pee without calling one of the administrative assistants to sit in her chair, because God forbid someone sneak into the company and steal . . . what? All their information was in computers. And the computers were protected with passwords. What were they so afraid of? Of course, you never knew when some pissed off person might come in with a gun. But if that happened, what about her? She was a well-placed target at the front desk. Maybe she should bring the gun to work. She laughed. Here she was thinking about it again.

She picked up her phone even though it hadn't alerted her of a returned text. The screen was dark. She got up and kicked her jeans and two shirts into a single pile, shoving them toward the closet door. If anyone looked inside now, she'd know. Her parents never went through her things, there was no reason to be concerned, yet knowing it was in there, bullets in the clip, called for extra caution. She had a feeling her mother would be furious if she knew of its existence.

The screen on her phone was still empty. She pressed the button anyway. No new messages. She shoved it in her pocket and went downstairs, trying not to think about whether her toes were drawn to curling over the edges of the steps, a genetic pattern she was powerless to control.

Dinner was wild rice and chicken-apple sausage. Tomatoes and yellow peppers for a salad were sliced on the cutting board. A bag of lettuce, an avocado, and a can of garbanzo beans sat nearby.

"Will you wash the lettuce and slice the avocado?"

"Sure." Ashley patted her pocket to make sure the phone was settled securely. Jack should have texted back by now. Unless he was in the car. Or talking to Krista.

"What are your plans?" Dana said.

"Probably watch TV."

"Not tonight. Long term."

"Every time I try to talk to you about it you shut me off."

"Well now I'm asking."

"It feels like you want to be rid of me." She tore open the bag of lettuce mix, emptied it into the colander, and turned on the water.

"I just don't like the drifting."

"Aren't you and Dad drifting? What are your plans?" She glanced over her shoulder. Her mother looked shocked.

"Our life is settled."

"I'm only twenty-three. Besides, it's hard. I thought I'd get a job right away." She patted the lettuce dry with a paper towel and dumped it into the salad bowl.

"You aren't putting in enough effort. I bet they have some full time positions open at TechGuard."

"I don't want to work there." She made a slice around the avocado, cutting deep until the knife touched the pit. She pried the pieces apart, removed the pit, and set one half on the counter. She made a cut in the thick skin and peeled it back gently, careful not to tear off the soft green fruit that was reluctant to let go of its skin. "I didn't think it would be like this. I have a great resume, awesome references."

"Not everyone gets to have a glamorous career."

"I know. But I worked hard for this. A degree from Northwestern should guarantee me something."

"There aren't any guarantees."

"I know that. I just didn't think it would be this hard." Another strip of skin came loose from the avocado. She dropped it into the garbage and picked at another spot with the tip of the knife. "I have an idea, though."

"What's that?"

"I was thinking I could make a video. Tell a story about someone who overcame a huge problem, something really awful, or was still in the middle of a horrible situation. I'd do some interviews and edit it with music and other images. And post it on YouTube. Maybe it would go viral and I could get some leads."

"That sounds like nothing more than playing the lottery."

"It's how a lot of things work now."

"It's a myth."

"Look at the musicians who've put their stuff up and got a following."

Her mother was silent.

Why did she have to be like this? Ashley wished she'd told her father about it first. He thought all her ideas were good. He didn't argue with every single thing she said. Sometimes she felt as if she didn't know her mother at all. Things had been one way, then she went away to school, and now they were completely different. She wasn't sure if her mother had changed or she had. Either way, it was maddening.

Her inability to comprehend her mother's passive acceptance of life frightened her. Although it was one of the things that made her long for a career as a journalist. She wasn't simply drawn to reporting facts and information about government or economics, she wanted to make people feel something — to taste and touch life, get angry, get excited, instead of plodding along. But she couldn't make her mother feel anything. If she couldn't do that, how could she ever impact another life?

She wanted to shock her mother, jar her out of her own aimless drifting, her lack of purpose, her willingness to plod through every day, every week, every month, never changing anything, as if she was a miniature train chugging around a track that was an oval one year, a figure eight the next, then back to an oval. Were all lives like this, except for the lucky few? Was it already too late for Ashley to be one of those lucky ones who didn't live on a tiresome suburban street, concerned with nothing more than what she was buying at the grocery store, planting in the garden, or wearing to her book club once a month? What if she didn't have that magic?

Maybe everyone was trying so hard to censor their words and feelings and every single thing they did, the color was leached out of their lives. Perhaps that should be her focus. Getting people to spill their guts, act out.

She yanked a big section of skin off the second half of the avocado. She was nauseous. She put the knife and avocado down and leaned her hip against the counter. She put her hand on the back of her neck as if to slow the rush of thoughts along her spine, in and out of her brain.

The gun and its hidden power wouldn't leave her alone. Something had to change in her life and the gun certainly promised that. Is that what caused people to go on shooting rampages, destroying every living thing in their path? It wasn't as if she wanted to kill someone. The thought was too awful — that she even had to make that clear to herself. She would never use a gun. Never. She'd never hurt another human being and she didn't understand where those thoughts had come from. She couldn't even step on a daddy long-leg spider without wanting to cry.

"What's wrong with you? You can't slice an avocado without putting on a show?" her mother's voice was higher-pitched than normal. She sounded angry, or panicked.

"I don't feel good."

"I already cut the tomatoes and the peppers. The lettuce requires no work at all. How difficult is it to finish making a salad?"

"Okay! I said I don't feel well. Why are you attacking me?"

"You said you would help with dinner and all you've done is peel half an avocado, come up with a delusional plan for finding a job, and swoon like you're seventy years old."

Ashley picked up the knife. Although her head was full of a bubbly sensation and her stomach loose and soggy as a bowl of oatmeal with too much milk, she hacked off a piece of avocado skin and peeled it away. She felt she was peeling the scalp off a human skull, wanting to peer inside the soft, pulpy brain, trying to figure out where such disturbing thoughts had come from. As if the gun had brought a shadowy presence into the house that was infiltrating her brain.

Without its skin, the avocado was slippery. She tried to hold it firmly, but if she squeezed too hard she'd either smash parts of it, or it would slither out between her fingers and splatter on the floor. The knife cut through cleanly, gliding through green flesh, cutting deep, sharp lines. She cut the sections into smaller disks and pushed them off her fingers into the bowl.

It would be better to return the gun to Jack. She didn't like how it was consuming her thoughts, glowing in her closet, casting light over her room, demanding attention.

He still hadn't returned her text. Did that mean Krista had gotten a hold of him? They'd met for coffee or a beer? Krista would have painted an ugly picture of Ashley, turned Jack against her. While Ashley was away at college she hadn't thought of him much. Only on the weekends when they talked or when she came home for holidays. Now, she couldn't stop wondering whether there might be a guy out there who was better suited to her. She worried that she didn't really love Jack. She felt that if she did love him, she wouldn't have to peel her feelings apart and inspect them. She'd know he was the one, without a hint of doubt. But now, when there was a definite possibility he would find out what she'd done, that he'd break it off in disgust, lose his temper, she ached with anticipated loss. Did that mean she really did love him? Maybe there was something wrong with her. She only wanted him when she thought he might slip away from her. She only wanted what she couldn't have.

Although that wasn't being fair to herself. She'd desperately wanted to get into Northwestern. And every single moment she was there, she'd loved it. Her classes were exciting, driving her to think and work crazy hard. The people she met were like her, most of them journalism majors, obsessed with success, thirsty to get recognition for their investigative skills, their compelling words, wanting to change the world. Although what they wanted to change it into wasn't always clear. They had varying opinions on that.

She washed her hands and left the water running. She poured the can of garbanzo beans into the colander and rinsed them. She dumped the beans on top of the salad. She should have added them first. Now the avocado would get smashed when she mixed everything together.

"It seems like you don't care if I'm happy," she said. "You just want me to hurry up. It doesn't matter to you if I find the right guy or a satisfying career, just so long as I'm out of your hair and moving forward, whatever that is. I don't understand why Daddy is so supportive and you act like you can't wait to be rid of me. You don't care if I don't use my education to my full potential and end up in a low-level job for the rest of my life."

Dana turned. She folded her arms across her chest. "What makes you think your father is so supportive?"

"Because he listens to what I have to say. He's not always telling me what to do. He hasn't asked when I'm moving out or anything. He knows what I want and he knows it takes time. He insisted I go to a good school and you acted like it wasn't that important where I went to college."

"Well maybe it's not. How is it helping you now?"

"It will help. This is just a setback, because of the economy. You act like you don't even care what happens to my career."

"And your father does?"

"Yes. He wants me to succeed."

"What are you saying? That he loves you more than I do, because he doesn't require anything from you?"

"No." Why was her mother re-shaping her words? "I wasn't saying that."

"You have a very narrow view."

"What does that mean?"

"You think he loves you more because he doesn't challenge you."

"I don't think he loves me more."

"Well you think I'm somehow less. He hardly notices you. He wanted a son, you know. All men do."

The phone buzzed in her pocket. Jack's text message. Maybe. But she couldn't look, couldn't think. She leaned against the counter. Her head was filling with tears yet none of them seeped out. Her vision was clear, her eyes dry, so dry she could hardly blink without being hyper conscious of the movement of skin scratching across her eyeball. "He didn't want me?"

"I didn't say that."

"What are you saying?"

"Stop thinking he's the hero and I'm your enemy."

Her mother seemed to be looking directly at her for the first time since she'd moved home. Dana's eyes were kind. They were rid of the vacant, staring-past-her look Ashley had seen before.

"He seems more supportive because he doesn't react to anything. I'm not trying to push you out or prevent you from chasing your dreams. I'm just giving you a nudge. That's what parents are supposed to do. Nudge the birds out of the nest so they try their wings."

Ashley cringed at the cliché. Her mother's eyes still looked kind. She didn't seem to be trying to inflict pain, but simply open a curtain. "I don't need nudging."

"Before you didn't. You were driven. You always knew exactly what you wanted and you took it."

For some strange, terrifying reason, taking the gun from Jack's closet flashed through her mind.

"But now, it's like you're sitting around waiting for a job to fall on your head."

Maybe she was. Coming home had been a mistake. Returning to Jack, re-connecting with her high school friends had been the wrong move. Krista's twelve steps wouldn't have affected her at all if she didn't live here. She'd had a chance to stay in Chicago with two of her roommates, but she'd stupidly thought it would be cheaper to live at home. She was saving money, yes, but it wasn't worth falling backwards into a past life.

Her mother moved closer. She stroked Ashley's arm. Her fingers were cold and unfamiliar. Ashley tried not to jerk away, tried not to let the cold fingertips cause goose bumps or worse, shivering.

After a moment, the stroking stopped. Ashley squeezed her arms.

"I love you, Ashley. Don't ever think I don't." Dana turned her back. She pulled open the oven door. Heat rushed into the kitchen.

"It's done," she said. "Finish up the salad."

Ashley tossed the salad and tried to sort out what had just

happened. The area behind her ribs echoed with the whisper of her shallow breaths. Her father seemed like a stranger. And her mother wasn't any more familiar than when she'd stood in Ashley's bedroom implying she could read her daughter's thoughts.

They were all seated at the table, her mother going on about her workday, before Ashley remembered she hadn't looked at Jack's text message.

AFTER A DINNER that seemed to go on for hours, all three of them worked to load the dishwasher, packaging leftovers in plastic containers, and scrubbing seared chicken flesh off the glass pan. Usually one of them cleaned up while the others drifted off to their evening activities. For Ashley, that meant going on Facebook, searching the internet for tips on launching the career of your dreams, or studying the profiles of popular journalists, looking for clues to their success. When she didn't find the secret she was looking for, she ended up in front of a mindless TV show with her parents falling asleep on the couch.

Her mother was right. The course of Ashley's life had turned into a wandering, slow-moving stream, barely a ripple in the surface of the water. What twenty-three year old woman sat on the couch and watched reality TV or legal dramas with her parents? The weather was nice enough now, she should be playing tennis. Living with her parents hadn't hampered her tennis games all through junior high and high school, why was it a problem now?

Jack's text had read — *Can you come over? We should talk.*

As her parents moved slowly, inevitably toward the family room and the TV, her mother's face blank, already thinking of other things, rather than her daughter's career, Ashley jogged up the stairs. She let her heels hang over the edges of the steps, running on her toes so her feet didn't thump. Her mother hated her thudding up and down, so instead she moved with the prancing, stiff-legged gait of a deer.

Even though the tank top and shorts she'd put on before dinner were clean, she pulled off her shirt and opened the closet door. It was important to look hot. If Krista had made her out to be a conniving bitch, it was important to remind Jack how lucky he was. One mistake didn't mean she was a horrible person, and if he saw her looking good, it would distract him from whatever lies, or exaggerations Krista had fed him.

She texted back that she was taking a shower. He didn't respond.

She dug through her drawer like a mad squirrel looking for a lost nut. When her feet were buried by bras and thongs and camisoles, she finally decided on navy blue. The color made her eyes look darker. That was assuming they'd get to her lingerie. What if he met her at the door, told her she was someone he didn't recognize, told her to take the few things she kept at his house, and sent her away. Then she'd really be without a life. In its place, she'd have a reputation for being cold and heartless, as Krista made the rounds trying to heal the past. She shivered and stuffed the discarded lingerie into the drawer.

After another ten minutes staring at the rack of jeans and tops, dresses and skirts, she decided on skinny jeans and a silky, low-cut mauve tank. Her toes still looked good from last week's pedicure, so flip-flops would be the right balance with the dressy top.

She took a shower and blew her hair dry slowly to maintain the silky texture even though she felt like leaving the underneath damp so she could get to his house before he had more time to think about what a horrid person she was. She'd been someone else then. A kid. She would never do something like that now. The dual lies had been a spur of the moment mistake, something she'd blurted out before thinking it through. Of course, if she explained that, it made her sound like her natural instinct was toward lying and cruelty. She honestly had no idea why she'd done it. She just had.

When her hair and make-up were perfect, she picked up a soft white sweater and slipped it on. The white created an aura of innocence and sweetness. And she was sweet. She was assertive and determined, but she was a nice person. Jack already knew that and she couldn't believe Krista had the power to wipe it out over a single cup of coffee.

JACK OPENED THE door. He was barefoot and wore cargo shorts and a 49ers t-shirt. He stepped aside. Ashley put one foot inside the apartment and leaned forward to kiss him. He turned his cheek and her lips brushed across bristly skin.

Okay. He wasn't furious, but there was definitely something wrong.

He closed the door. A baseball game was playing on the TV.

"Want a beer?" He crossed the living room and went into the kitchen. He opened the fridge and took out two bottles of Dos Equis.

She didn't like Dos Equis. Wine would be better than beer anyway, a nice glass of Sauvignon Blanc or Pinot Grigio, but he obviously wasn't offering and she didn't want to disrupt the apparent calm with a request he probably couldn't fulfill.

"What's new?" she said. She took a sip of beer. It foamed up around her lips and there was too much in her mouth to swallow gracefully. She coughed.

He went to the couch and sat down. He propped his feet on the edge of the coffee table and pressed the remote to mute the TV. She wished he'd turn it off. If he didn't, she'd keep glancing toward the images flickering at the corner of her eye. She needed all her energy concentrated on him, even though a small part of her mind kept wondering why she cared, if she cared. Maybe all she cared about was winning.

He took a swallow of beer. "Not too much."

She nodded.

He stared at the game. "Oh, Krista Miller called."

She licked the mouth of her beer bottle. He acted as if he'd just thought of it. Why would he summon her with a text that they needed to talk and then put on an act about the topic of conversation?

"I haven't talked to her since high school. She must be getting back in touch with everyone," he said.

"Maybe."

"It was weird."

"How?"

"She wanted to meet up for a glass of wine. Said she had to talk to me this week. *Had* to."

"Why?"

"I guess she's having surgery."

"Huh."

"But she acted like she was going to die and had to say good-bye. It was weird."

"So you didn't get together?"

He shook his head and took a gulp of beer.

"Why not?"

"I dunno. Seemed like a hassle. Maybe when I'm not working any overtime."

"She didn't say anything else?"

"Nope. Seemed kind of upset I couldn't meet her. She was sort of pushy about it."

"She can be pushy," Ashley said.

"I thought you two were good friends."

"We were. But I could tell when I saw her last week we're in really different places now."

"Whatever that means," he said.

She laughed. "So what did you want to talk about?"

He put his beer on the table. He stared at the TV as if he was watching the game. "Why'd you take my gun?"

For all her thinking about the gun over the past few days, she'd never considered this. What was she supposed to say? I thought you'd find out what a liar I am and shoot me? "I feel nervous with you having it."

"But it's okay for you to have it?"

"I know I won't shoot anyone."

"I said I didn't even think about it."

"Then how did you notice it was gone?"

"I just did. That's stealing."

"Not really. We're in a relationship. I didn't steal it. I was keeping it safe."

"Taking something that I don't know you took is stealing."

"It's not really."

"Whatever. I don't like it. I want you to bring it back."

"Why didn't you tell me that when you texted me?"

"I wanted to see what you'd say."

"Is this a test? I thought you loved me."

"Clearly more than you love me, since you refuse to live with me."

"That's not about love."

"It sure is. Anyway, it's not your gun."

"I know that." She shifted closer to him. "I love you." She put her hand on the back of his neck and flicked her tongue across his lips. He tasted like beer with a touch of mint. He must have brushed his teeth before she came over. She smiled and pressed her mouth into his.

He pulled away. "Why do you think I'd shoot someone? I'm the most low-key person I know."

"You are."

"Then what's up with you?"

She inched closer and leaned into him. "I don't know." She spoke more softly. "I'm just confused about a lot of things right now." In some ways, that was the truth. At least she thought it could be the truth.

He put his arm around her. "If there's a reason you don't want to live with me, you need to tell me. I don't want to just keep drifting along like this."

It was unsettling that he was accusing her of the same thing her mother had. She took a sip of beer and picked up the remote. If they were going to watch TV, she wanted something other than a baseball game.

Sixteen

THE TRAFFIC CONES stood like doughy security guards — mute and essentially helpless to offer real protection. Bob lit a cigarette. The prayer meeting would start in ten minutes. The sky was darkening but the streetlights hadn't come on. It had been a cloudy day and the thick covering made it seem darker. No stars, no moon, just heavy white stuff turning to charcoal gray.

It wasn't good for his health that he was getting precariously close to smoking a quarter pack every few days. Dana hadn't said anything recently, but he was sure she noticed. He'd come into the bedroom and seen her standing near the nightstand on his side of the bed. Her fingers had been curled around the drawer handle and the only things in that drawer were a flashlight and his back-up cigarettes and lighter. He pictured her counting the cigarettes.

Did all marriages turn into this silent observation of the other person, wondering who they'd been and who they'd become? Occasionally trying to figure out if there was any correlation between the younger self and the current self, trying to figure out whether you really knew each other at all?

He loved her. He really did. He didn't like the gaps between them, their satisfying but somehow not satisfying love-making twice a week. He wondered if she felt the same. There must be a way to go back. And maybe that was all on him. He'd never completely forgiven her and he wasn't sure if she knew that. If she even knew what she'd done.

"Smoking again?" Dana's voice was soft but it startled him.

He dropped the cigarette. Damn. What would she say if he immediately lit another? For half a second, he felt like a little kid, caught by his mother playing with himself in the bathroom, too young to realize he should have locked the door.

"Just one," he said.

"One and one and one. You're smoking a lot."

"Not that much."

"And what's with the cones? You're acting like a cranky old man."

"Maybe I am a cranky old man."

She grabbed her hair and stuffed it behind her ears. It didn't stay. She strode across the strip of grass, down the driveway apron, and into the street. She picked up the first cone. She scurried to the next, bent over, like an old woman gathering firewood, nesting the cones on top of each other.

He debated between lighting another cigarette and

grabbing the cones from her. She was pissing him off. The cones weren't hurting her. She was treating him like a child.

He decided against the cigarette. He walked down the slope of the driveway apron and into the street. He grabbed the top cone but she jerked to the side and his hands slid off the soft plastic. He tugged at the base of the bottom one. She twisted and wrenched herself away. She stumbled further into the street. "Go smoke your cigarette."

She turned and picked up another cone.

He didn't want to attract the attention of any neighbors, tussling with his wife in the middle of the street. Or the churchgoers. That was all he needed. Their interference in what they'd perceive as a domestic dispute requiring police involvement. He stepped onto the curb and walked back to his spot on the sidewalk.

Dana bent over and picked up another cone, even though the previous one wasn't firmly fitted on the stack. The two cones tumbled off and landed on the pavement. She bent over again. As she started to straighten, she glared at Bob and pinched her face into a scowl, looking more ominous in the growing darkness.

She shifted the armload of cones. A car roared around the corner, accelerated past the house next door, and plowed into her. There was a sound like someone falling into wet cement. The impact forced the cones out of her arms. They flew up and scattered as her body slammed forward and smacked the pavement.

Bob heard a bellowing, something that made him think of a wounded elephant. It came from inside of him, tearing at his brain, his throat, his chest. He lurched toward the street, skidded across the grass and stumbled into the gutter.

Dana's body was half under the car. He flung himself onto the ground, touching her, feeling thick, smooth blood coating his fingers, spreading through her hair. Her face was scraped and broken so she didn't look like herself. From some distant space he heard a woman screaming but he couldn't interpret the words. Something about god. Finally new words began to take shape. "I'm calling 9-1-1. Right now. I'm calling."

He knew it didn't matter. He could feel as he pulled Dana onto his lap that every part of her was broken. Her head was the most sickening, the way it flopped around like it wanted to remain on the pavement.

"Don't move her!"

He collapsed over her, pressing his face into her hair, missing the fruity smell, his nostrils filled with nothing but the odor of blood and something else he couldn't identify. The inside of his head was empty. He felt a silent, long, unbroken scream race through his blood vessels. It penetrated his bones and echoed inside his skull, yet no sound or tears came out.

He heard Ashley screaming behind him. Her voice mingled with the roaring of a train inside his head.

Ashley's body crashed into his, her hands pulled at his shirt, dragging him away from Dana. She forced herself between them, touching her mother's hair. She recoiled. She lifted her hand and held it in front of her as if she'd never seen it before, as if she wasn't really sure what the wet stuff was. It was bright red. He realized the streetlights had come on.

Tears ran down Ashley's face in black streaks, mixing with other colors on her skin, a pale pink, and something beige, like coffee. Despite all the colors, her skin was white and lifeless. She sobbed, her body shuddering as if the ground shook beneath her.

He should touch her, pull her close and comfort her, but he couldn't. The silent scream of pain continued to pulse through him, wiping out everything else. The meaningless thoughts of the streetlights, of Ashley's stained face, rising up one after another, seemed to be appearing on a giant screen, far away, something hanging from the dome of a stadium at a basketball game.

He heard sirens, cars, trucks rumbling. Dana's blood was already drying on his fingers. He'd been here for hours or only seconds, either way it was the same.

Meaty hands pulled him away, forced him to a standing position, and helped him to the curb where he was pushed back down. A woman dressed in blue slacks and a blue shirt with dark hair swept into a ponytail handed him a blanket. It fell out of his hands and she picked it up, partially unfolded it, and draped it over his shoulders. He wasn't sure why. It was a warm spring evening, he didn't need a blanket. But then he realized he was shaking. She must have assumed he was cold.

He wasn't cold, was he?

Ashley sat on the curb beside him, also wrapped in a blanket, crying. Her shoulders convulsed and tears dotted the tops of her dusty bare feet as she bent forward and let them fall from her eyes like raindrops.

For a long time, people darted back and forth. They put Dana on a stretcher and rolled it into the back of a blue paramedic truck. They drove away. Shouldn't they have asked him to go? He half stood, then sank back to the curb. His bones pounded against the concrete. Of course not. It was too late.

SOMEHOW, AFTER THE hospital and the police station, he ended up back at home. Ashley was sprawled on the living room couch in the arms of an Ambien-induced sleep. Her hair hung over the side of the cushion. Her lips were slack. He remained for a moment, remembering when he and Dana had stood by Ashley's crib, Dana's shoulder pressed against his, watching Ashley as she slept. Her mouth was like porcelain, her lips occasionally sucking unconsciously. He'd taken Dana's hand and laced her cool, slim fingers with his.

The house was far emptier than it ever had been when Dana was shopping, or out with friends, or gone for a girls' spa weekend. He went into the breakfast room and sat at the table. Everything looked as though it belonged to someone else — the pine table where he rested his forearms, wood pressing into the bones, the white refrigerator visible through the doorway, the glistening blue and white tile counter, and the blue tiled floor. There was a small sprinkling of damp coffee grounds on the floor below the spot where the coffee maker stood. A banana with two overlapping stickers on the peel sat on the counter near the stove. Ashley didn't like bananas. Dana must have planned to eat it. The thought made his throat feel as if the stem of the banana was lodged there.

They'd taken him and Ashley to the hospital in the back of a police car, in the space reserved for criminals. He didn't know if they'd taken Melody somewhere in the back of a police car. She was the one who belonged there.

When they'd arrived home, the street was empty, as if nothing had happened. The cones were gone. Two cars sat in the church parking lot. A single window facing the lot glowed with light.

Ashley had already been limp with Ambien. She'd barely made it up the front steps, leaning on his arm. At the hospital, they'd tried to give him drugs but he refused. They insisted he call someone. But who would he call? His brother? Not likely. It would be unhelpful in the extreme to listen to his brother's platitudes, watch him try to mask the pity lurking in his eyes. The person he would call, the person who would be most helpful, the only one who really knew him, despite the empty spaces between them, was Dana. He didn't mention that to the cops. The cop asked if there was a faith leader who could be contacted. The contempt on Bob's face must have answered that question because there were no further suggestions.

His arms ached from leaning so hard on the table, but if he sat up, he might fall off the chair. The unyielding surface was keeping his limbs from flopping about helplessly.

In three minutes, maybe less, they'd gone from a content — they were content, weren't they? — middle-aged couple, to nothing. He'd become an elderly man, cranky and alone. He could brood to his heart's content now. He could almost hear the words passing across her lips. He could smoke as much as he pleased. Yet right now, he had no desire for a cigarette. Maybe a small desire, but no will to carry out the task. It was too much work, his fingers wouldn't cooperate.

He ran through their list of friends, his co-workers. He should call someone.

He pushed back the chair and went into the kitchen. He picked up the banana. It was soft at one end. From where he'd sat in the breakfast room it had looked not quite ripe, but it was the opposite. Why hadn't she tossed it? Maybe she planned to cut it in half and eat the good part. He put it back on the counter. He walked into the hall and out to the front porch. The night was warm. The air smelled vacant. He walked down the path and stood between the two sides of the hedge.

The glowing light in the church window had gone out. The parking lot was empty. He wondered if any of them would try to use this to lure him through those strip mall doors. He shuddered. He hated himself for thinking about them when Dana was gone. Dead. His wife was dead and he would be alone for the rest of his life. He'd thought he was alone before, disconnected from her. He'd had no idea what alone was.

He went back inside, closed the door, and snapped the deadbolt into place.

In the living room, Ashley lay curled in the shape of an egg. She'd shifted the position of her head so that her hair now covered her face like a silky shroud. He should push it back, but he hadn't touched his daughter's face in nearly twenty years.

He sat in the armchair. There was hardly any movement of her body to indicate she was even breathing. A slight whisper of air moved in and out of her lips. He hoped they hadn't given her too much. An orange plastic bottle with a white cap sat on the coffee table. More pills in case she woke up and became hysterical again.

And how long would that go on? What was he supposed to do? He had no idea how to comfort her. Inside was a void so enormous he couldn't imagine forming words, much less speaking them. She was an adult. She'd have to figure it out herself.

It was far past the time he should go to bed, but that was impossible. The chair would be good enough. He had nothing to do but watch Ashley. He would be there if she woke and needed him. As along as what she needed was simple. A glass of water. A blanket. Something to eat — half a banana.

He pushed himself to his feet. He went to the dining room and removed the cork from the whiskey bottle. He couldn't remember the last time he'd had whiskey. Usually they drank wine, or he had beer while he watched a game. He poured two shots into one of the fancy glasses. Dana loved those glasses, kept them polished so they sparkled, sitting near the front edge of the shelf in the breakfront, glittering through the glass panes. She loved the glasses but hated whiskey.

He took two sips and trudged back to the living room. He set the glass on the end table and went back to the dining room for the bottle. It looked like the doctor had been right. He did need a sedative.

He collapsed in the chair, his legs sprawled, and let his head fall against the back. Tears formed deep inside his skull. The last time he'd cried was after the final miscarriage. Dana never knew that he'd cried over the boy's death. This was the second time in his adult life. God must hate him more than he'd realized.

Seventeen

"IT WASN'T MY fault. It wasn't my fault at all. I think it's almost like the Lord wanted to take her life and He used me. Maybe she was the one leading him astray, and that's why he wouldn't tell me what was bothering him. To protect her. Without her, he'll turn to the Lord," Melody said.

Sarah patted Melody's knee. "You don't need to speculate. Some things are inexplicable."

"Are you saying it's my fault?" Melody's eyes were blurred, making Sarah's eyes and the line of her lips look softer, friendlier than usual.

They sat in the prayer room, Sarah beside her on the couch, but far away so she had to extend her arm fully each time she patted Melody's knee or shoulder. Sarah's Bible was open on her lap, draped over her thighs. Several times it had started to slip through her legs so she had to re-position it between pats on Melody's various joints.

"It just happened," Sarah said.

"If God is in control, how can something just happen?"

The pages of Sarah's Bible crinkled softly as she brushed them forward, looking for something, an answer. Something reassuring.

"Tell me again what happened."

"I told the police," Melody said.

"Tell me. All they do is gather facts, without looking for insight."

"I was singing. Doing what you suggested, letting my tongue loose to say whatever it pleased, not trying to control it."

"That's good."

"I think I closed my eyes. It just feels better that way, you know? Like the Spirit is right there. When you have to look at man-made objects, God seems far away, but with my eyes closed, it's different."

"Of course. But not a good idea when you're driving."

"I know. I *know*! But it was only for a second and I knew right where I was headed, I always come around the corner from that direction, and I try to park in the same spot. On Sunday the cones were gone, so I thought he'd given up."

"Did you tell the police you closed your eyes?"

Melody swallowed. That was her secret. She shouldn't have revealed it to Sarah. Would Sarah tell the police, would they start blaming her?

It was not her fault. That woman, his wife, was standing in the middle of the street. Not just standing, she was bent over, so you could hardly see her. It had been almost dark. It must be God's will because she would never, *never*, deliberately run over a human being. Not over any living creature. Unless the Lord told her to run over someone. Unless the Lord told her that Bob needed a wake-up call, he needed everything stripped from his life, he needed to see how lost he was without God, and there was nothing like grief for making that clear.

But she hadn't done it deliberately. Her eyes were closed. Only for a moment, only when she felt there was something bubbling deep in her throat, ready to burst forth.

"What did you tell the police?"

"I told them I didn't see her."

"Because your eyes were closed?"

"I didn't specifically mention that, no."

"Do you think you should?"

"Does it matter? I didn't see her. Not really."

"What do you mean, *not really*?"

"It was dark. She was bent over."

Sarah nodded.

Melody's eyes were clearing, the tears retreating. The room looked sharp and focused. It was good of Sarah to sit here and help her through this. At first, when they took her to the police station, she'd been terrified they would arrest her, that everyone would blame her. But when they realized she was completely sober, that she had a good driving record, and the cones — they did seem to factor in the cones, they saw how those could be very confusing — they'd let her go home. Not for good. They were clear about that. There would be an investigation. A woman was dead.

"Should we pray?" Sarah closed the Bible and placed it on the coffee table.

"What for?"

"Guidance. We should be seeking guidance every moment and this is no exception."

Melody didn't like the condescending tone in Sarah's voice, as if Melody was a newbie in the ways of God, as if Melody was someone who needed an older woman to help her on her journey. She was just as worthy as Sarah. Although, she'd probably opened herself to that motherly voice by asking what they should pray for. The question had been a dodging tactic, if she was honest with herself. She didn't feel like praying. She didn't really want to know where God might direct her next.

The demands on her were too much. During that half second before her car slammed into something solid, yet soft and filled with liquid, she was certain she'd recognized the heavenly language, indecipherable words on the back of her tongue, the space where something might make her gag. For less than a breath she'd thought the Spirit had touched her, that God was finally accepting her as a woman worthy of His gifts, His unending presence, an intimate relationship that would fill her body with bliss every second of every day. And then, that woman, that couple really, because the woman wouldn't have been in the street if Bob hadn't put out his cones, they'd gotten in the way, ripped the Spirit right out of her heart.

It was possible she'd seen the woman, despite tightly closed eyes. She'd had a toehold on the precipice of rapture, but was denied the glorious release. She wanted to cry, she wanted to claw at Sarah's face. It was so unfair. As Melody had strained to see through the skin of her eyelids, the woman's skin glowed red. For a moment, Melody had wondered if the figure was Satan, trying to snatch her out of God's hands, feeding doubt into her heart. Had she pressed harder on the gas, just a little bit? She wasn't sure. Knowing it had been a human being, she absolutely hadn't done that. But for that instant, she hadn't seen a human being, she'd seen something else.

"You start." Sarah rested her hands on her thighs, palms up. She bent her head forward. Her hair covered the sides of her face so it was impossible to see whether her lips were tight with condemnation.

Melody put her hands on her legs, palms up, her fingers curled slightly. She closed her eyes.

The room was silent for several minutes. Sarah had given the command to pray and she wasn't going to say a word to get them started. *She who speaks first loses.* Melody wondered what that meant in this context.

Melody spoke the Lord's name. Then she began talking rapidly, softly, mouthing Bible passages, phrases from songs, declarations of regret and sorrow that were written by strangers. She held herself off from revealing any of the thoughts plaguing her. She wondered if Sarah noticed.

Finally, she paused.

The couch squeaked. Her breath was loud in her ears, echoing through her head. She took in more oxygen with each inhalation until she felt lightheaded. She blew out air, a long steady stream, paying attention to her lungs squeezing down until they were empty. She took a shallow breath. Why wouldn't Sarah take over? Melody took another deep breath. There was a faint release of oxygen in her intestines. A car drove past outside. The muscles at the base of her skull creaked, trying to unknot themselves.

"Oh, Lord," Sarah said. "Forgive Melody for her uncontrolled behavior. Remove her willfulness, her refusal to surrender."

Melody felt a hot pebble inside her chest. It grew like flames spreading over coals, the heat increasing until it burned her lips and the tip of her nose. Sweat on the back of her neck crept up into her hair. She took her hands off her legs and clenched them, shoving them between her thighs, trying to drive the anger out of her arms.

Sarah went on praying, skipping from Melody's flaws into words of praise, then back to Melody's weakness, her lack of devotion. Sarah gave lip service to her own, minor, acts of disobedience, her own faults that were more like pats on the back — begging forgiveness for not noticing how deeply in need Melody was, chastising herself for spending too much time alone with God rather than opening her eyes and giving others the benefit of her wisdom.

Noodles and leftover peas from dinner swam in Melody's stomach. The food pressed up into her esophagus until she tasted the half-digested mass. She swallowed. It would be terrible to vomit all over her jeans and sandals. Worse, she might lurch to the side as heaves wove through her body, covering Sarah with the unwanted contents of her stomach. She straightened, trying to calm the sloshing food.

It wasn't her fault that the car had struck Bob's wife. She shouldn't have been standing in the street at dark, shouldn't have been bent over — almost invisible. Sarah was supposed to be comforting her and instead she was blaming her! It seemed as if the women of Triumphant Life Tabernacle belonged to a private club, just like the groups of girls in high school who looked past Melody when she spoke, who stared down at her large feet, or glanced with barely concealed contempt at her clothes that weren't quite right, although she could never figure out what, exactly, was wrong with them. She shopped at the same stores. Maybe trendy clothes just didn't look as good on her as they did on the others.

She had done everything they told her to do. She read her Bible every day. She spent at least half an hour in prayer every morning and joined the Wednesday prayer group. She listened exclusively to religious music. She read Godly books and watched very little TV since most of it was trash and offensive to the Lord. She didn't insist on having things of the world or wear clothing to attract the attention of men or make women envious. What else did God want from her?

The room was silent. At least her stomach had stopped threatening to explode. Was she going to be arrested? Would they decide it was her fault? Was it her fault? She didn't think so, but another tiny voice told her everything had happened on purpose. She was so willful, so determined to take control, to maybe hurt Bob so he would lose that arrogant, mocking smirk.

If Sarah would just wrap it up, speak some concluding words, it would be so much better. More than a touch from God, more than a half-hearted, yet half-afraid desire to understand what had really happened in those few fleeting seconds that were already growing dim in her memory, she wanted a cup of tea. She wanted to take off her sandals, curl up on her couch, turn on the TV, and let her mind drift without trying to think, without always trying to figure out what God wanted and why He didn't seem very interested in her.

She could speak some concluding words and phrases herself, thank God for being present, lie to His face that she was grateful for His insight and guidance, the bliss of His love. Or she could sit here forever, feeling every throb of blood moving through her veins, every twitch of muscle, and every step in the digestion of her dinner.

Why wouldn't Sarah break the silence? Why did it all have

to be on Melody's shoulders?

"The Lord is trying to touch you," Sarah whispered. "Why won't you let Him?"

Melody said nothing. Let Sarah feel some discomfort for once. Let her be confused, wondering if she'd misread the signs, if she wasn't as connected as she thought she was.

"We're listening, Father," Sarah said. "We're waiting."

Melody burped softly and tasted vomit in the back of her throat. She'd changed her mind about throwing up. At this point, anything to stop the torture of not knowing what was expected would be welcome.

She wasn't sure why she'd come to this church. Of course, that wasn't exactly true. She knew why, she'd come thinking everything would be different. She'd start over. The experience at Mt. Olive Sanctuary would be buried forever. She'd thought she would emerge like a butterfly in her new environment, belonging to the group, accepted, all her awkwardness falling away like a stiff, cracked cocoon.

Now, memories from her old church rushed forward like a crowd waiting for the start of a sold-out concert surging when the barricade was removed.

There had been so many prayer meetings like this one she'd lost count. Every week they met. They crowded around her and laid their hands on her shoulders and arms and back. They didn't lay hands on the top of her head like they'd done for others, she was too tall for most to reach. She could have been seated, but they never suggested that. Standing was uncomfortable, especially when the meetings went on for thirty minutes or more, sometimes an hour. Was she the only one whose feet ached?

The final prayer meeting at Mt. Olive stood apart from the rest. After that, she'd known she could never go back there, even though the members had been friends for years. She'd eaten dinners with them, cared for their children, gone out for coffee, gobbled up over-cooked hamburgers and corn on the cob at backyard barbecues. If she'd been asked, she would have called them her family.

The final attempt by the members of Mt. Olive to rouse the gift of tongues inside of Melody had taken place on a cool August evening. Because the fresh cut grass smelled so sweet, they left the doors to the sanctuary open. But it was cold as the breeze filtered into the building. Melody shivered even though she wore jeans and slip-on shoes and a long-sleeved t-shirt.

Seven people had shown up. Melody's failure to speak in tongues had made her an object of pity and concern. Sometimes, they glanced at her and she imagined they were thinking she wasn't a believer at all.

There had been three men and four women. Two of the women — Jeanine and Paula — she'd considered her best friends. In fact, she and Paula had joined the church at the same time. Paula had been a friend since high school, had helped Melody through the ending and the extended pain of her breakup with Bruce.

The very good looking Pastor David had taken her elbow and led her between the railings surrounding the altar area, up two steps, and stopped a few feet from the marble altar. For a moment, it flashed through her head that he liked her as someone more than just a fellow believer, that he didn't have to take her arm. He was letting her know he had an interest in her. She realized they would take those same steps, in the same way, if they were approaching the altar to get married. Her face flamed with heat and she wondered if he noticed. She moved further to the left and his hand fell away from her elbow.

She placed her palms on the cold surface of the altar. Despite the chill, her fingers were damp. She wasn't sure how she would prevent them from sliding around while they prayed, but he insisted she stand close to the altar and keep her hands fixed to it, as if God might enter her body from out of the stone.

The others closed in behind her. She felt their heat even before they rested their hands on her body. As fingers and palms began to press against her, she tried to discern which belonged to David, but she couldn't. So, there was nothing there after all. If there had been, she was sure his touch would have been recognizable, warmer and more tender.

The men's hands were strong and insistent, the women's light, making her flesh tingle. She worried that it wouldn't take long before her skin started to itch.

For a good portion of time, easily twenty minutes, Paula

and then Pastor David and then a woman whose voice that Melody couldn't identify, spoke in tongues, the words filled with *g*'s and *l*'s and too many vowels, words that sounded as if they repeated often and were perhaps invented on the fly. She quickly dismissed the blasphemous thought.

They urged her to speak, to open her mouth, to let the sounds come out. Why did it always seem to be her responsibility? Wasn't God supposed to speak through her? Why did she have to *let* the sounds come out, as if it were a failure on her part that the gift refused to manifest itself? She tried, but nothing was there.

Her feet grew numb, for a while she was light headed, but it passed. Her shoulders ached and she longed to pull her fingers away from the altar. Then, she needed to pee.

Before she'd arrived at the church for the prayer meeting, she'd stopped for a beer. The Bible frowned on drinking. She never drank, but she'd thought it would help her relax. Just a little. Her body wasn't used to alcohol. She should have remembered that beer seemed to double in quantity inside her bladder. How did she gracefully interrupt their prayers and mention something so earthly? They were here for *her*, caught up in the rapture of seeking the presence of God, and she was thinking about her bladder.

"Believe," someone said.

"Praise God."

"Let him fill you."

"Hallelujah."

"Thank you, Jesus."

"Amen."

"Let go."

The words spun around her. She forced her mind to pay attention to each one. To not think that they might be getting impatient with her. They didn't seem to be. Their voices sounded cheerful, happy to be where they were, their minds caught up in the experience, not thinking of beer and the need to urinate.

"Let it go," David said. His voice was easy to pick out from the others — that preacherly resonance, the commanding tone.

A bit of urine leaked out. Her thighs grew warm and damp as liquid seeped through her jeans, soaking the crotch, spreading to the back. Her underwear was sopping wet. Tears ran down her face at the same relentless pace that urine spread down her legs. Her shoulders and back quaked.

"Yes!"

"The Spirit is filling you, Melody. Praise God."

She cried harder. Her shoulders convulsed as if someone was holding her by the hair and shaking her body. She yanked her hands off the altar and turned. She opened her eyes and looked at their shocked faces. She stumbled down the steps to the stone floor and ran up the aisle, a bride fleeing from an ill-advised marriage. She grabbed her purse off the last pew and plunged through the open doors, out into the cool evening. After stopping by the church kitchen for a towel to sit on, she got in her car and drove home.

When Paula called, Melody didn't answer the phone. It was three weeks before she spoke to any of them, and by then, she was looking for a new church. She still had faith. Someday, God would give her the gift of tongues.

Melody forced her mind back to Sarah and the silence in the prayer room. "Thank you for your care and for leading me every step of the way," she said. "Amen." She opened her eyes and stood. "I need to get home."

"That was sudden. Do you think it's a good idea? To be driving?"

"How else am I going to get there?"

"You should stay with Gordon and me."

"I don't know."

She wanted the freedom of being alone. Yet possibly, she'd misread everything. Maybe Sarah really cared about her.

Sarah looked up at her, wide hazel eyes, full of concern and caring. But how could Melody know that tender look was the truth? Sarah might be putting on an act, going out of her way to make Melody feel loved and cared for.

"I'm worried about you," Sarah said.

If she was so worried, Sarah should stand up, not sit there with that pleading expression, making Melody feel huge and out of place.

Sarah stood and brushed a loose strand of hair off her face.

"We'd love to have you. I don't think you should be alone.

You had a traumatic experience. You need people around you."

"I have to go to work in the morning."

"We'll get up early and I'll drive you back here to get your car."

"I don't have anything with me."

"That's easy. I have extra jammies."

"I'm too tall to fit in your clothes."

Sarah smiled but her expression was kind. "Night shirts are one-size-fits-all. Please."

Melody wondered why she would say please, as if she needed Melody's company. But that couldn't be right.

"You'll feel better."

"I need some time to think."

"There's plenty of time for that later. Come over. Tim's at the house too. It will do you good to not think about anything, just being with other people, getting something to eat, and a good night's sleep. In the morning I'll make pancakes."

Melody hadn't had pancakes in ages. Did Sarah know that? Thick soft pancakes, butter soaked into them, warm sweet syrup. The nausea had disappeared completely. It would be nice to be taken care of. Almost like being a child, not a woman who'd destroyed a human life. She started to cry. "That really does sound wonderful. Thank you."

Tears shimmered in Sarah's eyes. She looked down and tugged on her shirt, stuffing part of it that had come loose back into the waist of her pants.

"People care about you, Melody. Don't close yourself off so much."

How did she know? Maybe she really did have a gift of insight.

Eighteen

ON FRIDAY AT nine-fifty, Bob walked into St. Joseph's Catholic church on the corner of Winchester Road and Carroll Avenue, the first time his hard-soled shoes had echoed on the stone floors in over fifteen years. It was the kind of church that looked and smelled and sounded like a real church. It was quiet except for the naturally mournful tones of Amazing Grace coming from a small organ in the balcony overlooking the altar.

When the priest had asked what music he wanted, Bob told the blonde guy in a black suit and black shirt with a white plastic collar it was his choice. Dana loved everything from classical to country western, but did it matter? She wouldn't be there to enjoy it. Whatever songs were chosen would be nothing more than a collection of notes, noise to mute the coughs and sneezes and shifting of bodies in stiff, unfamiliar clothes.

In some ways, it was is if he'd been entering churches his

entire life, one long, unbroken stream, the fifteen years not believing in the notion of god, gone, as if he'd never lived them. His marriage dissolved into nothing but a vague memory, and his wife, dead. He'd never see her again. Already he was having trouble remembering what she'd felt like as her breath faded to nothing and her body grew heavier in his arms. Or maybe she'd already been dead the moment the car slammed into her. It was possible her weakening breath was his imagination.

The cold dimly lighted building and colored glass in the windows made him feel as if he were under water. The candle flames hardly flickered. Rows of people sat waiting to observe his grief. Of course they were there to comfort him, but comfort wasn't possible. They were there to remember Dana, but if he couldn't remember her, how could they?

Did she know he loved her? Even now?

Hundreds of people. He had no idea where they'd come from. He wasn't sure he knew more than fifty people, but maybe that was an illusion, like everything. If he browsed the employee directory at work, he would recognize more than a hundred names, so he guessed he'd spoken to or exchanged email with all of them. And there were the people scattered throughout Dana's life. But how many were friends? His parents were dead, hers were gone. The Lambert family was shrinking. Weren't families supposed to expand over the generations?

Most of Ashley's college friends lived in other states, other countries, but there were quite a few younger people — her high school classmates. How had they all received the news so quickly? The accident had been less than forty-eight hours ago. Email. Facebook. Instant everything.

Maybe it was a mistake to have the funeral so soon. They'd hardly absorbed that she was gone. But the church couldn't accommodate them on Saturday, and waiting until Monday seemed like too much. Sooner was better, get it over with, cope with things on his own — he and Ashley, without all of these spectators.

He turned and walked back outside to wait for Ashley. She was having trouble entering the building, as if remaining outside would freeze time. Had she been inside a church since she became an adult? He suspected she hadn't, but who knew what she'd done when she was gone for four years. She'd lived a whole life without his knowledge, so it was within the realm of possibility that her other life contained religious rituals.

She looked so grown up. The sunlight on her blonde hair was the antithesis to what they were doing. She looked like she belonged at a job interview, or a political convention, not her mother's funeral. Her face was pale and there were gray shadows around her eyes. She didn't seem to have as much stuff painted on her eyes as usual. He hoped that didn't mean she was planning to cry. Not that anyone planned something like that, but she'd obviously thought about it. He couldn't deal with it when she cried. He had no idea what to say, couldn't manage to do anything but cough or put his hands in his pockets. Yesterday when she'd cried, he'd patted her back but she stopped suddenly and her head jerked up. They stared at each other. After that, he kept his hands securely in his pockets.

He knew how to relate to Ashley around a basketball or a tennis ball, he knew how to talk to her about school, her classes, her career plans. But as he watched her now, he realized there were only a few small touch points in their lives. It had been that way from the very beginning. When she was an infant, he'd felt left out of the mother-daughter bond. Jealous, if he was honest with himself. It was almost sexual, the way Dana gazed at her daughter, watching the baby suck on her breast. The look on Dana's face bordered on rapture, and it was mirrored on Ashley's round, perfectly formed lips, her tiny nose, her delicate eyelids. He couldn't watch, and he wondered if there was something wrong with him.

As he waited for her to walk up the steps, his gaze wandered out to the tree-lined street — suburban tranquility at its finest. But there was nothing tranquil about the coffin that stood waiting for him and Ashley at the front of the center aisle. He closed his eyes for a moment, but that made the image more vivid.

When he opened them he saw Melody. She stood behind a tree, as if she could hide herself. The tree was younger than she was, with a narrow trunk and only a thin web of branches, a sparse covering of leaves.

"Hey!" He took a step down, moving around Ashley who was coming up the second step.

Ashley jumped and wobbled on her heels. He grabbed her upper arm. She pulled away and steadied herself.

"What are you shouting at?" Her eyes were watery. The floating look of her eyeballs frightened him.

"That bitch who murdered your mother is stalking us."

"Calm down, Dad."

He pointed and Ashley turned to look. "At least she's not coming inside," she said.

"But she might try. Hey! I see you. Get the hell out of here." His voice was rough and deeper than normal, strained as if from hours of yelling.

Melody remained behind the tree.

He walked down to the concrete area that joined the church steps and the sidewalk. "Get the hell out of here."

Melody moved out from behind the tree. "I'm sorry. I wanted to offer . . ."

"I don't want to hear a word you have to say and I don't want to see your face. If there was any justice, any god, you'd be in prison."

"It was an accident."

"Get out of here."

She backed up to the sidewalk. Her dress brushed against a shrub with rough, thorny branches. It grabbed at the fabric. She turned and fought to release the skirt from the branches.

Bob walked to the center of the street. A dumb, stupid

human being who didn't deserve to live. He'd known from the first time he saw her that she couldn't handle that car. What seemed like petty annoyances had turned into something deadly and he hated himself for not seeing earlier that it wasn't petty at all. Any moron was allowed to own a car and the requirements for getting licensed were pathetic. Memorize a bunch of meaningless rules, and manage to drive for fifteen minutes with an equally stupid person, proving you could stop at traffic lights and change lanes without running into someone. There was no guarantee you had any control of the vehicle or that you'd adhere to any of the rules or even remember them once you were on the road.

A car rounded the corner and he was forced to decide whether he would pursue her or make it into the church in time for his wife's funeral. He would deal with her later.

He turned and walked back to the church and up the steps. He put his hand in the center of Ashley's upper back. Together, they walked through the doors.

ASHLEY HATED HERSELF for noticing she looked good in her navy blue dress and navy blue pumps with the three inch heels. What kind of girl admired her looks when she was standing in a condolence line at her mother's funeral?

When she'd woken that morning, her transition to reality was sudden. *Today is my mother's funeral.* She'd cried in the shower and had gone through seven tissues clearing her nose afterwards. Everything was so wrong — hot water running over her skin, blow-drying her hair, putting on her almost new navy blue bra, and tugging up pantyhose. Stepping into her pumps, admiring the smooth leather — all of it made her feel mean and small. Each movement, every choice, being alive, finding even a thread of pleasure — the strong, dark taste of coffee — was a betrayal of her mother.

People she'd never seen before shook her hand. Some hugged her. Men and women her father worked with? Teachers from her mother's school? People who made a hobby out of attending funerals? There was no way to know. Some of them introduced themselves and identified their relationship to her mother. They said her mother was a wonderful person.

So happy.

So friendly.

So easy to know.

A great friend.

A huge loss.

So sorry.

Such a tragedy.

They insisted Ashley should comfort herself with knowing how proud her mother was. *She talked about you all the time.*

That part was a surprise. Her mother talked about her? What did she say? Of course, Ashley couldn't very well ask. The mourners were clearly anxious to say something meaningful. At the same time, their eyes darted to the parking lot, desperate to walk away from death on this warm, pristine, seventy-four degree day.

She wished she and her father had stood inside the building to greet people. It was getting hot, despite the breeze. She didn't want her face red and her armpits and back wet with perspiration. She wished she didn't have to do this at all. But she was an adult, her father said. It was expected. That sounded like her mother more than her father. Maybe he just didn't want to stand there alone. Fair enough. But right now, nearly three hundred people were inching their way out the doors, clumping up, waiting to shake the hands of widower and near-orphan.

Finally it was over. She couldn't wait to get home and change her clothes, but that wasn't meant to be. People were coming to the house. Her mother's book club friends had brought food. Ashley would have to continue nodding and listening, noticing that each stab of hunger and need to use the bathroom and thought about wanting people to leave was part of an unbroken string of selfish human needs that her mother would never experience again.

She regretted thinking that moving back home was a failure, a return to childhood. Now, it seemed like a final chance. At least they'd talked, traded scraps of information about their lives.

Mostly, she tried not to think about how annoyed her mother had been. How not proud, but frustrated and distant and wanting Ashley out of the house, not caring if she achieved her dreams now or in ten years or never. Was her mother sorry? Did she feel anything? Think anything? Did she know what was going on in the lives she'd left behind?

AT HOME, SHE decided the hell with it. She was not going to sit around and stink up her dress and watch her mother's friends cry and listen to them repeat over and over how they just couldn't believe it. She ate a small plate of pasta salad then slipped out of the living room, kicked off her shoes, and carried them up the stairs. In her room, she put them in her closet. She glanced at the glossy black shoebox.

When her father had shouted at the woman who ran over her mother, an image of the gun had slipped through the back of Ashley's mind. Obviously there wasn't going to be any kind of punishment. The so-called accident had happened at dusk, her mother had been in the middle of the street, bending over, not visible in the driver's line of sight, blah blah blah. They'd determined the driver was going the speed limit, there was no *crime* — just a terrible accident.

Would her father file a lawsuit? But for what? Since the police concluded the driver hadn't done anything negligent.

She stripped off her pantyhose and dropped them on the floor of the closet. She should put them in the laundry basket so they didn't get snagged, but it was too much work. She unzipped her dress and stepped out of it. Her heart was like an iron ball inside her chest, weighing so much more than her frame could bear. Nothing could penetrate that thick, solid mass, not even a bullet.

The sagging flesh of her father's face, his empty eyes, made everything worse. It wasn't fair that a stupid woman, unable to master the basic skill of driving a car — no matter what the police said — possessed the power to destroy three lives. A hard piece of her brain knew she'd return to some sort of normal, eventually. But it hurt worse, thinking how her plans for the future had never even considered that her mother might not be part of the picture. She'd been robbed. Other girls her age got to live in blind happiness, not realizing how everything could change in half a second. She'd never get a chance to prove to her mother that her dreams weren't too big.

She tugged on jeans and a tank top. It was an inappropriate outfit for a funeral lunch. That's what her mother would say. Comfort shouldn't always be the first choice, sometimes you dressed for others. Her mother had never actually said that, but Ashley could imagine it. She could almost hear her mother's voice. How long would that last? Would it all fade into nothing?

She shoved her feet into flip-flops and pulled out the shoebox hiding the gun. Jack was downstairs, waiting for her. Now that this had happened, she assumed he'd forgotten about his demand that she return it.

She sat on her heels, the fabric of her jeans pulled tight over her knees. She lifted off the cover and placed her hand on the towel. The metal was so hard, so powerful. What would her father think of it? Maybe he wanted revenge. He'd hated that woman from the get-go, although Ashley still wasn't sure why. There was so much she didn't know about either of her parents. The disgust that steamed off his skin when he watched the woman lurch across the street, slamming in and out of her car, was like something solid. Maybe there was more to it than she knew.

Nothing was what you thought it was. Like that bomb her mother dropped. That her father preferred a son, that Ashley wasn't enough, that his interest in her was really disinterest. On some level, she'd known that. The memory was a tiny needle prick at the back of her brain, nearly forgotten. One of those memories you thought you remembered but weren't really sure if it was accurate, whether it had changed shape over the years.

She'd been small, she wasn't even sure how old. Although not a preschooler, because she'd walked home from a birthday party three houses away after a girl she didn't like soaked her with a water balloon. The front door was locked. She'd gone around to the backyard and into the house. For some reason, she didn't call her parents' names. She climbed the stairs, stopping near the top step when she heard her father's voice behind the partially closed bedroom door.

"Come on. Don't make me beg."

Her mother laughed but didn't sound very happy.

Ashley walked toward the bedroom. Her father stood with his back to the door, naked. Through the opening, she could see her mother standing just outside the bathroom, wearing nothing but a coffee-colored bra.

Ashley's eyes filled with tears, fear, maybe, that they might see her, that she didn't belong there, but she couldn't turn away.

Her father walked toward her mother and pressed her against the wall. He groaned.

Ashley closed her eyes.

"Not now," her mother said.

"But I need you."

"I said, no!"

Her father's voice sounded so different, like nothing she'd heard before. She felt sorry for him. Why was her mother being so mean? It was the same voice she used when Ashley pleaded for a Popsicle before dinner.

"Let's make a baby," her father said.

"How many times do I have to say it?"

"Don't you want a little boy?"

"It's too late."

After that, the memory faded. She was pretty sure they never knew she was there. She couldn't remember if she'd stayed, watching, or if she'd gone back downstairs, or down the hall to her room to take off her wet sundress.

Maybe her father would view her differently if he knew she had the gun. He'd be impressed with her strength, with her bravery in possessing something so dangerous. If he hadn't been paying attention to her all these years, this would get his attention. She smiled. The change in the shape of her lips felt strange, the skin pulling, her cheeks tightening. She hadn't smiled since . . .

She lifted the towel off the gun.

The stairs creaked. She moved the towel back into place and put the lid on the box. It was probably Jack, coming to find out where she'd disappeared to, leaving him alone and not knowing what to say to anyone, all complete strangers who kept saying, *So, you're Ashley's boyfriend?* Then they paused. It was uncertain territory.

Footsteps thudded softly down the hall. She looked up. Her father stood in the doorway.

"You need to come back downstairs," he said. "I can't deal with this alone."

Nineteen

BOB WAS WISHING he'd gone into the office, but he was off work on bereavement. He didn't want to be in his ten-by-twelve-foot white-walled space. That would require politely responding to condolences from the same people who had attended the funeral, as well as the casual ghouls who were compelled to tell him how sorry they were even though they were not sorry, they just felt awkward and wished he wasn't around, reminding them death might come sooner than they'd planned.

But drifting through the empty rooms, seeing Ashley, a pale ghost haunting the backyard and the living room or collapsed in front of the TV, not bothering to turn on the sound, was worse. Watching as if she were dead herself, observing the world from far away, her eyes traveling across flat, glowing images.

He wanted to help her but he hadn't a clue how to do that. He couldn't even get his own brain on track. It was like someone had placed a vacuum cleaner hose in his mouth and sucked out every bit of brain and muscle, blood vessels and bone, all the pieces that made him a solid presence, leaving nothing but a shell. And pain. He alternated between pain that made him double over as if he'd been kicked in the balls, and that floating empty space, like watching the sky when you were thirty thousand feet in the air, flying through wisps of cloud.

He went to the cubby in the kitchen and pulled out the pink binder full of Dana's dream bathroom plans. He took it to the breakfast room and placed it on the table.

It was almost eleven-thirty. Not too early for a beer. Drinking in the middle of the morning on a Monday was a bad habit to start, but it wasn't as if he'd be home on weekdays from here on out. Just today and tomorrow. Maybe Wednesday. He'd see how he felt by then.

Four beers stood on the top shelf of the fridge. He hoped there was more in the pantry. At some point he'd have to go to the grocery store. Or maybe Ashley could do that. He wouldn't know what food to choose or how much was needed for a week. He pulled out a beer and twisted off the cap. If it were Saturday, no one would think anything of him having a beer on a warm weekend morning after working in the yard. Something about indulging in one before noon on a Monday continued to feel wrong. But then, there was no one to notice his bad behavior, so it didn't matter.

He sat at the table, took a long swallow of beer, and

flipped open the book. The first page was an image of a woman's back. She was looking out a picture window at a dense forest — trees laced with flowering vines. She wore a floor-length white silky robe and her hair hung straight to her shoulders. She looked very much like Dana, although Dana didn't own a robe like that.

"What are you doing?"

He looked up and took another swallow of beer.

Ashley stared at him. "Beer in the middle of the morning?"

"It's eleven-thirty. Probably eleven-forty now."

She glanced behind her into the kitchen. "Eleven-thirty-four."

"Same difference." He took another swallow.

"Can I have one?"

"You're an adult."

She disappeared into the kitchen. He looked at the image of the woman in her bathroom — Italian tile, graceful faucets that were works of art in themselves, an enormous vase of freshly cut lilies on the counter. The tub looked like an outdoor hot tub, although not quite as deep.

He closed his eyes and pictured the robe sliding off the woman's shoulders, slithering down her back, pooling on the floor like milk.

He opened his eyes. Ashley stood in the doorway again. She took a sip of beer. When she pulled the bottle away from her mouth, a few bubbles of foam stayed on her lips. She flicked her tongue across her upper lip.

"What are you looking at?"

"Your mother's pictures of exotic bathrooms."

"Why'd she have pictures of bathrooms?"

"She wanted to remodel the master bathroom."

"Oh. When were you planning to do that?"

He shrugged.

"I guess it doesn't matter." She took a long swallow of beer, walked into the room, and pulled out a chair.

The chair he'd chosen was Dana's. He usually sat at the other end, facing out the front window. Ashley was in the spot opposite from where she usually sat as well.

He flipped the page, suddenly ashamed of looking at the picture of the woman, as if it were some kind of porn. No, that wasn't right, as if he were staring at his wife getting into the bath and Ashley had blundered into the room, interrupting an intimate moment. Except there'd never been such an intimate moment. There was no exotic bathroom, no white robe, and no Dana. Tears clogged his throat and his nose filled with mucous. He lifted his head, trying to get it to drain without Ashley noticing he was falling apart.

The next page was a plastic sleeve that held a brochure from a tile store.

"It's okay, Daddy."

"What's okay?"

"It's okay to cry."

"I'm not crying."

"You should."

He stared at the tiles. They all looked pretty much the same. One had a bright blue felt-penned ring around it. The tile had more of a gold tint than the others. Although if the ring wasn't there, he would have no idea which one she'd chosen. Had she chosen it? Or was she just leaning in that direction? He flipped the page. There was a series of diagrams from a magazine demonstrating how to cut a hole in the wall to enlarge a normal bathroom window, creating a picture window. He would need to hire a contractor if he was going to knock a hole in the wall. Or maybe he could figure it out himself. It couldn't be that difficult if he had a decent instruction guide. There were probably videos all over the web explaining step by step what was needed, what to watch out for, how to work around a beam without compromising the integrity of the structure.

The next page was filled with more photographs cut from magazines, the corners held with glue. It was difficult to tell what the appeal was in each setting. Was she simply collecting every attractive photograph of a spiffed up bathroom, or was there something specific in each one he was supposed to notice? There was no way to tell. He could study the images forever and not know if it was the brand of fixtures, the color of the tile, or simply the dish of decorative soaps she wanted to include in her fantasy project.

The beer was still cold, but it had that too-foamy texture which gave it a slightly soapy flavor, or was it thinking about the perfumes in those tiny soaps that created the sour taste on his tongue? He took another sip anyway.

"What are we going to do?" Ashley said.

"About what?"

"Without Mom." Her voice was weak, tired, as if she'd just now realized her mother was gone.

"I don't know."

"Why aren't you angry anymore?"

"At what?"

"That stupid woman who can't drive a fucking car!" She took several long swallows of beer. When she was finished, her lips were wet.

"I am."

"You don't seem like it," she said.

"I can't un-do it."

"All you do is mope."

"What else is there?"

"I don't know. She should be punished." She stood and took several more swallows of beer.

"That won't bring back your mother. It's done. She's gone." The rage he'd felt earlier, the constant chewing over what that rude, stupid woman had done, how he despised her, had dried up. It might return, it might not. For now, he was consumed with a numb calmness; maybe the need to be there for his daughter had taken over.

She put her near-empty bottle on the table and walked to the doorway. Dana would tell her to put something under it, that the moisture was going to damage the finish. Now that

Dana was gone — *gone*, he hated that word — all the furniture would have rings from beer bottles and soda cans and coffee mugs. He was sure of it.

"It's not fair." Ashley put her hands over her face. The tip of her nose, turning red, poked through the space between the sides of her hands. "It's not fair! She ruined my life and now she's just driving around and going to church like nothing changed. She belongs in prison! She should be suffering."

He nodded.

"It's so un-*fair!*"

"Everything's unfair."

She collapsed against the doorframe. With her hands still covering her face, she slid down until she was seated, her knees bent. She took her hands away from her face and hugged her legs close to her, leaning her head against her knees.

"Why is God doing this to me? To us?"

"There is no god. You're smart enough to know that."

"Before, it seemed like there might be. Everything was going so good in my life, sort of. I mean I had a great life and now, I can't do anything."

"They say it gets easier. After a while."

"Who says it gets easier?"

"People. I guess people who have lived through it."

She let go of her legs and thrust her upper body toward him, her face turned up. The skin was red, her hair damp around the roots. Her eyes looked like they'd collapsed inside the sockets, the whites blurred, and the tender part of her upper and lower lids a brighter red than her nose and cheeks. "My life was good, and now it's all screwed up. And you . . . you!"

"What about me?"

"I thought you loved me. I thought you supported me and wanted me to succeed."

"I do."

"That's not what Mom said." She stood and tugged her t-shirt down but it stopped short of her belt, leaving a line of exposed skin. She moved closer to the table, staring into his eyes, not blinking, defiant and demanding.

He swallowed. "What are you talking about?"

"She said you didn't want a daughter."

"That's not true." It sounded like a lie to him. But it wasn't true. It wasn't that he didn't want a daughter, that he didn't love his daughter. It was something else, something deeper . . . he couldn't explain it.

"That's what mom told me."

"She did?" His own mother had insisted a son was an emblem of manhood. Without a son, a man didn't see himself live on, she'd said. That was the best thing she'd given Bob's father — multiple reflections of himself. She'd reminded the family often, and she didn't stop repeating her proclamation when Ashley was born. On the other hand, what guarantee was there that a son would turn out as you hoped? Besides that, it was an antiquated belief from a world where male children were needed to give a family physical strength against other clans. Still, it wouldn't release its grip.

"Was she just trying to hurt me? You think she was that cruel?"

"I wanted you."

"She said you wanted a boy." The word came out of her mouth like she was spitting a wad of tobacco.

Hearing Ashley voice his desire when he'd never spoken of it, never said anything to Dana . . . or had he? It was difficult to remember after all these years what they'd actually talked about and what was left unsaid. After the third miscarriage she'd said, *I'm done*. At least that's how he remembered it. Sitting by her bed in the hospital, not wanting to see the five-month-old fetus they'd removed. But wanting to see it. Not wanting to know if it was a girl, or a boy. And then he did see it — him. The memories were cloudy. He didn't understand why some memories remained distinct and others turned murky as a dream, making him wonder if he'd imagined it, interpreted it from things she hadn't mentioned. Did she mean she was done getting pregnant? Later, in the months following, she'd been very clear. But what if she'd changed her mind? He didn't know, because after a while, he'd stopped asking. Begging, really.

"So I guess you did," Ashley said.

"I did what?"

"Wanted a boy. Instead of me."

"That's not how it was at all."

"You didn't disagree."

"I was thinking."

"About what?"

He took a swallow of beer. He gagged on the warm liquid. "We wanted more children."

Ashley pounded her fist on the table. Her beer bottle skittered on the wood surface. "That's a lame answer. Why are you lying to me? On top of everything else, you have to lie?"

"I'm telling you the truth."

"Not all of it. Did you want a boy?"

"Yes."

"Oh!" She grabbed her stomach and bent over. Her hair fell over her shoulders, her scalp a thin line of red where her hair was parted. Her shoulders trembled and she half-sobbed, mostly gasps of air.

"Are you okay?" He pushed out his chair.

"I'm fine. Just fine. No mother, no father. Nothing."

"I'm your father. Of course I wanted you. Wanting a son doesn't mean I didn't want you."

"That's not how it sounds."

Her voice was soft and cold, a paper-thin sheet of ice layering the space between them. She straightened. Her eyes were still red, the pupils shrunk to tiny specks.

"I wanted you. I . . ."

"How pathetic. To have to tell me you wanted me. When

all these years I thought you were my biggest fan. It was all a lie."

He stood.

She turned and went into the kitchen. She opened the refrigerator door and grabbed the last two beers by their long necks. She slammed the door. Jars and bottles rattled against each other. He shouldn't let her drink by herself. She'd already polished off the first beer in less than fifteen minutes. But she was an adult. He could complain that the beer was his.

What a mess. She had it all wrong. It wasn't really clear what Dana had said to her, or even that Ashley heard it correctly.

She didn't understand. There was a primal need to see your life go on in another male. It was so natural, and so easy. Men fathered boys every minute of the day, spreading their seed and going about their business. Boys popped up all over the place. They became delinquents and geeks, rapists and businessmen, priests and lawyers, ballplayers . . . Everywhere he looked he saw men with their sons, something that was received without thought by nearly every man on the planet had been denied to him.

Ashley's feet thumped up the stairs. The sound of her door closing pierced his chest — she didn't slam it, or close it softly so he couldn't hear. There was just the sound of wood meeting up, the latch clicking into place. Or maybe that sound was only in his head. Surely he couldn't hear the door latch down the length of the hall, through the kitchen walls.

Twenty

MELODY TOOK A BLOCK of cheddar cheese out of the refrigerator. She put it on the cutting board and shaved off six pieces. She cut them in half and placed each slice on a whole-wheat cracker. Since the accident, her appetite was tiny. A few pieces of cheese and a handful of crackers, a cup of yogurt, a strand of grapes or half a cookie made her stomach ache as it did after a Thanksgiving dinner of turkey and stuffing with mashed potatoes and gravy. She dreaded going back to church. Her mind circled endlessly from one unpleasant scenario to the next.

The first bite of cheese and cracker tasted salty and crunchy and smooth. She chewed slowly. It was the swallowing that was difficult. Even the smallest bite, a third of the cracker, caught in her throat like an un-chewed spoonful of overcooked rice, thick and pasty. She forced herself to swallow. She picked up her coke can and took a small sip.

It wasn't good to stand at the counter and eat dinner, if you could call it that. She should at least put her cheese and crackers on a plate and sit at the table. But sitting at the table highlighted everything wrong in her life — she wasn't eating an actual meal, she had no mate, she had no close friends to listen and offer comforting, reassuring words, even if they were partially false.

The evening at Sarah's after the accident had been her only contact with other human beings for five days. She'd called in sick at work. They understood — her nerves, a raging headache, her unstable stomach. She hadn't attended the worship service last Sunday. The thought of walking into the hall, faces turning to look at her, or possibly not turning to look, trying to suppress their ungodly desire for scandal and gossip, terrified her. Between the incident with the baked beans and the accident, she'd become an object of ridicule and horror. Even when they'd patted her shoulders and lifted their hands in silent pleas to God that night while the lights of the ambulance blinked red in the gathering darkness, she'd known they weren't sympathetic. They were shocked.

Watching Bob and his daughter shun her at the funeral delivered the first stab of anger she'd felt in a long time. Maybe that was why all these humiliating things kept happening to her, she drew them to her by never fighting back, by letting people treat her badly, as if deep inside she knew she deserved it. Was that an ungodly thought? To reject constant humiliation and attacks on her personhood? God required submission, accepting what came your way. But why did it all come to her and not to the others at Triumphant Life Tabernacle? It wasn't right that she was the only one to suffer like this. Unless God had a much higher calling He was preparing her for. But if that were the case, how was she supposed to figure out what it was?

She hadn't intended to hurt the family when she showed up at the funeral. She wanted to let them know how deeply sorry she was. If they saw her, they might realize how kind and full of love she was. They'd recognize the hand of God in all of this, even if it was a heavy, unjust hand.

The street in front of the church had been lined with cars, glittering in the April sun like lines of soda cans waiting to be recycled. Huge pieces of tin — black, red, blue, silver, and white. Weapons of death. She'd never looked at a car that way before, but that's what they were. Enormous machines with too much power and the ability to kill so easily. They lulled you into thinking they were tools of convenience, simple to manage. With just a few fingertips on the steering wheel, you could maneuver around corners and into parking spaces. Even with your hands off the wheel, the car would proceed on course for a moment or two.

She put another cracker and slice of cheese into her mouth, chewed it quickly, and stuffed in the next cracker before she'd swallowed the previous one. As she followed that with another cracker and cheese combo, her cell phone rang, imitating the melodic chords of a harp. She swallowed and sipped her coke and picked up the phone. "H'lo?"

"Melody?"

"Yes."

"This is Tim. Gordon Wilson's brother. I met you a few times, at . . ."

"I know who you are."

"Do you have a minute?"

"Yes."

"Uhm, this is kind of awkward."

"What is?" She took another sip of coke. It fizzed across her lips and dribbled on her chin. A few bubbles landed on her phone. She strained to touch the screen with her tongue to make them disappear, but couldn't reach. It sounded like he was going to ask her out. Dating hadn't been on her list of things to do for a long time now, but that didn't mean she'd slammed that door forever. She hoped Sarah hadn't said anything to him — *poor Melody, she really needs a man. A godly man. She was so hurt by her fiancé* . . .

"I don't know how to start," he said.

"At the beginning."

He laughed.

"It's not really funny. It's an old joke."

"I laughed because it doesn't apply here. There is no beginning, since I don't know you."

She went to the table, pulled out a chair, and sat down. She picked up another cracker with cheese and put it in her mouth. She chewed quickly and swallowed.

"Sarah asked me to call you."

"Oh? Why?"

"She thought you'd be more inclined to listen to someone you didn't really know . . . uh . . . that you might pay more attention to a guy."

"What are you talking about?"

"She wanted me to give you a message."

"Then why didn't she call me?"

"Because of what I said. That you needed to hear a guy's voice." His voice was rough. He obviously needed to clear his throat, but didn't want to stop until he got to the end. "She thinks you're bringing an unholy presence into the church. She wants you to stay away until you give up your, uhm, willfulness. She thinks the accident, killing someone, is going to damage the church's ability to keep its message pure and . . ."

"Why would you call and tell me this? And who does she think she is? She's not the minister. She . . . you . . . why would you agree to call me about this? What kind of person are you?" She stood and carried the last two crackers topped with cheese to the sink and stuffed them down the disposal. She should hang up. She lifted her shoulder to press the phone against her ear. She wrapped plastic around the block of cheese and put it back in the refrigerator.

"I know. I'm sorry. I kind of owe her."

"It was an accident! It has nothing to do with my faith or anything else. A woman was bending over in the street and it was dark and it was an accident."

"I'm sure. I know. Sarah can be a little intense."

"Intense? What kind of slimy doormat are you that you'd call a total stranger and say things like this? You know nothing about me."

"I'm sorry. Really I am."

"Then why did you agree to call?"

"She's very . . . she's . . . she loaned me some money a while back, a lot of money, and I don't want my brother to know. She threatened to tell him about it."

"You're a weak man." She was glad he hadn't asked her out now that she saw what he was like. Not a man at all. She remembered meeting him, thinking he could hold her head in the palm of his hand, almost like God.

"I had a good reason. I'm helping my little sister. She's an alcoholic and Gordon thinks I'm enabling her, but I can't let her live on the street. Sarah understands. Or I thought she did."

"You make it sound like she's blackmailing you."

"Maybe. A little. Anyway, I'm not trying to hurt you. I'm really not. I know some churches can be vicious if you do something they don't like. The church I go to is quieter, not so . . . enthusiastic."

"I like enthusiastic churches. If God doesn't deserve all of our energy and devotion, who does?"

"I don't know. But anyway, I'm sorry. If you want to know the truth, she can be a bit of a bitch."

Melody felt something in her chest, as if she'd been singed with a sparkler. Thin, hissing flames buzzed through her blood vessels. A tiny thrill of excitement. She wouldn't use the word he had, wouldn't be so harsh, but it was true.

"I shouldn't say that about her, she's been good to me."

"But not so good to me." She giggled. "The word fits." The fizzing sensation behind her breastbone continued to spread. It was fun to say what she really thought. This was what the Bible meant, that the lure of sinful behavior was exciting. That was it — she felt excited, like she could say anything, let go and speak her mind. Should she?

"She's telling me I'm not welcome until I pass some magical test?" She laughed again. She felt like a teenager on Halloween, hurling an egg, enjoying the explosion of shell, the splattering of clear fluid and thick strings of yellow. "I've done everything God asked of me. Everything! She has no right to tell me I can't go to church. It was not my fault that woman died. Does she think it was my fault Mike dumped beans on my head?"

"She didn't mention that. She did say I should remind you about closing your eyes."

"Is that a threat?"

"I don't really know what she means, she just told me to mention it."

Melody slipped off her shoes and twirled around. Her hair flew out from her face. "Sarah and the others made me feel like there's something wrong with me. But there's not. I love

God and I've done everything the Bible asks and everything the Spirit has led me to."

"I know."

"You don't know. How could you know? You've only met me twice."

"You seem like a very godly woman."

"Is she kicking me out?" She laughed. "She thinks she can kick me out of the church? And what a two-faced bitch. You're right. She's a bitch. She sat there and acted all concerned about my life last week, and then she was all comforting after the accident, and then she puts you up to calling me because she doesn't have the guts?"

"You have a right to be upset."

She laughed. She felt drunk. Not that she knew exactly what that felt like. It had only happened twice in her life and it was so long ago. But she remembered the giddiness and absolute sense of not caring what anyone thought, even though behind that sense of freedom was a second self, observing her uncensored words, her high-pitched laugh, sharp and too loud, like a myna bird trying to mimic human laughter.

She stopped suddenly. And that too, reminded her of her long-ago drunkenness — the sudden crash, becoming nauseous and dizzy, no longer amused. "I really don't know what I've done wrong, and I don't understand why she's being so cruel. Is that her opinion, or does everyone at the church agree with her?"

"I think it's mostly her."

"But you're not sure?" She turned off the kitchen light and walked into the living room. She sat on the edge of the couch. The cushions were thick and soft and she sank down so that her knees jutted up, too high to rest her elbows on them. She shifted back and moved the phone to her other ear.

"Look, I'm really sorry," he said.

"You should be."

"It's not like she wouldn't have gotten the message to you if it wasn't from me. I only did what she asked because I owe her."

"So you said."

"You could visit my church. Any time. It's Quaker and everyone's friendly. They don't judge."

"The Lord is the judge of us all."

"Yes, but we shouldn't judge each other."

She knew he was right, but she wanted to argue. "I don't understand why she didn't call me herself. If she thinks God wanted to deliver a message."

"She cares about you, and she feels bad."

"Ha."

"I'm not saying I understand. Just telling you what she said."

"Well she can't prevent me from attending church. What's she going to do, have the elders drag me out the door and toss me to the curb?"

He laughed. "I need to get going. But like I said, you could visit my church . . ."

"I know. Sure."

"Bye," he said.

She clicked the button to end the call. She tossed the phone on the couch. It slid away from the edge and wedged itself between the seat cushion and the back. She got up and went into the bedroom. She stripped off her jeans. The tails of her shirt hung down to her thighs. She had nice legs — long and lean. A shower would rinse away the sticky film of sweat that appeared during her conversation with Tim, but she wasn't sure she had the energy to stand under the hot water soaping her body, then observe herself in the mirror, drying her hair.

She flopped on the bed. Her Bible sat on the nightstand. Usually she read a chapter and spent time praying every night. Instead, she pulled the comforter over her legs and closed her eyes. If she fell asleep, she'd regret it because she'd probably be sleepless sometime after midnight. But all she wanted was to escape her thoughts and the menacing voice of God.

WHEN SHE WOKE, she had the urge to hurl the Bible at the mirror. She'd fallen asleep with it in the crook of her arm, although she didn't remember taking it off the nightstand. The clock said eleven-forty.

She'd dreamt she was standing at the back of the church hall. It was much longer in her dream, the size of an airport concourse. At the far end was a tiny circle of chairs and a small group of people with their heads bent forward, their hands lifted in prayer. Lying on the stage beyond the ring of bowed heads was the woman she'd killed. The dead woman's limbs twisted like clumps of vines and her head hung over the edge of the stage, her hair coated with blood.

Melody had tried to turn and run out the door, but she couldn't move. Neither could she seem to approach the group.

Suddenly, Sarah had lifted her head, turned, and stared at her. Her eyes were like rays of sun forcing themselves through window blinds on a hot summer afternoon.

Sarah stood and went to the stage. She lifted Dana's body and cradled it like she was carrying a child, the body suddenly much smaller than it had looked initially. She walked around the circle of chairs. As she approached, Melody strained to reach the panic bar on the lobby door but she still couldn't move. She didn't want to see the corpse, didn't know how Sarah could bear to touch it. Melody saw the face had been eaten with decay. The toes were missing and the flesh on the fingers had fallen off, the bones visible, but the skin was still there on the upper part of her hands, torn and bloody.

Melody strained toward the door but her body seemed to be encased in something thick.

Sarah drew closer. The body looked worse with each step, the eyes still there, loose and floating in their sockets, the optic nerve visible as the head lolled over the side of Sarah's arm.

When Sarah was a few feet away, she held the body out for Melody to take it. Melody clenched her arms to her sides, tried again to turn, but somehow, Sarah managed to transfer the corpse into Melody's arms. She couldn't look at it. The weight was more than she would have imagined. She felt her legs giving out. The eyes turned and looked at her.

As she stood there, trying to get rid of it, the skin began to blister and melt away.

Melody screamed. When the body convulsed, she'd woken.

She put her hand on the Bible, ready to throw it, but her fingers slid off the leather, leaving a smear of oil.

She sat up. Even with her eyes open, all she could picture was that woman's body decomposing in her arms.

How would she ever erase this from her mind? Would she be tormented with nightmares for the rest of her life? She sat up and flipped open the Bible. She picked it up. "God, please. Please. It wasn't my fault. I didn't mean to step on the gas. Or maybe I did. But you were there with me, weren't you? It's not my fault. Please help me. Please."

Her eyes flooded with tears so she couldn't read the words. She grabbed the bed sheet and pulled it up to her face, dragging it across her eyes. She moved it away and read — *Do your best to present yourself to God as one approved, a worker who has no need to be ashamed, rightly handling the word of truth.*

So nothing had changed. The only way to escape her shame, to obliterate the nightmare, the only way to receive the gift of tongues and be welcomed into the sisterhood formed by Sarah and the others was to deliver Bob into the family of God. Bob and his daughter. That's why they had to suffer, so God could bring them home. Melody was His instrument, removing something precious from their lives so they could turn to the source of life.

Twenty-one

ASHLEY HAD BEEN back at work for two days now. Sitting at the reception desk, she felt like her brain was split in two. With one half, she greeted visitors, checked them in, scheduled conference rooms, answered phones as if nothing had changed. Life was normal, simple and constructed of small tasks. The other part of her, as if she were standing a few yards away, watching, wondered if her life had ended.

Sometimes she found herself thinking she'd imagined her mother's death. Unless sitting at the reception desk was in her imagination. Every so often, the watching part of herself shut off and she'd find herself making plans for the future, surfing the web for opportunities, talking to her friends on Facebook. Her life might be an illusion, unfolding inside her head but looking entirely different from the outside. She wasn't sure if her mother's death intensified that feeling or if everyone felt that way. It certainly wasn't discussed on Facebook.

Tonight she was going to Jack's, another betrayal. She'd take off her clothes and feel his hands on her skin. They'd eat dinner and she'd savor the tastes and the warm thudding of her pulse, the softening of her brain as wine wound its way through arteries and blood vessels and the tiniest veins.

At three minutes to five she locked the desk drawers. She set her computer password, which in some ways felt more secure than the drawers, since the drawers could surely be pried open from behind. Yet the computer wasn't really locked. There were still probably ways to get around the window demanding a password.

She picked up her purse, walked across the lobby, and out the main door. Most days she stopped by her supervisor's office to say good-bye, but she couldn't manage another inquiry about how she was doing, how she was holding up, to just *say the word* if she needed more time off.

Outside, the air was cool. That was fine with her. She was no longer anxious for summer, preferring the wet, dreary spring to continue for quite some time. At least until that day arrived, the day when everyone promised she would feel normal again.

The drive to Jack's passed without her awareness of turning the wheel, accelerating and decelerating, braking, following the map in her mind. She parked in one of the guest slots and walked through the garden area. The sharp colors of daffodils and cyclamen and the scent of freshly cut grass paved the way to his apartment.

She knocked and Jack opened the door. He stood back to let her in.

She went inside and dropped her purse and overnight bag on the couch. He put his arms around her waist and pulled her against him. They weren't quite facing each other and his belt buckle pressed against her hipbone. It hurt, but she didn't want to adjust her position, which he would interpret as a signal that she wanted to hurry to the bedroom. She definitely wanted a glass of wine first. She needed to find a way to put her head back into the normal world. Wine would help. Dinner too. And listening to Jack.

His arms were stiff on her back. His body wasn't melting into hers like it normally did. He didn't pull back his head to kiss her. His ear touched the side of her face. His breath was warm on her skin, but he didn't burrow into her neck, touching each part with warm, firm lips. An aroma of grief must be coming off her body, pushing him away, or at least holding him apart from her, a gossamer wall between them.

He let go and stepped away. "Want a beer?"

"I'd rather have a glass of wine."

"I don't have any."

She pouted and looked up at him through her lashes. It was the first flirty, normal thing she'd done in ten days and although it was followed quickly by a whisper of sadness for her contrived actions, she didn't feel the wave of despair that had accompanied each hint of normality. Was this how quickly it would all fade? Every day, there'd be a new moment where her mood was microscopically lighter? Each day more moments, every moment less darkness? "I thought you'd buy some since I was coming over."

"I thought you were real with me."

"What?"

He went into the kitchen and pulled out two beers. He twisted off the caps and walked back around the counter. He handed a beer to her. He returned to the counter between the kitchen and living room and took a long swallow from his beer. "I don't even know who you are."

"What are you talking about?" She put the beer on the coffee table, shoved her things to the side, and flopped on the couch. She pried off her high heels and sat cross-legged.

"I saw Krista."

Ashley picked up her bottle. She tipped it against her lips and swallowed carefully.

"You told her I said she was gross because she had big boobs? Had! She got them cut off you know."

"She didn't get them cut off."

"Well made smaller. She looked fantastic and now she mutilated herself because you lied? And you put it on me?" He slammed his beer on the counter.

"I was a kid. I had a crazy crush on you."

"That's no excuse."

"You sound like my mother." She winced. There was a tightness in her throat like a fishbone poking the tender flesh.

"You are so cold."

She blinked, trying to stop the tears. She lifted her head. She closed her eyes so the light didn't make it worse. She couldn't deal with this. Her mother, what he'd just said, the hatred forming a thin white line around his lips. Krista must have told him a completely different story. And it wasn't mutilation, what a drama queen.

She got up and went to the window. She pulled the cord to open the drapes. She hated that he kept them shut all the time. Sure, there were a lot of people walking by, but the path was at least ten feet from his window, and only occasionally did they turn to look inside. And so what if they did? "I'm not cold. I wanted you to myself." She turned. "Is that so bad? You know I love you." She took the drape in her hand and ran her fingers down, feeling the bumpy weave rub on her skin.

"Do you? How would I know that?"

"Because I . . . because we're together. I'm with you."

"How are we together?" he said.

"What do you mean?" She pulled on the drape. The bar holding it in place gave way more than it should have. She let go. She didn't need the drapes crashing down on her head, but she wanted something to hold onto. She plucked at the fabric but kept her grip light.

"You refused to live with me."

He couldn't be breaking up with her. He wouldn't. Yes, she'd had doubts, didn't know for sure if he was her one and only, but she didn't want to break up! She liked him a lot. And if anyone broke up, it should be her! But she wanted to be with him. They didn't have to decide anything right away. They had years. Why couldn't he see that? Especially now. "We're talking about too many things at once."

"No we're not. We're talking about us. You think you're better than me," he said.

"I don't."

"Yes you do. You think I won't go as far as you, whatever that means. That I'll drag you down."

"I don't think that at all."

As he drank his beer, he looked at her over the top of the bottle, holding his gaze steady. He was in control of the conversation and he knew it.

Each denial on her part led to disagreement on his side — a ping pong ball smacked back across the table, tapping the wood, the rubber-coated wood paddle deflecting it as if it knew where the ball was headed before it arrived.

"I'm pretty sure you have no soul. At least Krista has a soul, feels things, gets hurt, like a normal human being."

"I have a soul."

"Did you even cry when your mother was buried?"

"That's not fair!" She yanked on the curtain. The rod tore away from the plaster and part of the drape fell on her shoulder.

"Hey. Watch out. Don't start trashing my apartment."

She pushed the drapes away.

"You don't know what I do when I'm alone, and you have

no idea what I feel for my mother."

"Exactly. I have no idea what you feel about anything."

"Why are you doing this to me?" She moved away from the window and sat in the armchair. A chair they never used. The cushions like a stack of cardboard, the back and arms too stiff, it was like sitting in a chair made of concrete.

"Why didn't you cry at her funeral?"

"Because I don't cry in public. That's how I am. It doesn't mean I don't feel anything."

"Even your father was crying, but you stood there like an ice goddess. Prancing around in your high heels."

Her eyes watered.

"*Now* you're crying? You can't cry for your mother, but one tiny criticism and you get all sad?"

She folded her arms around her waist and closed her eyes. She wasn't going to give him the satisfaction of crying, or shouting, or doing anything more to let him see how badly he was hurting her. She stood and went to the coffee table. She picked up her beer and took a long swallow. If she could finish it quickly, she could have another and then she might feel calmer, buff off the edges of the sharp blade pressing on her heart.

She took the bottle away from her lips. It was still a third full. She put her mouth around the opening and leaned her head back. Her throat narrowed at the coldness but she kept drinking until she felt the thin foamy layer at the end fizzle across her tongue.

"You look exactly like your father when you do that."

"Oh really?" She walked to the counter and put the bottle near his elbow. She stepped around him and opened the fridge. Ten dark brown bottles stood on the top shelf, shoulder to shoulder, challenging her to drink all of them. Or at least half. She took one, twisted off the cap, and put it with the others on the counter. The bottle was so cold her fingers stung. Her stomach was heavy with the beer she'd chugged, but it was worth it. Everything seemed less important. She really could care less about Krista and whatever exaggerated sob story she'd told Jack. So he'd rather believe a girl he hardly knew instead of his girlfriend of six years.

"Your father drinks beer the same way. I noticed because when you disappeared after the funeral, I was sitting next to him. Listening to him not talk about your mother, so maybe you two are the same in more ways than one. Soul-less and chugging beer, your eyes all bulged out like the beer is filling your head instead of your gut."

She laughed. "Whatever."

"It was weird how he wanted to talk about the woman who ran over her instead of actually missing your mom."

"You can't judge him on a five minute conversation at my mother's funeral. He's all over the place. We both are. You have no idea what it feels like."

"Maybe not. But he was obsessed. And it was more than five minutes. You were gone for like twenty minutes or more, and he went on and on the whole time."

"About what?"

"About how he hated himself for going into the church for the funeral. God didn't exist anyway, why did you have to go through the motions, then talking about how stupid that religious woman is, how she can't drive, how she ran your mother down like she was a varmint in the street, how God was a myth and he only had the funeral in a church because it would have made your mother happy, but what did that matter because it wasn't like she was there to thank him for following her wishes. If those even were her wishes, he didn't know for sure. And how that woman showed up, lurking across the street like some kind of rubber-necker wanting to see what she'd caused. And how he was sure he knew her from somewhere else and it was making him crazy trying to remember. Then he'd circle back to God again and how stupid people were who believed that shit."

"What did you say?"

"He didn't give me a chance to say anything. He hardly took a breath. Except when he drank his beer. And then I'd say, *wow, sorry,* and *it's tough* and lame stuff like that. He seems messed up."

"Of course he's messed up. His wife is dead."

"Yeah, so why is he more worried about God and some stranger who had a terrible accident? It's not like she tried to kill your mother. It wasn't a hit and run."

Ashley slammed her beer on the counter. Golden beer splashed out on the white Formica. "She killed my mother."

"Not on purpose."

"She should still be punished." She picked up the beer, licked off the liquid around the top and took a swallow. "My father said he knows her?"

"He did know her. Or met her before."

"He didn't mention that."

"Maybe he was drunk. Just rambling."

She didn't want to talk about her father. How had they even gotten on the subject? "So are you breaking up with me?" She put her beer on the counter. It wasn't very good, too gamey tasting. A nice glass of cold white wine would be so nice. Or warm, silken, heart soothing red. She walked into the living room. She picked up her purse. She stepped into her shoes and turned. "Are you?"

"I feel like I don't know you. That we're just going through motions, playing parts. Boyfriend. Girlfriend."

"That's a *yes*, then?"

"I don't know."

"Do you love me?"

"That's not the question."

"What is the question then?"

"Do *you* love *me*? Can you love anyone?"

Those words should hurt, but they didn't. "I think I should leave."

"I think so. We need time to figure things out."

"Whatever." She picked up her overnight bag. She didn't want to go home, but she surely didn't want to stay. She could call one of her friends, meet for a glass of wine and a nice dinner. She didn't want to think about anything at all. Except maybe how to get the kind of job she deserved, something that would consume all her thoughts and energy and make life seem more real.

Twenty-two

TWO OR THREE finches were trapped inside the cavernous Home Depot. With the warehouse doors continuously open during business hours, it was surprising more birds didn't wind up inside, chirping, not immediately alarmed, but flapping their wings a little too fast, trying to find their way out.

Knowing how often birds needed to eat, Bob figured their panic would escalate quickly. But they must eventually escape, or the building would turn into an aviary. Instead, there were never more than a handful, and he'd never seen one that had dropped dead of hunger or sheer terror. Unless the workers scooped them up so quickly, customers never had the opportunity to stumble upon one. On the other hand, knowing how long it took to obtain help, he doubted they had a lot of spare cycles for removing bird corpses to ensure customers didn't have horrifying experiences in their warehouse. He could stop worrying about the birds.

Still, he felt their rapidly fluttering hearts inside his own chest, the anxiety of darting around the rafters, landing on a beam, looking around and not seeing sky or grass, and nothing edible except the occasional broken piece of potato chip purchased from the curbside vendor.

He decided not to take a cart. This was an exploratory trip. He'd pursue the project in small steps. Dana's pink binder was tucked under his arm. The biggest jobs would be enlarging the window and that Jacuzzi tub. He might need to hire help for the tub. He'd start with the tile and then look at the fixtures to see if the things she wanted were available or if he'd have to do more research online, or visit a store that specialized in bathroom remodeling rather than a general purpose warehouse that included tile and tubs alongside everything from lumber to light bulbs and insecticide.

He walked to the tile section and flipped open the binder. The brochure in the binder was from a tile store, but he preferred to get it here, if he could.

He walked slowly past the shelves. There were several tiles that looked similar to the one she'd circled — various shades of pinks and browns with hints of gold. He stopped and knelt on one knee. The concrete floor hurt, but he needed to hold the brochure up close to see if it was the same pattern.

"Can I help you, sir?"

He looked up. A clerk pushing a handcart had stopped behind him. The clerk shifted the stack of boxes off the cart.

Bob stood. "Just trying to find this tile."

"Do you know the manufacturer?"

Bob looked at the brochure. "San Marino."

"We don't carry that style, but we can order it for you. When do you need it?"

"I haven't started the demolition. There's plenty of time."

"Do you want to place an order? Do you have the square footage?"

"I don't. I'm just getting started. But good to know I can get it here. I need to figure out everything — fixtures, sinks."

The clerk nodded. "Let me know if you have more questions."

"Sure." Bob flipped the binder closed.

The clerk grabbed the handle of the cart and walked to the end of the aisle. The stack of boxes remained in front of the shelves behind Bob. It looked like actually filling the shelves was someone else's job — a precise division of labor.

Bob knelt in front of the tile again. He touched it with the tip of his finger. It had a satiny finish. He stroked it again. It looked natural and earthy, handcrafted, instead of stamped out of a machine. It was very similar to the one in the book. Did it matter that he had exactly that pattern? Maybe she hadn't seen the one he was looking at. Maybe she only circled it because that was the one she liked most in the brochure.

He shifted from sitting on his heels and lowered himself to the floor, crossing his legs at the ankles. He was unable to stop touching the smooth surface of the tile, tracing his finger along the faint blue lines that split through it like veins on the back of a woman's hand.

"Excuse me."

An oversized shopping cart appeared in his peripheral vision. He inched closer to the shelf.

"There's still not enough room."

He looked over his shoulder at the stack of boxes behind him. He wanted the woman pushing the cart to recognize that in the time it would take him to get to his feet, she could back up and find an alternate route. He inched closer to the shelves.

"That's not a place to be sitting. I can't get past you."

He pushed himself to his feet, bent over, and picked up the binder. The woman wore jeans faded to the color of a summer sky and flat leather sandals. Her hair was light brown with strands of gray that sparkled under the florescent lights like Christmas tinsel. Her ponytail had pulled loose so a few strands of hair hung over her shoulders. She had dark-framed glasses sitting like a second pair of eyes on top of her head.

"Thank you." She thrust her head forward. The glasses slid toward her forehead. She pushed them back. "You live across from my church. You're the man whose wife died."

"She was run over," Bob said.

"Yes. I'm so sorry."

"Thank you."

"I know the Lord will see you through this."

He waited for a moment. "Is that so."

Her lips parted slightly. She plucked her glasses off her

head and put them on her face. "If you ask for help, you'll receive it. I've experienced it in my life and seen it in so many others." She wiggled the cart between him and the stack of boxes.

"What do you think god's going to do, resurrect Dana and give her back to us?"

She smiled and tipped her chin down to show it was a smile of sympathy.

"I know how hard this must be. And with a young daughter to help through her grief, when you're trying to bear your own. If there's anything we can do to help. We'd love to have you join our prayer group, or worship with us."

"Sing songs and wave my arms? How will that help?"

"It's not like that."

"Am I supposed to dance and praise the lord with the woman who murdered my wife?"

Her smile tightened, her teeth disappeared as her lips pressed hard against each other.

"It was an accident. It's understandable that you're bitter. But is that how you want to live?"

"I'm not bitter."

"You sound very bitter."

"One of your friends murdered my wife."

"I know you're just venting, trying to find words to express your pain. It's okay."

He clenched the binder.

"She's hurting terribly."

His laugh sounded harsh in his ears, echoing up to the ceiling.

"Not like you, of course."

He glared at her. "Are you stupid? That's one of the most insulting, thoughtless statements I've ever heard."

"I'm trying to be kind. It doesn't help anything to lash out at me."

"Your friend murdered my wife."

"She's not really my friend."

He took a step toward her. His hip bumped the shopping car and it jittered a few inches to her right. The front end tapped the boxes. "Did she get kicked out of the church for breaking one of the commandments?"

"She didn't hit your wife on purpose."

"How do you know?"

"I just know. But if it makes you feel better, we've asked her to take some time to think about her life. To be alone with the Lord and sort things out."

"Nice group. Someone screws up and you kick them off the team."

"That's not how it is."

"That's the second time you said that."

"Is it?"

"If that's not how it is, explain it to me. Are you worried about liability? Worried I might sue you for not providing adequate parking?"

"You can't do that. I don't think you'd do that."

"So why'd you kick her out?"

"We didn't kick her out."

"Because she murdered my wife?"

"No. There were other issues."

"Such as?"

"I don't think I should talk to you about her personal relationship with the Lord."

"Why would you even be involved in her personal relationship?"

"I think we're off track here." She pulled the cart closer to her hips.

He could tell she wanted to get going, regretted acknowledging she knew him. Or maybe she didn't. Maybe she was angry that he didn't jump at the chance to attend her church. She couldn't add him to her list of people saved, her street cred in heaven, or wherever they tracked that sort of thing.

"You need to know that God wants to help you. He'll bring something good out of this. You can't see that now, but you will."

"If god wants to help out, shouldn't he mention it to me, rather than sending you like a mafia courier to deliver the news?"

"That's not how . . ."

At least she had the self-awareness to realize she was headed toward repeating the phrase again. Red spots sprouted over her cheekbones. He waited for her to fish around inside her head for something to bring him over to her way of thinking. It was almost funny, and he realized he'd crept out from under the oppressive emptiness while he'd been talking to her. Once again he was alive, eager to prove his point, even though he never could. Maybe the battle was enough, you didn't have to win, you just had to keep parrying your sword. "Was kicking her out your way of punishing her?"

"We didn't kick her out. We asked her to take some time for reflection."

"Sounds to me like she was kicked out."

She fiddled with her glasses, although he couldn't see that they'd slipped out of place.

"She deserves more punishment than that," he said.

"It was an accident. She's not being punished."

"She should be."

"Please don't be so angry. You need to forgive her."

"If it was an accident, why does she need forgiving?"

"It's about your heart. You can't hold onto this bitterness and blame or you won't be able to heal. You'll be stuck in this state for the rest of your life."

"What state?"

"Bitterness. Grief."

"Maybe I like this state."

"How could you?"

"If I'm not angry, then it will seem like it doesn't matter that Dana's gone." He couldn't believe he'd said that. And especially to her. He didn't want to think about Dana being gone. He was here to focus on remodeling the bathroom, doing something to please her, not spend his time dwelling on the fact she was dead. Evaporated into thin air as if she'd never existed.

"Well it's not a good way to live. And it's definitely not good for your daughter."

"Maybe my bitterness will go away when that woman is punished."

The cords of her neck stood out. She must be gritting her teeth, wanting to smack him as much as he wanted to smack her. Maybe he wanted it more, a solid punch to the mouth, break a few teeth, knock her brain back on top of her spinal chord so she could think straight.

He turned and walked toward the front of the store.

No one ever got punished. They were all about forgiving and letting the murderers and freeloaders and liars and cheats off the hook, but never about equalizing the suffering. He was supposed to weave his fingers together to keep him from hitting someone, bow his head, and forgive and accept and let it all go. The hell with that. Someone should be punished. That might prove there was a god.

Twenty-three

SARAH COULD BREATHE fire out her nostrils for all Melody cared. She had no right to dictate who attended Triumphant Life Tabernacle. Melody had been too long without the companionship of other believers. She was going to the prayer meeting. No matter what happened, she wasn't leaving. They would not shut her out.

While the invitation to attend Tim's church had a certain appeal, she was still drawn to the loss of herself in rhythmic music, dancing and shouting praises, wild clapping. Standing in front of a long wooden bench, holding a heavy book, singing plodding songs that all sounded like dirges from the eighteenth century, led her to feel she was attending God's funeral.

Before she got in the car, she reminded herself to approach Calliope Avenue from the opposite direction, both to wipe out the memory of the accident, and to avoid Bob, for now. She'd deal with him later, when the timing was right. That had been her problem all along. She was running ahead with her own plans and not waiting for the whisper of guidance. Her own voice had been too loud in her head. She hated to admit it, but Sarah had been right about that. You didn't *demand* gifts. You received them graciously, with gratitude. You couldn't lead someone into the arms of God on your own strength. The Spirit had to prepare the way, make his heart ready, open the door, or at least crack a window.

She'd arrive at prayer meeting early so there would be plenty of space in the parking lot. She hoped Bob wouldn't be out in the street lining up the cones, reminding her of that night. Surely he'd given that up. He must see that his own pettiness had contributed to the tragedy.

She pulled the front door closed, stuck her key in the deadbolt, and turned it. The air smelled like jasmine, but the exhaust from an idling truck was working hard to crowd out the sweetness of the moist, white flowers that clung to the post supporting her porch roof.

She walked down the steps and past the rumbling truck. A guy stood with his elbow on the window frame, talking to the driver. They reminded her of the guys who'd assaulted her at the park. Of course they weren't the same, they looked nothing like those others, but they were the same age, had the same bored, surly glare circling their eyes. Was that only for her, or did all men in their twenties have that look? They seemed to hate the world.

She hit the remote to unlock her car and swung open the

door. Inside it smelled like hot plastic. She climbed in, closed the door, and started the car. She backed out slowly, checking each mirror two or three times, twisting her head left and right to survey the surrounding area without the aid of the mirrors. The bottom of the car scraped on the drive as she went down the incline. The driveway designed for smaller cars, and trucks with large wheels that lifted the body high off the ground. She was beginning to get the feeling the whole world just didn't like her very much.

When she neared the church, the traffic cones were not in the street. Only the pastor's car was in the lot. She chose a parking space close to the sidewalk and got out of the car. She stuffed her Bible in her purse and closed the door.

The bench in front of the lobby doors looked inviting, not speckled with water from the sprinklers or night dampness or morning dew like it often was. She sat down. She put her purse on her lap. It was so quiet. Not a single car had passed down the street. A thread of music came from the downtown area where the main street was closed to traffic every Wednesday evening during the late spring and summer. Residents gathered to listen to live bands, dance in the street, and eat at sidewalk tables in front of the restaurants. It would be so different if her life included dinner out, dipping spring rolls into a spicy red sauce, crunching through fried layers of delicate flour and egg sheets stuffed with bean sprouts and celery and bamboo shoots, sipping wine, a man at her side. They'd watch couples and groups and children walk past, bare legs in shorts and skirts, bare feet decorated with toe rings and painted nails, bare shoulders. Everyone letting warm air wash over them, feeling safe and free and unconcerned about trying to please anyone but themselves, and possibly their mates.

Instead, she was heading into a drab building where she'd sit on a metal chair, nothing to eat but a cookie or two. Prayer meeting was supposed to offer an encounter with God that transcended any lowly physical pleasures offered by a street party. Prayer should banish any thought of food or desire for a mind-relaxing drink. It was the ultimate human experience — touching the Divine. But every week that transcendence was denied to her. She was getting a little tired of trying to understand why.

She stood and hoisted the strap of her bloated purse onto her shoulder. She walked to the doors and pulled the one on the right. It gave way too easily and she stumbled back. She went inside. The lobby was filled with shadows, the only source of light coming through the glass doors.

She opened the door that led from the lobby into the main hall. The circle of chairs was arranged near the front, a tray of cookies sat on the lone table at the left. Even from where she stood, she could see they were store-bought. Not the kind from a grocery bakery either, but the kind that came in a box, which meant they'd be hard and crumbly and taste mostly like sugar.

It was ten minutes to seven. She walked toward the circle

of chairs. Her soft-soled shoes tapped the linoleum, loud and insistent and corporeal. If God was in the room, He was strangely unavailable. She felt nothing. She pulled a chair a few inches from the others and sat down. She took out her Bible and put her purse under the chair.

The door opened and Elise and Jennifer walked into the room. When they reached the ring of chairs, Jennifer smiled and took a seat. Elise patted Melody's shoulder. "Nice to see you."

Apparently Elise knew nothing about Sarah's directive.

A few others arrived and took their seats.

It was five past seven when Sarah and Gordon walked through the door. They were never late, but they took their seats without explanation.

Melody felt as if she'd floated up near the ceiling and was looking down on the small, awkwardly arranged circle of people, feet pointed at one another, hands knotted on their knees, fingers twisted around each other. She saw the scuffed toes of her red ballet slipper shoes, her anklebones jutting out to the sides, her skirt draped over her thighs. There was nothing heavenly or otherworldly about any of it. Nothing about their posture or the arrangement of chairs hinted that God would enter this room.

Gordon suggested they begin. He lifted his hands. Melody closed her eyes.

Voices washed over her, asking for healing, employment, the repair of marriages, safety, the rescue of children that were headed down the wrong path, more healing. Interspersed were voices speaking in tongues.

She wasn't planning to speak at all, so it didn't matter whether her words came in a heavenly language or English. Nothing mattered.

The moment that thought passed through the front of her brain, she felt something sharp stabbing behind her ear. The pain spread across her scalp. The voices drifted to the back of her mind, swallowed by a rushing sound, like trying to walk in a strong wind as the roaring and pressure of it pelted her eardrums.

She felt as if she continued to float above the group, outside now, looking down on the building. She saw the empty white bench, the small patches of grass on each side of the path, the parking lot. Her car was the only red one.

Out in the street, the woman's body lay sprawled on the pavement. There were no emergency vehicles, no other people, just the empty shell of a body, blood on her face and neck, her mouth wide open as if she'd been screaming.

While Melody looked down, Bob emerged from behind the hedge. He stepped onto the sidewalk, put a cigarette in his mouth, and lit it. She smelled the smoke. At the same time, the bitter taste of blood filled her mouth.

She observed Bob as he walked to the center of the street. He didn't seem to notice his wife, her body now melting onto the blacktop. He drew on the cigarette, removed it from between his lips, blew out a cloud of smoke, and tapped his finger near the end. Ash fell into his wife's open mouth. Melody was sure she heard a sizzle as the hot ash touched her tongue.

Now her body seemed to be dissolving into raindrops, falling on Bob and his wife's corpse. Their skin began to run like candle wax, seeping into the ground, sucked down into the lake of fire where they'd live in eternal torment.

A voice spoke. It wasn't one she recognized. It was softer than the others surrounding the shell of her that remained seated on the metal chair, as if the speaker was seated right next to her, leaning toward her, breathing into her ear. *Save him. Even if it takes another violent act. Whatever it takes to wake him up.*

She stood. The hard rubber tips on the legs of the chair screeched against the floor. No one opened their eyes. She picked up her purse and walked across the hall. Although her shoes made the same distinct tapping as before, no one noticed she was leaving. Maybe they hadn't recognized she was there to begin with. In fact, maybe she hadn't been there. Nothing felt real, not the linoleum floor, not the doors to the lobby, or the pebbled concrete outside the main doors. The street was empty.

The blue pickup truck sat in front of Bob's house. His daughter's Prius was in the driveway, the back end almost at the sidewalk.

Melody crossed the street, walked along his front path, up the steps, and across the porch. Only the screen door was closed. The window to the right was open a few inches but the room was dark and silent. Maybe the open window was a sign. She rang the bell. She didn't know what she'd say, but the words would be given at the right time. The full power of God pouring forth, like those boys that had jumped her car that day. Back then, God had been telling her to use violence, but she hadn't recognized it. Not the violence of weapons or a car or fists. But the Word of God — sharper than a sword. She'd been too kind, too gentle with him. She recognized that now. The sword of God wasn't sweet and delicate. It was fierce and unyielding.

She rang the bell again.

The daughter appeared behind the screen. She pushed the door open, forcing Melody to step back.

"I'd like to speak to your father," Melody said.

"I don't think he wants to talk to you." She started to pull the door closed.

Melody grabbed the handle.

"Hey!"

"I have to talk to him."

"You killed my mother. We don't want to see your ugly face ever again."

"I have a message from God."

The girl laughed. "He doesn't believe in God."

Melody stepped over the threshold. She put her fingertips on the girl's shoulder and pushed. The girl stumbled back. Her bare feet squeaked on the wood floor.

Melody stepped into the foyer and let go of the door. It clattered against the frame. "Where is he?"

"Leave him alone. Get out of my house."

Melody took a few steps forward. A mirror hung on the wall to her left. Her hair was disheveled, and her skin very pale, although that might be the lack of light in the hallway. Past the mirror was the doorway to the kitchen and beyond that she saw part of a breakfast room. The house was as big and old-fashioned as she'd guessed from the exterior with its wide porch and wood-frame windows.

In front of her was the staircase. Near the side of the stairs was a narrow table with a jumbled collection of photographs. She didn't pause to look. If she didn't move quickly, she might lose the fire of her mission. The girl might call the police. Bob might emerge and drag her down the hall and back out the front door.

She walked past the staircase and the door to the dining room. Deep inside was a massive chandelier and a mahogany table with six matching chairs. Behind the staircase was a darkened office and beside that, a family room that opened onto the back porch.

Bob sat in a wing chair, his feet propped on a puffy footstool. The TV was set to a news channel, the volume turned down low. The indistinct words of the talking heads sounded like the hiss of people whispering.

Bob was drinking a beer and staring out the back window. The yard was now in almost total darkness, the large trees blocking light from neighboring homes.

She went into the room, sat on the couch, and glanced at the doorway. The girl hadn't followed her. That was surprising, but good.

Bob put down his beer. "How did you get in here?"

"Your daughter let me in."

"Get out."

"I just want to say something simple. I want you to know that God wants to make you his own and he'll keep taking things out of your life until you turn to Him."

He grabbed the beer bottle, lunged out of his chair, and splashed beer at her face. "Go to hell."

She blinked beer out of her eyes, but remained motionless, her hands folded in her lap. Beer dripped down her nose and onto her lip. It tasted stale and smelled vile. "You say you don't believe, but your first thought is of hell."

"Get out of my house. I don't want anything to do with a god that murders a woman to get another person's attention."

"It was His will."

He walked to the couch and grabbed her upper arm. He yanked her to her feet.

"Ow."

He dragged her across the family room into the hallway. Her foot caught on the wood piece that held the carpet in place in the doorway.

"God is in control of everything. Nothing happens that isn't His will. If you yield to Him, you'll see that. If you turn your life over . . .""

"Shut up!"

"Your wife's death is part of His plan. You'll see."

He let go of her arm. It fell away from him like an inanimate object, flopping against her hip. "Get out of my house. Now."

She remained where she was. This was her last chance. All she needed to do was listen to her own words. *Nothing happens that isn't God's will.* "Accept that he took your wife, accept that everything in your life came from His hand. Can't you see that? It's not like you could have stopped her from dying."

"You could have."

"If you let go, you'll find peace."

"I'll find peace when you're rotting in prison, or dead. An eye for an eye, isn't that how it goes?"

"In the Old Testament. That's not the life we should aspire to." She was a bit of a hypocrite for saying these things. She was so far from peace with God it felt like she was mouthing lies. But God wanted her to say these things. She was sure of it, no matter how hurtful. "There's peace with God, if you just let go, you'll see. He loves you and loving Him is all that matters."

"I loved my wife! Not a figment of collective human imagination."

She could see the pain slashed across his face as clearly as if someone had taken a knife to his flesh. It was so raw, she had to look away from the gaping wound. She lowered her voice. "And I'm sure your wife knew that. When she died. It's the only pure thing and she has all she needs — knowing you loved her, your daughter loved her, and now she's resting in God's love. As long as she was saved, if she had a chance before her last breath."

He shoved her toward the front door.

She stumbled back but didn't lose her balance.

He shoved her harder. The palm of his hands dug into her ribs.

"Get out or I'll call the police."

"You can see how He controls everything. Just open your eyes." She felt as if her own eyes were opening. The hallway looked brighter, luminous. The cream colored walls pulsed with life. Every hair on Bob's head and his long, thick sideburns glowed. That was how God saw them, noticing each hair, the follicle, the way the individual hairs merged with the others to form a unique human being.

He grabbed her wrist and dragged her down the hallway. She didn't resist. His fingers pinched her skin. Her bones hurt. Surely he didn't have the strength to break her wrist? He opened the front door and shoved her onto the porch. "Don't come back here again. I'm finished arguing with you. If I have to, I'll get a restraining order. I don't want anything to do with you and your perverted ideas."

"He wants to give you so much." She grabbed the edge of the screen door.

He pulled on the door but she resisted and he couldn't

manage to get it closed.

It was time to change course from promises of knowing His love to painting the picture of what waited for him if he continued this way. "You don't know when it's your last day on earth. Your wife didn't know. Do you want to take your final breath and end up separated from Him forever?" Her voice caught and the final word ended in an airless squeak.

If Bob repented right now, she'd have confirmation that God had used her for the most important task in the universe. She could go on from here in peace, knowing she mattered. "You think hell is about fire and physical suffering. But it's so much worse than that. The pain is inside of you. Worse than knowing your wife is gone, worse than being alone in your house. It's being alone forever. Never having contact with another human being, your soul ripped out of you but you never get relief, you live with searing pain for eternity. Think about that. Eternity! It's not too late!"

He let go of the screen and she fell back, sitting down hard. Pain shot up her spine. He slammed the door. The deadbolt clunked into place. The screen remained open, standing silently.

This was no different than when her father had died. She'd been shut out then, too.

According to her brother, Melody's theatrics were too upsetting for their father. If she wasn't so shrill, so unstable, so obsessed with freakish beliefs, they might have let her say goodbye. It was her fault they'd been forced to move her father to another hospice facility, keeping the location hidden from Melody. The man was in pain. He didn't need a wild-eyed daughter, foaming at the mouth about hell and sin, fire and demonic beings. Her brother had laughed when he said that. A cold, knowing laugh. Brian told her she should accept it was the best thing for their father. Saying good-bye was a myth anyway. The loved one was there, nearly unconscious, and then . . . gone. No one said good-bye. She should comfort herself with that. But the worst part hadn't been not saying good-bye, it was knowing her father was condemned to hell and she hadn't been able to save him.

She stared at Bob's front door. Slowly, she pushed herself to a standing position. She closed the screen door, turned, and walked down the porch steps. Something darted past her, the buzzing of an enormous insect rattled in her ear. She ducked and almost tripped on the edge of the lawn before she realized she was imagining things — it was the whir of a hummingbird's wings — harmless.

Twenty-four

ASHLEY'S BODY FELT like vapor. When she ate, the food dissolved into nothing. There was no taste, no fullness in her stomach, no satisfaction. She missed Jack's voice and the pressure and softness of his mouth on hers. She'd taken his devotion for granted. Maybe he wasn't the *one*, but he'd adored her, made her feel solid and noticed.

She and her father ate in front of the TV without talking. He didn't offer to help when she cleaned up the dishes. When she got bored with the infinite stream of world information and basketball games, she slipped out of the room without him noticing she was gone.

She had to do something to make herself alive again. Her mother wanted her to take charge, move forward. She missed Jack, but it was his presence, his body, the way he filled her weekends that she missed. He really wasn't much more than a habit. College was over. Jack was over. Her mother was gone. Only one thing remained. She had to do something unusual to make the world notice her. People did it all the time. They got themselves in the news and then the offers came — interviews, speaking opportunities, a book deal. Why not job offers? You had to stand out from the crowd. Filling out online applications and attaching electronic resumes was like blowing soap bubbles into the night sky.

She closed her bedroom door and pulled out the desk chair. She sat down, tucking her foot under her thigh. She swiveled the chair slowly while she moved the mouse to wake her computer. She clicked the tiny button to close the tab displaying her Facebook page. When she figured out a way to make a splash, then she'd go back to Facebook, announce her presence and watch it spread like a disease eating its way through the body, attaching itself to other organisms, unstoppable. That's why they called it viral. Nothing took over as quickly as disease, or a rumor, or a scandal. It was the truism they referred to in school all the time — if it bleeds it leads. She needed to create something with that potential. Good things didn't go viral. Sure, they got a moment of attention. If a ten-year-old kid sketched a charcoal portrait of a homeless man that looked like Leonardo da Vinci drew it, he received media coverage. A clip on the news, or a blog mention. But then it sank and the ocean of human activity closed over it forever.

She'd thought about starting a blog. She could interview local people and blog about . . . what? Where was the viral potential in that? There were hundreds, thousands of people posting local stories, their reactions to hurricanes and snowstorms and earthquakes. Crazy stunts. In some ways, you couldn't predict a viral reaction, but for sure you couldn't get one uploading videos of a suburban college grad trying to find a career. She laughed to herself.

After her glass of wine with Maggie a few days ago, talking mostly about dumb things people posted on Facebook, lying in bed pleasantly buzzed, she'd thought about going to clubs and interviewing tipsy people. She'd ask complex, philosophical questions. That could be funny. Sure, eighty percent of the responses would be lame, but if she did enough of them, she might produce something outrageously hilarious that could be the start of a series.

She clicked to the Huffington Post home page. Another shooting. It wasn't a rampage this time, just two guys who got into it on the campus of a junior college.

She glanced at the closet door. She should have given the gun back to Jack. It was strange that he hadn't asked for it. Was his desire to avoid her greater than getting what belonged to him? She shoved the thought to the side. He hadn't acted like he wanted it all that much, it seemed more that he was making a point about their relationship. But she didn't want it either. She hated how often it flickered through her mind. Having it there had changed her life in some small, imperceptible way. Was that how people ended up shooting each other? You bought a gun and it crept into your mind, always there, like a tumor behind your eye, pressing against the nerve, occasionally subsiding. Then, when something drove your anger beyond mild irritation, the gun led your thoughts in an entirely new direction.

Amateurs with phone cameras, taking stills and video footage, covered all the news. Bloggers and tweeters said everything there was to say. It was as if every single breath of the human race, each first date and wildly entertaining marriage proposal was already covered. Seven billion people on the planet. Every one of them had a story and a reaction to events around them. The digital world was exploding with news and anecdotes so that she felt her brain was going to explode. Maybe the world had reached the point where there was no place for a professional journalist. The topic had been discussed at school, but only in theory. Now it seemed she might have chosen the wrong career path.

She pushed her chair away from the desk. Staring at the computer wasn't going to give her fresh ideas. It was narrowing her brain into things that had already been done. She'd spent hours trolling YouTube. Seventy percent of the videos were either concerts and TV show excerpts or lame crap. Maybe she should take time off work, or even better, quit her job. She could take a road trip to open up her mind. Stop thinking about Jack and her mother and watching her father mope.

The closet door wasn't fully closed, stuck on a pile of laundry that needed to go into the washing machine. She opened it and took out the shoebox. She lifted off the lid.

A crash jolted the house. The walls shuddered. She dropped the lid. It didn't feel like an earthquake. Although there hadn't been one in ages, maybe she'd forgotten what they felt like. It sounded more like a car slamming into the side of the house. Could that woman at the church have truly lost it? Was she coming back to run over the rest of the family?

She picked up the lid and put it on the box.

Another crash shook the walls. The window rattled.

She opened the bedroom door. There was a third crash, followed by a thud. It came from her parents' room.

She hurried down the hall. The carpet in the master bedroom was soft and comforting. The bathroom light was on and she could see her father's back. He was bent over, leaning on something. She walked toward the bathroom doorway.

There were three large holes in the plaster around the small window that looked out onto the backyard. The paint was chipped and the sheetrock exposed — bright white, like bone, as if a person's skin was cracked and falling off, the bone protruding. Her father was leaning on the handle of a sledgehammer.

"What are you doing? You scared the shit out of me."

"Don't talk like that."

"Why are you smashing up the bathroom? I thought we were having an earthquake."

"I'm starting the remodel."

"The remodel?"

"Your mother wants a new, nicer bathroom."

Ashley leaned against the doorframe. The edges of her vision blurred. She couldn't see the walls. She pressed her fingers to the bridge of her nose and bent her head forward. It was difficult to tell whether he was playing a mind game with her, or he'd momentarily forgotten her mother was dead, or maybe he was going insane. "But mom is . . ."

He lifted the sledgehammer and swung it at the wall next to the window. Paint chips dropped to the floor, the sheet rock buckled, and a cloud of white powder flew into his face. He turned his head to the side and swung.

"Daddy! What are you doing?"

"I just told you." He hit the wall again. The impact created a space between two of the existing holes, joining them into a large opening where she could see the frame of the house. The wood was streaked with black. The house was ninety years old, but she'd never thought about what it was like behind the walls. Her parents had always kept it freshly painted, inside and out. It looked like they should have investigated further to make sure they weren't just coating over something that needed work deep inside.

"Stop!" She stepped into the bathroom. The linoleum was cold. Moving closer was risky because at any moment he might wind up his arms for another assault on the wall. The random spacing of the holes proved he didn't have a plan.

"She's wanted this for so long. I keep ignoring her. I was

lazy, or something."

He swung the sledgehammer. A two-by-four cracked as plaster shattered around it.

"Please stop."

"I need to get this done."

"Mom doesn't care about it now."

"How do you know? She's wanted this since you were twelve. Maybe younger." Sweat streaked his forehead, mixing with the white flakes of sheetrock.

"She can't see it! She can't use it. She's dead!" Tears clogged her throat and spilled out of her eyes. She couldn't see anything but the holes around the window. She lunged at him.

He shook her off. "Don't get in the way, you'll get hurt."

"Please don't destroy the bathroom."

"I'm not. I'm just making space to enlarge this window."

"You don't know what you're doing."

"I'll learn as I go."

"You're crazy. You're making a mess and it's pointless."

He lifted the sledgehammer. She grabbed his lower arm. He wrenched away from her and swung the tool underhand. The wood handle slipped as his arms came up. He stepped hard to one side, off balance from the awkward movement. The iron mallet slammed into the window frame. The glass cracked. A large line ran from the lower left up to the center where it spiraled out like the rings that form around the spot where a rock has been tossed into a lake.

"Put it down. Stop before you destroy everything."

"That window has to go anyway, so it doesn't matter."

She sat on the edge of the tub and pressed her face into her hands. "Can you please stop? I don't understand why you're doing this."

"Your mother wants a nice bathroom and I'm going to make sure she has what she wants."

"She's not here."

"It needs to be done."

"Can you maybe hire someone?"

"I want to do it myself."

She rubbed her face, pushing her hair back. She grabbed her hair and twisted it around her hand and wrist like a boxing glove.

"Why?"

"What else am I going to do?"

"You look like you want to kill someone."

"Maybe I do."

"That woman?"

He leaned the sledgehammer against the counter and folded his arms across his chest.

"It was weird that she barged into the house," Ashley said.

"She doesn't deserve to live."

"You're just talking. You wouldn't really kill her. That would ruin everything."

"What does it matter now? My life is finished."

She felt tears gather behind her eyes. "Don't I matter?"

"Of course you matter. But there would be justice in the

world if she was punished."

"I have a gun." She swallowed. She didn't understand why she'd told him. Like a zit she couldn't stop touching, the minute he started talking about punishment, she'd thought about it.

"Where did you get a gun?"

"Jack's father gave it to him."

"Why do you have it?"

"It's kind of complicated."

He raked his fingernails through his sideburns. A few of the hairs, gray mixed with brown, stood out from the rest, the whole thing in need of a trim.

She waited for him to ask why it was complicated, or express shock.

The glass in the window crackled, the fracture spreading further under its own volition.

"Do you want to see it?"

"Sure."

This was the first real conversation they'd had since her mother died. This was the first time he'd looked her in the eye since her mother said he hadn't wanted her. Was that really what her mother had said? It hadn't been quite that harsh, had it? She'd said he wanted a boy. That he wasn't interested in her. No, that wasn't right either. She couldn't remember. She couldn't remember most of the things her mother had said, on any topic, as if all their conversations were transparent words circling their heads, cartoon characters trying to talk to each other, letters and phrases in a cloud of nonsense.

She stood. He followed her out of the bathroom and down the hall to her room.

When was the last time he'd entered her bedroom? Surely not since she'd returned home with a college diploma but nothing else to show for four years and over a hundred thousand dollars in student loans.

He pulled the chair away from her desk and sat down. He kept his gaze on her computer, not looking at the unmade bed, the pile of drip-dried lingerie on the window seat, the tiny stuffed animals filling the other half of the window seat so there was barely room for her to curl up with a magazine. He didn't seem to notice the posters of the Chicago and New York City skylines, the framed photographs from senior sneak day at the Santa Cruz Boardwalk and the spring beer bash during her freshman year at Northwestern. He didn't look at the trashcan near her bed, filled to the brim with wadded tissues and a few Snickers wrappers.

She lifted the gun out of the shoebox. She carried it to the bed and smoothed out the comforter to make a place for it. She unfolded the towel and handed the gun to her father.

"It's not loaded, is it?"

"Actually, it is. But it's locked."

"So why do you have it?" He turned it over. He ran his finger down the barrel. He wrapped his hand around the grip and pointed it at the floor.

"I guess I didn't trust Jack with it. A guy at work told me when he had a gun, it was the only thing he could think about when he got upset."

"How is it any different if you have it?"

"I don't know. Because Jack couldn't give me a straight answer when I asked if he'd ever use it. Or maybe I trust myself more than him. If I have it, I know where it is. And I know I wouldn't use it."

"What about me?"

She looked at him. He handed the gun to her. She held it in one hand and wrapped the towel around it. "What about you?"

"Aren't you worried I'll use it?"

"No."

"Why not?"

"Because you wouldn't. I know you." Did she? This was the man who acted like her biggest fan her entire life, until she found out she was only a poor substitute for what he wanted. Why had she shown him the gun, just to get his attention? To shock him? How had the conversation evolved to this?

"I have a lot of hate inside me, Ash."

"I guess we both do."

"At the whole mass of them, squealing how Jesus loves them and everything is all fine and happy rainbows and unicorns."

She laughed. "I don't think they believe in unicorns."

As if he hadn't heard her laugh or registered her correction, he went on. "All my life they told me if I trusted god he would give me what I wanted. And it's been the exact opposite." He stood and glanced quickly at the computer, the towel-wrapped gun in her hand, and then her. But his gaze didn't rest on her face, it slipped off and ran toward the window. "Don't take that personally." He walked to the door. "You should put it somewhere that's not so accessible." He disappeared into the hallway.

A moment later the house shook as the sledgehammer hit the wall, possibly another beam because it sounded less giving than when he'd been smashing the sheetrock.

Twenty-five

BOB DRANK A FOURTH cup of coffee, double his usual amount. It tasted sour from sitting too long on the warmer. He hadn't made it strong enough and the thin texture intensified the sourness. Not the satisfying bite of coffee that had a higher grounds to water ratio, the robustness that made him believe life had a lot of pleasure to offer.

His whole body felt sour and weak, but he had to push past it. He needed to make the most of his Saturday. He'd decided not to go back to the Home Depot. This would be an upscale bathroom. None of the brochures in Dana's binder had come from multi-purpose chain stores. Most of the stuff would have to be ordered anyway, so it was better to go with the experts. He had what he needed from a warehouse store — construction guides, plumbing books, tiling manuals. When he needed sheetrock and grouting material and nails, he'd return, but for the tub and toilet and sink and fixtures, and the right tile, the specialists were the way to go.

He buttered a toasted bagel and stood at the kitchen window eating it. The breakfast room did nothing but serve up images of Dana sitting across the table. He was done eating in there.

Why hadn't he ever noticed the view out the front windows was confining. All that was visible was the porch, the small lawn, and the back of the hedge. He supposed that was a good thing, because he sure as hell didn't want to look at the church. Still, he had a slight feeling of claustrophobia looking at the hedge, like the thick walls of a castle grown over with thorny branches.

THE *WATER WORKS* bathroom shop was darker than he would have expected, especially on a May morning. A woman wearing low-slung jeans and a sea green tank top that exposed her black bra straps stepped out from behind the counter before the shop door closed behind him.

"Hi, can I help you?"

Although the jeans looked good, she was closer to forty than thirty. Her hair was blonde, streaked with copper, black, and dark brown. The streaks of color left him wondering what, if any, was real.

"I'm remodeling my master bathroom."

"Fantastic. Have you been here before? Do you have a documented plan with us?"

"My wife might have been in."

She tilted her head and her long bangs fell across her eyes.

She brushed them to the side. "You don't know?"

"She has a brochure from here."

The woman zipped behind the counter and put her hands on the computer keyboard. "What's her name?"

"Dana Lambert."

She typed quickly, using only her index fingers. "Nope. Who did she say she talked to?"

"She didn't."

"Well can you call and ask?"

"No. If she's not in the computer, it doesn't really matter."

"But how can we make sure the designs she discussed are lined up?"

"I know what she wants."

"Let's sit down." She gestured toward two small couches set perpendicular to each other. Between them was a six-foot square coffee table. In the center was a glass bowl filled with stones and brochures fanned out around it.

"I don't need to sit down. I already know what I want." No matter how unmoored he felt, he wasn't going to be strong-armed into hiring a designer and a contractor and all the associated workers. This was his project and he was going to hammer every nail and twist every pipe fitting himself.

"We should look at design options, if you're sure your wife doesn't have a plan."

"I'm doing all that myself."

She crossed her arms. "Have you remodeled a bathroom before?"

"Yes."

"Okay. And you did all the work yourself?"

"Yup."

She looked doubtful. He was certain he sounded confident, she had no reason to be so suspicious.

"It's a lot of work. Most people can't do it properly unless they have a construction background. And if you're getting a new toilet and tub and sink . . . oh boy, you have no idea. Unless you've done it before."

"I can handle it."

"Then why are you here?"

"I want to order what I need."

She stared at him then glanced at the binder. "It's all in there? All your measurements? Do you have a permit?"

"I have everything handled. I just want to order the tub and sink and toilet. After they're installed, I'll be able to measure more accurately for tile."

"That's not how it's usually done."

"Are you here to argue with me, to try to sell me on design services, or are you going to let me buy what I'm looking for?"

"I'm just getting a weird vibe from you."

"So what? I want to buy a damn bathtub. Why is that so hard? It's not like I'm buying pipes that could be used in a bomb."

She held up her hand, palm facing him. Her fingers were thin. The index finger curved toward the center finger, making it look like she was signaling him. "I think we got off on the wrong foot and I'm not sure why. I'm happy to help you order whatever you need." She smiled and lowered her hand. "Your wife must be very excited. It would be great to have a husband who's willing to spend money on a new bathroom, and do all the work himself. How intimate."

"She's excited."

"What made you decide to do it?"

"If I don't do it now, it'll never happen."

She smiled. "I like that take-charge attitude."

He smirked.

"It's not flattery. I do."

"Uh huh."

"Should we start with the tub? I assume she wants a Jacuzzi style. Do you have the model in your book there?"

He set the binder on the counter. He opened the cover and ran his finger down the brightly colored numbered tabs. She had the tub and sink info under number five. He flipped to that section and turned the binder to face the woman. "I didn't get your name."

"Miriam."

There was something soothing about her name. It sounded peaceful, as if she belonged to a quieter time in the history of the world, even though that wild hair and her clothes planted her firmly in the twenty-first century. She stared at him with dark brown eyes and pale, inviting lips that didn't rely on a glossy coating or unnatural colors.

"Why do women want palatial bathrooms?" he said. "Why do they want enormous tubs and fancy fixtures and high-end lighting and huge windows in a room that's about privacy?"

She leaned her elbows on the counter. "Why don't you ask your wife?"

"I want to hear your answer."

"It's not as if all women are the same. And if you don't know why she wants it, why are you putting in all this money and effort to remodel?"

"Because she's been asking for it. For a long time. And I never did it." His throat tightened. He didn't want her to see the hollowness inside of him. He wasn't crazy. He knew Dana was gone, that this was absurd. He knew how it would sound to Miriam, if she knew — a husband mad with grief, thinking he could please his wife, confused about whether or not she was dead. He was pretty sure that's what Ashley had been thinking too. "I know all women aren't the same. But they're similar in some ways. I've never heard of a man wanting a luxury bathroom, but lots of women seem to want them. Why?"

"I can only tell you why I would want one."

He was surprised. Working in this place, he would have thought she had everything in her home remodeled. Maybe she was just a clerk, not a decorator or owner as he'd originally thought. Or maybe it was the old stereotype of the shoemaker's children going barefoot.

The partial walls displaying various bathroom features

surrounded them, dark and spotlessly clean, but sterile. It reminded him of the room where they'd gone to choose Dana's coffin. A large empty space, silent, coffins with their tops yawning wide to display satin and ruffled fabric, designed to remind you of luxurious sleep when the thought of their contents elicited horror rather than rest. The fancy bathrooms gave off the same feel, promising elegance when really they were designed to dispose of all the waste and decay, the constantly dying cells of the human body.

He shivered.

"Are you cold?"

"Are you going to tell me why women want Taj Mahal bathrooms?"

"A big bathroom is unnecessary space so it seems indulgent. And it feels like a setting from the ancient world — imported tile and beautifully formed stainless steel, steaming water to wash away all the sweat and dirt so you're clean and pure. It's all for you, to make you beautiful and desirable. And it's soothing — scented oil and soap, candles, flowers. You don't have to do anything. No laundry or dishes. Nothing but self-pampering. It makes me feel like a queen."

"So women all want to be queens with a bunch of servants combing their hair?"

"I shouldn't have used that word."

"I guess not."

"Haven't you ever washed your wife's hair, or taken a bath with her?"

He hadn't. Was that what Dana wanted? He supposed he'd spent far too much time thinking about what she'd failed to give him — a son — he hadn't considered what she wanted from him. He held his breath for a moment, overwhelmed with a desire to be with her. Maybe god would let him die too. It was all he really wanted right now. He wanted to see her, if that were possible, to tell her how he'd wasted their lives, that he loved her.

"Don't take it wrong, my comment about queens. I don't mean women want to be waited on. But they want to be cherished and desirable. A beautiful bathroom makes you feel like you can become that perfect woman — a goddess, and your man will worship you."

"That's a lot of imagining for a bathtub and toilet and a bunch of towels."

She turned toward the rack of brochures on the counter, tilted her head back and shook her hair off her face so it fell between her shoulder blades. Her narrow back was like a culvert with all that shiny hair rippling through it. "You asked me why women want exotic bathrooms. I told you. Don't imply that I'm making it up."

"I didn't say you were."

"You said I had a big imagination."

"I don't think I did."

"Well that's how I feel about having a nice bathroom and I think other women feel the same."

"Why?"

She turned back and rested her elbows on the counter. Her shoulders curled forward and he could see the tops of her breasts at the edge of her shirt. "Not everything can be explained. Stop over-thinking it and build the bathroom your wife wants."

"I'm trying. It would just be easier if I understood the appeal."

"I told you."

"Women want to be worshipped."

"Yeah. I guess so. I do."

"Really. So you think you're a god?"

"A god-*ess*." She laughed and straightened. "You look so confused. Like a little boy."

The conversation had taken a weird turn and he couldn't figure out when that happened, or why, and he wanted to get back to business. But he also wanted to figure out this worship thing. He'd never gotten even a hint of that from Dana.

"Why haven't you asked her why she wants a new bathroom?"

"I don't know."

"It sounds like your communication could use a little work."

"How would you know? You just met me. And you sure don't know anything about my wife."

"It's just strange that you're so curious about why a woman would want a nice bathroom, and you're obviously ready to spend money and a lot of time to give her that, but you've never asked her why she wants it."

She was right, and it made him angry.

"So why haven't you asked her? Do you have kids?"

"A daughter. What does that have to do with it?"

"Kids get in the way of couples talking, don't you think?"

"Sure. But she's an adult."

"They still get in the way. Only the one?"

He nodded.

"How come?"

"None of your damn business."

She jumped back from the counter. She grabbed her hair and twisted it around her shoulder like she was clinging to a security blanket. "Okay. Sorry."

"No. I'm sorry. It's been a long week. I wanted a son but it never happened."

"You don't get to pick children like you would a Porsche."

"I know. Let's just say I wanted more kids and hoped we'd have a boy. Eventually you have both, if you keep going." Why was he telling her this? He'd never discussed it with anyone. Spending most of the day by himself was doing a job on his brain. He turned. "I'll look around at the displays." He moved away from the counter and she went to work, tapping at the keyboard.

Maybe he was losing his mind. Standing here right now, it was hard to believe Dana was gone. He felt he was actually getting ready to remodel the bathroom, that she'd be so surprised he'd finally started work, so excited to see the results. But then, wouldn't she be here with him, picking things out together? He wouldn't be talking to this woman with the multi-colored hair and nice tits.

Now that he'd started talking, he didn't want to stop. Dana was gone, what did it matter if he told this stranger about the big disappointment of his life? So what if Miriam thought he was nuts, or maybe she would agree that god was a prick for promising to answer prayers and then withholding one of the most basic human desires. God planted a genetic need in your brain and then withheld it. Other men got sons. His brother had four of them. It was normal to want a son. It wasn't like he'd asked for too much.

The moment when Dana had told him she was done getting pregnant lurked in his memory, emerging to torment him when he least expected it — while he was watching a basketball game, or mowing the lawn, or helping her with the dishes. It would ooze through the twists of his brain like toxic waste creeping to the surface years after officials thought a dumpsite had been cleansed. There it was. Dark and ugly.

Without a son, without a legacy, the potential for a chain of male descendants, he felt as if he hadn't existed. When he'd allowed Dana even a glimpse of those thoughts, she went on the attack. *He had a wonderful daughter. They were so blessed. How dare he wish for something different. What did he expect of her? That she would subject her body to pregnancy and loss over and over again to satisfy his ego or some other prehistoric drive? And it wasn't just her body. It was her soul. She couldn't do it any more. She accepted God's will for her life.*

And now that capricious god had taken his wife. It was almost ridiculous. He laughed.

"Are you okay . . . I just realized I don't know your name."

She'd come out from behind the counter.

"Bob," he said.

"You sound a little crazy."

"Sorry. Just thinking."

"So it was a good laugh?"

"Sure. A good laugh." He shoved his hands in his pockets. "I should order the tub and all the other stuff. I need to get going on this or I'll lose the whole day."

"Right. Let's go have a seat." She gestured at the couches. "I'll use the laptop to place your order. I'll be right back."

She trotted to the far wall where a door led out of the showroom.

He sat on one of the couches and put his hands behind his head, stretching. His body felt like he'd been hunched over his desk all day.

So Dana had wanted to be treated like a goddess. Instead, he'd treated her like a horse put out to pasture because she could no longer breed.

Twenty-six

BLUE THE COLOR of a mountain lake filled the sky. A few stars glittered like tiny eyes watching in the darkness, winking and pulsing as they took it all in. The air was still warm enough for Melody to recline in the lounge chair on her back deck, wearing only a sleeveless top and shorts. Her legs were so white they glistened in the semi-darkness. It wasn't good to suntan, to expose her skin to infiltrations of cancer, but the white looked equally unhealthy.

She sipped her coke. The fizzing sweetness calmed her. There'd been a church dinner but she hadn't gone. She didn't know what to do with herself. Trying to rescue Bob had ended badly. His heart was the consistency of granite, and now she questioned the vision she'd been given. She wasn't sure if this meant she was unworthy to ever receive the gift of tongues, but at this point, she wasn't sure she wanted it.

The more she thought about it, the more she felt like God wanted nothing to do with her. Other people didn't have to turn over their whole lives, all their earthly desires, convert the most stubborn men in order to prove themselves. They just knelt, lifted their arms, opened their mouths, and a heavenly language burst out of their souls, making them feel as if they walked and lived on a different plane from the rest of humanity, confident they were loved. God's love was supposed to be taken on faith. Some people appeared to find that incredibly easy, while others, possibly herself, demanded proof. She hadn't started out looking at it that way, but it was where she'd ended up.

She leaned her head back and closed her eyes. After a moment she opened them. The sky looked so soft, the air felt as if she were soaking in a cosmic bathtub. The ice rattled in the glass as she lifted it to her mouth.

It wasn't fair that one person could ostracize her from the church. She'd done nothing wrong. She no longer knew for sure what she'd seen that night, and couldn't remember the small details of her actions — at what point she'd stopped singing praises, when she'd hit the brake, the moment it dawned on her that it was too late, whether or not she'd heard a thud, a scream, Bob roaring with grief. Any of it.

The doorbell rang.

She closed her eyes. People rarely came to her door unless they were selling or otherwise looking for ways to get money out of her, whether to support after school programs or services for the elderly or the environment.

She sat up and put the glass on the table. The bell rang

again. A persistent salesman.

She stood, picked up the coke, and drank the remainder. She sucked a half-melted ice cube into her mouth and bit down hard. Ice shattered inside her mouth, tiny explosions of cold on her tongue.

The bell rang a third time.

As she pulled open the screen door, it screeched along the metal track. She stepped inside. A third ring might mean it was someone she knew, although she couldn't imagine who that might be at eight on a Saturday night. She put the glass on the kitchen counter and crossed the living room to the front door. She looked out through the tiny window. Sarah and Elise. She opened the door. "Hi."

"Hi, Melody," Elise said. "Can we come inside for a minute?"

"What's up?"

"Can we come in?"

"I guess." Melody stepped back. Their smiles were small. They didn't have cookies or another prop to suggest a friendly visit. After what Sarah had done, she couldn't imagine any friendliness in the reason for their unannounced appearance.

They stepped into the living room and walked side-by-side to the couch as if they had choreographed each step. Amplifying that impression, they turned at once and seated themselves about three feet apart.

"Have a seat," Elise said.

Melody closed the door but remained where she was. "What do you want?"

"Please have a seat. This is very difficult, but it will be easier if we can look at each other, feel the oneness we have in the Lord."

Melody laughed.

"What's so funny?" Sarah folded her hands in her lap.

"Nothing."

Elise nodded. "Will you have a seat. Please."

"I've been sitting all evening. I can stand."

"It's not very conducive to conversation."

"I'm not in a very chatty mood. I assumed you weren't staying very long."

"That might or might not be true," Sarah said.

"Aren't you mysterious." Melody folded her arms and smiled. For the first time she felt like she had the upper hand. It was a pleasant feeling, although possibly not one God wanted her to indulge.

"This is important," Elise said. "We really would prefer you sit down."

"I'm standing. Get to the point." Where was this voice, this attitude coming from? She felt like laughing again but managed to suppress it. She hadn't been happy to see them at the door, only invited them in out of a sense of social obligation, but now she was enjoying herself.

"We're concerned about the accident," Elise said.

"What about it?"

"Have the police talked to you any more?"

"No."

"Have you talked to Bob Lambert about it?"

"I don't think so. Maybe."

"We heard you went over there. That you barged into his house."

"Where would you hear that?"

"Did you?"

"Yes. You told me to."

Elise and Sarah opened their mouths, staring. "We absolutely did not," Elise said.

"You told me I needed to bring Bob to the Lord."

"That's different."

"He wasn't responding so I was a little more aggressive. That's all."

"You shouldn't have. It's not your doing. The Spirit has to plant the seeds and make the ground ready."

Melody smiled.

"It's not funny," Sarah said. The barrette was slipping out of her hair, bumping against the nape of her neck. Her ponytail drooped, emphasizing the shadows around her eyes.

Elise looked as glamorous as ever, her hair smooth and silky, her dark blue eyes outlined in charcoal, and her lips glossy with coral lipstick. "You shouldn't have any more contact with him."

"You told me God wanted me to save him."

"It's too late. At least for you," Sarah said. "But that's not the only reason we're here."

"Oh! There's more?" She giggled.

They pulled back as if her giggle was a slap across their cheeks.

"I'd asked Tim to let you know you should stay away for a while until you could get yourself right with the Lord, regarding your recklessness. Your inability to yield."

Melody gripped her upper arms and pressed her forearms harder against her ribs. "I'm completely yielded."

"That's what we'd asked." Sarah kept talking, as if Melody hadn't spoken. "And it wasn't good that you showed up at prayer meeting."

"Is it a private club now? I thought everyone was welcome. Sinners and thieves. Everyone."

"Well, yes, but . . ."

"We're worried there's going to be a lawsuit," Elise said.

"A lawsuit for what?"

"Dana Lambert's death."

"What does that have to do with going to church?"

"There's concern that he's a very angry man. A man who wants revenge. Since you weren't arrested," Sarah was breathing hard, her words rushed out faster, "He might sue the church because we don't have enough parking, and we know he tried to block you from parking in front of his house. We think you should stay away. The best thing overall would be to find another church. It's not like God is limited to Triumphant Life. You can find another community."

Melody tried to think which part to address first.

The women looked at her, their faces like carved wood.

"If he's going to sue the church, it won't matter whether I worship there or not. It won't matter if I never attend church again or if I live out of my car in the parking lot."

"It might help. It's the only thing we can think of. To protect the church from the scandal."

"What makes you think he's going to sue?"

Elise leaned forward. She put her hands on the coffee table as if she was trying to prevent herself from falling on her face. "His daughter was hanging around the church. Filming. She was walking around the parking lot, up to the front doors, looking inside, talking into the camera, and recording everything. Then she went into the street and filmed while people were arriving to worship." Elise paused. She swallowed. "I asked her what she was doing. She said she was interested in our mind-set, whatever that means. She said she wanted to know what kind of beliefs you'd have to have to force your way into someone's home."

Melody glanced at the back deck, now covered in darkness. She could see why they'd be worried. But still, it didn't seem likely. Although what did she know about grounds for lawsuits.

"Anyway, we don't want the stain."

"The *stain?!*"

"Of taking a life. You took a woman's life, Melody, and you don't seem very upset about it," Sarah said.

Melody unfolded her arms and stepped to the side. She opened the front door. "Time to go."

They stood. "We really think you need to find another church," Elise said.

"We're not asking you, we're telling you." Sarah crossed the room and stopped a few feet from Melody. She looked up. "Do you understand?"

"I hope he does sue the church!"

"You should not hope that at all. He'll come after you too. We're having a prayer vigil to bring the concern to God," Sarah said.

"I guess I'm not invited."

"It's for the best," Elise said.

"Good-bye." Melody opened the door wider. A breeze floated into the room. It was cool. She shivered, regretting the lost time sitting alone on her back deck.

"You understand, right?" Elise said. "You won't pop up at the worship service tomorrow?"

Melody laughed.

"Is that a yes?"

Melody smiled and shoved her thumbs behind her belt.

"It would help if you showed remorse for killing her. It would help if you'd turn your life over to the Lord," Sarah said.

"I've already done that. Several times."

"Think about it," Elise said. "Seriously."

"And find a new church." Sarah stepped outside. She

turned. "Remember what you told me. I haven't forgotten."

"What?"

Sarah closed her eyes. She opened them and gave Melody a knowing look.

Elise stepped off the porch and started down the path. Sarah remained, presumably waiting for Melody to acknowledge her threat.

Finally, she turned. They walked down the front path and along the sidewalk to Elise's Audi. The remote chirped and they opened the doors simultaneously. It was fascinating to watch their movements mirror each other, as if they shared a brain. Maybe they did. Brainwashed by a warped interpretation of what they read in their Bibles.

She closed the door. She went into the kitchen and got out the step stool. She climbed up and reached into the cabinet above the stove. She felt around toward the back. Somewhere, there was a bottle of sherry she'd used once to make a sauce for Cornish Game Hens. Her fingertips brushed across a bottle with dust glued to the label by grease that had filtered up into the rarely used cabinet. She nudged the bottle forward and took it out. She stepped down.

She uncorked it, sniffed to make sure it hadn't turned to vinegar, and poured half a cup into a glass. She went out to the back deck. It was dark now, but there didn't seem to be any new stars poking through. The same ones as before winked at her. She raised her glass at the paper-thin sliver of moon and took a sip.

What was hidden behind those stars? Was there a God out there, or not? Bob sure didn't think so. But as she tried to comprehend the void of space, without the warm presence of an intelligent Being, her brain refused to grab onto the idea with any conviction.

She sat on the lounge chair and took another sip of sherry. Despite gathering dust in the cabinet for how ever many years it had been, it was quite tasty. Smooth and rich.

As the alcohol made its way into her bloodstream, the knots between her shoulder blades loosened themselves. Her neck felt pliable yet strong. It was strange to wonder about whether or not God existed. It wasn't a question she'd ever considered, and it was satisfying to know that maybe He was right there, proving Himself by the very fact that she couldn't erase her belief. That must mean it was true. And maybe He didn't mind if she had a glass of sherry or wine now and then, and maybe He loved her large awkward body, and maybe speaking in tongues was as silly as it sounded — a desperate grab for an ecstatic feeling that didn't last anyway. It wasn't like you could walk around all day babbling nonsense so you'd feel confident God was right there with you.

Tomorrow she would sleep in. She smiled and ran her finger around the lip of the glass. She licked her finger and took another sip. Next week, she might call Tim and check out his church. There were hundreds of churches. She could try them all, like going to a wine tasting party.

She closed her eyes. She imagined a church where people

actually listened to each other and didn't make you feel like you didn't belong.

It had been a mistake to push her way into Bob's house. But she'd had that vision, or whatever it was. Maybe she'd misinterpreted the meaning. Their bodies had dissolved like candle wax. She'd thought that meant they were losing their souls, being pulled into the pit of hell. And what about that voice? Telling her to save Bob, even if it required violence. What did that mean? Had she conjured up the whole thing, her mind warped by peer pressure and the intensity of all those people praying, making her feel like she'd failed, like God demanded something remarkable from her?

She took the last sip. Maybe God forgave her for the accident. For being stupid and foolish. And for letting those women, that whole church, those teenage thugs, her brother and his creepy friend, bully her.

WHEN SHE WOKE on Sunday morning, she had a different thought. She *would* go to church. After letting people bully her all her life, why was she allowing it again? They had no right to block her from a public worship service. This wasn't high school where the popular clique controlled access to the quad and another group commandeered one of the girls' bathrooms for smoking and bragging about their shoplifting skills — no weak girls allowed.

Besides, she was curious to see what it would be like to sit in one of the chairs, listen to the preacher, close her eyes and notice the strange languages around her without wanting anything. It would be a completely new experience now that God had hinted He was a different kind of Being than she'd been led to believe.

She got up and boiled water, added grounds to the coffee press, and made two super strong mugs of Sumatra roast. It was warm enough to sit on the back deck in her t-shirt and sweat pants, her feet bare. The coffee burned her tongue and lips with its aroma. She flipped open her Bible and looked for underlined passages about going into battle, facing down enemies and emerging victorious. God probably didn't like His children viewing each other as enemies, but the verses she selected gave her the same feeling she'd had the night before when she stood up to Sarah and Elise — *He gives us the victory . . . We are more than conquerors . . .*

Of course it wasn't their fault she'd been cowed by them for all this time. She'd sought them out. But they'd taken advantage of her, played on her neediness. They'd used her for some sick game of power. If she forfeited the game, she'd be free.

Twenty-seven

THE CAMCORDER HAD been a birthday gift from her parents on her nineteenth birthday, instigated by her father, offering a small token to encourage her dreams. Or so she'd thought at the time. Now, all memories of her parents were suspect.

She unplugged the charger. Those two women from the Triumphant Life Tabernacle had been a little unnerved when she'd filmed them. This next step would be perfect.

A faint whisper hovering at the base of her skull accused her of exploiting her mother's death. But was it really exploitation when a woman had died for no reason and it was their fault and no one took responsibility for it? People didn't accidentally slam their cars into other people. She was speaking out for both her parents, getting at the truth — the journalist's job. If she could poke that woman until she lost her cool, get her to admit on camera that she'd committed murder, there would be justice for her mother, closure for her father, and a compelling, dramatic story to put out there into the world.

She glanced in the mirror. The smile playing at the edges of her mouth had blossomed into a grin. This was the first time she'd caught herself smiling since her mother's death. And the smile wouldn't go away, even thinking about her mother being gone, didn't cause it to fade, because the thrill of knowing she could create something that would get all kinds of voyeuristic attention on YouTube generated a thrill that made her feel like she had a map spread out before her. Finally. She could build a career off this, and then her mother's death wouldn't be for nothing. Her mother would be proud, relieved that Ashley was no longer *drifting*.

Possible music clips played through her mind. She'd need rights, though, and she probably couldn't afford those. Once the video hit critical mass, any copyright violations would emerge from the shadows. She'd have to find unknown musicians offering their talent for free on the web, trying to gain fans. Maybe she'd build several careers with this — hers and a deserving band or two.

She set the camera on the bed and buckled her feet into flat, sturdy sandals.

She looked out the bedroom window. The orange cones weren't there. Her father had given up on that. Maybe he secretly blamed his actions as a contributing factor to the accident. But she suspected he was smoking, hidden on the other side of the hedge. He wouldn't give that up. If not this week, then next, he'd be out there, blowing out streams of smoke, watching.

She picked up the camera and hurried down the stairs.

The odor of smoke was strong on the front porch. She went down the steps and along the path. As she emerged from the opening between the hedges, her father turned. "What are you up to?"

"I'm asking the church members a few questions, trying to provoke them a little." She giggled. "And filming their reactions. I did it last Sunday. One woman got kind of wound up. She thought it meant we were going to sue them for Mom's death."

"Really?" He dropped the cigarette on the pavement and smothered it with the toe of his work boot. He smiled.

It was a relief to see his expression change to resemble the father she remembered from before her mother's death. There was nothing like a little revenge, no matter how mild, to wash over the grief that had left his mouth sagging and his eyes vacant and obscured by shadows, as if most of the lights had been turned off.

He pulled out another cigarette and lit it. She plucked off the lens cap and stuffed it in the back pocket of her jeans. She pressed the power button and took a few steps away from her father. She pointed the camera at him and spoke softly. Her voice wavered, then grew stronger.

This is a man who haunts a quiet suburban street. Bereft since his wife was brutally killed, run over by a crazed fundamentalist, his only comforts are his cigarettes, an occasional beer, and home improvement projects. His footsteps echo inside the turn of the century house that used to be filled with the quiet, settled love of a couple married for twenty-six years.

She took a few steps toward the curb and then moved to the left. She pressed pause and turned, aiming the camera through the hedge, up the path at the house. She pressed record and panned the house, letting the silence speak to her mother's absence. Later, she'd put her mother's sun hat and some gardening tools on the porch and take another clip to edit into what she'd already filmed.

The lens moved slowly past the front porch, across the width of the house, up to the second floor, lingering on her bedroom window then moving higher, capturing a beautiful image of the roofline against the cloudless sky, she pressed pause.

She turned and looked at the church. She already had plenty of footage of the building, both from a distance and up close. The week before, just as she'd pulled open the front door, trying to get images of the lobby, a woman with long gray-streaked hair had asked her what she was up to, and demanded she turn off the camera.

The parking lot was filling up. A few people stood around the entrance. A woman in a turquoise dress with a white collar and enormous white buttons running down the front was talking, gesturing wildly with one arm while the other cradled her Bible. Her light brown hair was piled into an elaborate swirl, but it had shaken loose and toppled sideways so it looked like a stack of pancakes ready to slide off her head. She touched her hand to her hair and shoved it back into place.

Ashley lifted the camera and let it crawl over the small group — four women, two children, and a lone man, who looked to be observing her father in the same way her father watched the churchgoers every Sunday. She smiled.

She spoke into the mic. *The members of Triumphant Life Tabernacle are clearly excited to enter the building. Their beliefs give them so much enthusiasm, it spills out the doors of the church and follows them like a swarm of bees everywhere they go. It doesn't take much to prompt a religious conversation. They're eager to retell their experiences, to persuade anyone who will listen to turn to God and give up their old lives.*

She pressed the pause button. It was fun narrating. The ideas formed themselves into words without any effort. Even though most of this might not make it into her final video, she wanted a lot of material to work with. Ideally the piece she posted online would be three minutes or less. Five minutes would give her more meat, but she'd watched enough videos herself to know that unless it was outrageously funny or made her blood boil within the first fifteen or twenty seconds, it was too easy to click away before the video was finished. The last few seconds of her clip would display her name as well as her degree from Northwestern and her email address. It was too bad she didn't have a website. She should work on that too, but one thing at a time. Maybe she could get a simple website launched before she posted the video.

The woman in the turquoise dress opened the door and held it while the others entered the building.

Ashley pulled her phone out of her pocket. Nine-twenty. She hadn't seen the dark red car that belonged to the woman who'd killed her mother. She should be here, begging God to forgive her.

Ashley stepped into the gutter and sat on the curb a few feet in front of her father. Smoke drifted over her head. She wondered what had he thought of her narration. Did he realize the words that had appeared fully formed in her mind came in part from his rants and complaints about the church? She needed to take a step back when she edited, to think about her own views, not just parrot his opinions. A journalist either dispassionately stated the facts or clearly spelled out her recommendations for change, rather than letting biases subtly twist the story. In this case, she wasn't sure she was capable of being a neutral reporter. That might make her appear cold, recalling her mother's death without emotion — soul-less, according to Jack.

She gripped the camera. Although she didn't want to appear icy and heartless, she also didn't want to start crying. She couldn't lose the confidence required to create interesting theater, to go head to head with that woman, shattering the carefully constructed armor to reveal her true nature.

The red car sped up the street. It lurched to the curb and

stopped. The rear protruded slightly and the front tires touched the concrete. She must have had bodywork done because there was no sign that it was a traveling murder weapon.

Ashley stood and hit record. For nearly a minute, there was no movement. A large magnolia tree hung over the hood and windshield. It blocked any view of the interior. Had the woman seen her? Did she plan to remain in her car until Ashley lowered the camera? Worse, maybe she'd restart the engine and continue on down the street.

The car door opened and Melody climbed out. She closed the door, opened the back door, and leaned in. She emerged holding a tiny purse with a long strap that she flung over her shoulder. The purse bounced off her thigh as she leaned back inside. She straightened and turned, clutching a Bible to her chest like she was afraid it might slip out of her arms and run screaming down the street. She slammed the door.

She hadn't even glanced toward the scene of her crime.

Ashley no longer smelled her father's cigarette smoke. It seemed he was complicit in not wanting to attract attention. He was so quiet, she wondered if he was still there.

Melody walked along the side of her car and up to the sidewalk.

As Melody approached the small fence that surrounded the patch of grass and the rarely used bench, Ashley started across the street, moving cautiously so the recording didn't get jerky. The slightest movement became an earthquake, but hopefully she could at least avoid the swaying that made viewers feel nauseous. She quickened her pace. She glanced down to make sure she didn't trip on the curb, then stepped up onto the sidewalk a few feet in front of Melody.

"Excuse me," Melody said. She moved to the left to go around.

Ashley matched her move, keeping the camera pointed at her. Melody's face was only three feet from the lens, raw and full of . . . something. It surely wasn't guilt. If Ashley didn't know better, she'd think the expression was pride.

A red bump on Melody's chin was in the center of the frame. There was no makeup covering the grayish skin under her eyes, and not a fleck of mascara to darken her lashes. The pupils of her pale gray eyes were dilated, despite the bright sun. Yet she wasn't squinting as her eyes adjusted.

"What are you doing?" Melody ducked her head and turned to the side.

"What do you hope to find inside your church?" Ashley said.

Melody stopped. She kept her head turned to the side, obviously more concerned about her face being recorded than her voice. It was almost as if she didn't realize her voice was being captured.

"What kind of question is that? I'm here to worship God."

"But are you looking for a vision? A message?"

"I'm not looking for anything."

"Then why bother?"

Melody inched to the side, but the fence blocked her way and Ashley stood between her and the opening. "Please stop filming me. What do you want?"

"I'm asking the questions. Do you know who I am?"

"Of course I know who you are."

"I think I have a right to ask a few questions. I want to understand your beliefs."

"Really?"

Ashley almost laughed. Melody sounded as if she thought Ashley was being friendly, possibly interested in converting. How gullible was she? Of course, you had to be gullible to think God was talking to you, that a guy standing behind a podium plucking words out of a book full of strange stories and rules, laced with inspiration and the occasional word of comfort, was speaking for the creator of the universe.

"Do you get a message from God every Sunday?"

"Not always." Melody pressed her hip against the fence. "I'm going to be late."

"Just give me a few minutes."

"Why do you have to film me?"

"So I don't forget what you say."

Melody nodded. "Okay. That makes sense."

So she did know her voice was being recorded. Yet she still seemed more concerned about her appearance. She licked her lips and pushed her hair behind her ear, then plucked out a few strands to curve across her jaw.

"Does God really talk to you?"

"It's not so much talking, more of a feeling, and a conviction about what you should do."

"Like what?"

"And it's not just on Sundays. He speaks all the time. He's always trying to communicate with his children — even those who haven't found Him yet. You too, you know."

"What kind of messages? Has he already spoken to you this morning?"

"Actually, yes. He told me to come to church."

"That's kind of obvious."

"I wasn't going to. But then when I woke up, I knew I should go."

"It still seems obvious. You changed your mind."

"It's hard to explain. It's a feeling. And these words forming in your head that don't come from your own thoughts or your mind."

"That's confusing." Ashley tried to keep her voice steady. She could feel Melody's excitement, the collapsing of her inhibitions. It wouldn't take much to lead her into a trap, to stimulate her emotions until she cried out like the crazed zealot she was.

"What's confusing?"

"How do you sort out the voices? Your own versus God's?"

"The more you listen the more clear it becomes when a voice is not your own."

"How do you know it's not the voice of the devil?"

A tiny squeak came out of Melody's throat. Her mouth remained open. She'd allowed her face to get too close to the lens so that her lips and nostrils were distorted. She licked her lips. Her tongue lingered at the corner of her mouth. "I would never listen to the voice of Satan."

"But how do you know? I don't understand how you can tell the difference."

"I'm late."

The sound of electric guitars and snare drums wafted out through the narrow space between the front doors.

"Please don't go. I really want to understand."

"You can just tell if it lines up with the Bible."

"Did God tell you to run over my mother?"

"No! God had nothing to do with that."

"Then it was the devil?"

"No. No! Why would you say that?"

Melody squinted at the camera. Her lower lip trembled. She bit it but the edges continued to shake.

"You killed her."

"It was an accident!"

"How can you just plow into a human being? It wasn't that dark. It wasn't raining."

"It wasn't my fault. I didn't see her."

"If it's not your fault, whose fault is it? God's? The devil's? Or there is no God and it just happened? A random world with random events and nothing makes sense?"

"I'm sorry. I'm so sorry."

"So you do know it's your fault."

"It's not. There are accidents."

"You said you were sorry. You must know it's your fault or you wouldn't apologize."

Melody's face was bright red. Her eyes filled with tears. "Turn that off."

"I need to know whose fault it is that my mother is dead." Ashley's finger hovered over the pause button. This had gone horribly off course. This was not a dispassionate interview she could post to get attention for her career. Her voice sounded as hysterical as Melody's. She should turn the camera off. This wasn't going to work, but she couldn't bring herself to stop. "Why weren't you paying attention?" Her voice was so quiet it sounded as if the words were simply an exhalation of breath.

Melody looked into the camera. The tears were gone. She squinted as if she expected to find something glittering in the depths of the lens. "You should come to the service. God will heal your pain and give you a purpose in life."

"I don't think so."

"Trust me. You should trust me. I've had terrible things happen in my life, and those wounds have been healed."

"Someone killed your mother?"

"I didn't kill your mother! You're twisting it around. It was an accident! Why can't you see that?" All her features pressed into a knot at the center of her face. "If you thought you were going to use that to make me look bad, to have some kind of evidence to sue me, or the church, you're wrong. It was an accident and the police agree with me."

Without pressing the pause button, Ashley lowered the camera. She glanced across the street. Her father was smoking. She couldn't read his expression, but she wasn't sure she'd ever been able to do that. He put the cigarette in his mouth. Smoke trailed out of his nose as he continued one unbroken cycle of inhalations and exhalations. She couldn't tell whether he'd heard the entire conversation.

Ashley started to cry. She wondered whether the camera was recording the sound. Her mother was gone. Dana would never see Ashley succeed in her career, find her soul mate, get married. Her mother would never cuddle a grandchild. Her father apparently had never been that thrilled with his daughter, always looking at her and seeing that she wasn't a boy. For all his declarations of love, Jack couldn't overlook a small mistake from a long time ago — a teenage prank. She'd always gotten what she wanted and now, suddenly, she had nothing.

She was used to having the upper hand. Why wasn't she able to force Melody to splinter into a thousand pieces? She hated herself for crying in front of this awkward, clueless woman who refused to feel guilty for what she'd done. This was all wrong.

Melody shoved her purse toward her back and spread her arms, the Bible flapped from her left hand like a large trapped bird. She leaned toward Ashley.

"God will help you. Just let go."

As Melody's body closed over her, the sharp smell of cheap shampoo filled Ashley's nostrils. She tried to wrench away but Melody's grip was too strong. "Get away from me."

Melody's arms tightened.

Ashley bent her elbow slightly, pulled it back, and shoved the camera into Melody's ribs.

Melody cried out. She pulled away and clutched her stomach.

Ashley swung her other arm and punched Melody's shoulder. It was a weak hit. Melody winced and moved to the left.

Ashley stepped to the side and blocked her way.

Across the street her father was silent. Was he hoping she'd beat Melody until her eyes were swollen closed, her teeth loose, her lips bloody? It wouldn't do any good. She pressed up against the fence and let Melody pass.

Melody hurried along the sidewalk, through the open gate, and up the path. She yanked open the door. The sound of singing and the beat of a base that dominated the other instruments burst out then faded quickly as the door slammed closed.

Ashley turned off the camera and walked across the street.

"What was that all about?" Her father dropped his cigarette on the sidewalk. It burned slowly.

"I don't know." She couldn't tell him what she'd planned. He'd think she was a loser. A stupid girl who had such grandiose dreams but seemed to have hit her peak in college. Knowing he'd never truly been behind her, that he'd simply tolerated her, always wishing she were someone else didn't hurt the way she would have expected. Instead, she felt hollow.

She looked at him. He didn't want to know what that was about. He was too busy mulling over everything that had slipped through his fingers. She was not going to live her life filled with regret.

She took a step back. He reeked of smoke. It was kind of disgusting. Was that his life plan now — smoke himself to death?

Twenty-eight

BOB STOOD IN the doorway of the master bathroom. The sky beyond the cracked window was black, darker than usual because it was the new moon. Most of the sheetrock was torn off, exposing wires and pipes. Removing it had been harder than he'd expected. The floor was bare plywood, a few shreds of pale green linoleum stuck in corners and hard-to-reach spots. Crumbled tile was everywhere.

Seeing the effects of the iron mallet, even though it was destructive rather than creating something new, he realized how disconnected his life was from the physical world. Explaining technology to customers, all his knowledge and life's work housed on a computer, rarely even touching the products his company sold, meetings conducted through faceless conference calls added up to a life that lacked substance.

His daughter was a stranger. He'd never have a son, although right now, he wasn't really sure why that had been so important. He couldn't remember what Dana's voice sounded like, couldn't remember her smell, or the feel of her skin. He had no idea what she'd spent her life thinking about, had never seen her at work, and didn't know what she and her friends discussed at their book club meetings. Had she loved him? Had she known he loved her? How did you ever know?

It was possible he could put things back together, try to make something different out of his relationship with Ashley, but when he tried to think how to do that, his mind took on the consistency of a wet sheet. The only things he enjoyed were wielding the sledgehammer, drinking beer, and smoking. How long would it be until he started smoking in the house?

Removing the bathtub and counters was a two-man job. An entire wall had to be taken out to allow for the expansion. He wasn't up to it in terms of skill or energy. There was no doubt he should have hired someone, but he owed Dana his hands-on involvement. He stepped into the bedroom. The bed was perfectly made, the comforter centered and smooth, as always. His mother had taught him the proper way to make a bed and it had been his task over the years. Dana had smiled at his ability to produce a showroom-quality effect, while her own efforts were lumpy and uneven. He walked through the room and into the hall and pulled the door closed behind him.

At the opposite end of the hall, Ashley's door was wide open, her bed unmade. It looked like she'd inherited her inadequate bed-making skills from her mother.

She was downstairs, staring at the TV. Since her encounter with Melody, she'd gone back to doing little more than sprawling on the couch watching so-called reality shows. She still went to work, but the minute she arrived home she changed into jeans and an oversized t-shirt and flopped on the couch with two slices of microwaved pizza or a corn dog.

He knew he should talk to her, try to help her out of her funk, but he had no idea where to start. She seemed angry with him. Maybe she was angry at the world. It was understandable. He felt the same way. Angry at the world, angry with god. Of course, he'd been that way most of his adult life.

He walked down the hall. Did she still have that gun? It wasn't good that she kept it in her closet, especially as she walked around in a cloud of depression, or rage. It was a little unclear why she'd taken it. Because she didn't trust Jack, she'd said. Right now, she shouldn't trust herself.

He went into her room and opened the closet door. There were so many shoeboxes. The one with the gun had been black. Shiny. He pulled it out, removed the lid, and picked up the gun. He unfolded the towel, put the towel in the box, and replaced the lid. He put the box back in the closet, stacking two other shoeboxes on top of it.

He stuck the gun in his waistband. It was cold and hard and didn't feel like it was securely in place. Movies and TV dramas made it look simple. He took a few steps, but his legs were stiff, his hips moved awkwardly. Maybe his pants were too loose. He tightened his belt a notch. He pulled his shirt over his belt and walked down the hall. The short stroll gave him a sudden sense of control over his life. Was that the implied power of a gun? The feeling you were in a superior position to any human being you encountered? No one could hurt you. Or you could punish them for hurting you. Too bad there was no way to punish god.

He started down the stairs. The gun pressed against his groin with each step. He was being foolish, a high tech geek acting like a cowboy. Dana would laugh.

When he reached the bottom of the stairs, he glanced at the front door. A shadow wavered beyond the leaded, textured glass. He waited. Sometimes the movement of the Japanese maple next door caused eerie looking changes of light across the front porch, caught in the already distorted view caused by the glass. The shadow flickered again, then remained steady. Someone was standing there.

The bell rang.

He waited to see if Ashley would make a move off the couch. It had to be one of her friends. Since the funeral, two of the couples he and Dana socialized with had stopped by, but they hadn't stayed long. He realized how much Dana carried the weight of entertaining guests, maintaining friendships.

He preferred the figure outside the door to be a friend of Ashley's. There wasn't anyone he wanted to talk to. He wasn't interested in answering any questions about how he was doing. In fact, the only relaxed and somewhat interesting encounter he'd had since Dana's death was that woman at the bathroom store — Miriam. Her name sounded biblical. Was he doomed to be haunted by hints of religion the rest of his life? Or maybe that name wasn't in the bible, it just sounded like it was because of its archaic quality.

The bell rang again. He walked to the door, turned the deadbolt, and opened it.

"You." He started to close the door.

"Wait." Melody put her palm on the door.

He pushed harder but the door didn't budge. It didn't help that he was holding his lower body in an unnatural position, trying to prevent the gun from sliding down his leg.

"Don't shut me out. Please. I felt bad about your daughter. She was hurting so much. I should have been kind and instead I made her cry. I've never made anyone cry in my life. I need to ask her forgiveness."

He laughed. "Her forgiveness? For being unkind? How about for killing her mother?"

"It was an accident! I don't need forgiveness for a terrible, horrible accident."

The gun handle pressed against his belly. Could she see it? She didn't appear to be looking down. In fact she didn't appear to be looking anywhere. Her eyes were coated with a film of tears, focused on something he couldn't see, or nothing at all. She was bordering on madness. He should have seen that from the beginning. They all were. Would it make him feel better if he pulled the gun out of his waistband and shot her? She was trespassing. Almost. Wasn't it justifiable to shoot someone who entered your house? But not an unarmed person, not a woman. He relaxed his pressure on the door and it opened wider. He moved his hand to the edge to give himself better control while he reviewed his options.

"Can you go get her? Or can I come in?"

"I don't want you talking to her."

"You've poisoned her against the Lord. The Bible speaks to that — if you turn a child against God, it would be better for you to have a stone tied around your neck and thrown into the depths of the sea."

"She isn't a child."

"Yes she is."

He shoved the door. Her arm collapsed and the door started to close. She lunged forward and wedged her body between the door and the frame. She winced as the door dug into her shoulder and hip.

"God told me to ask her forgiveness. To reach out to her."

"God didn't tell you anything. That's in your own head. God doesn't give a shit about you or me or Ashley."

"Oh. That's not true at all. He loves us. You just have to accept His will. He gives life and He takes life."

That tall, lanky body, those arms with the knobby wrists, her feet as big as his. He knew where he'd seen those gray, filmy eyes and those crocodile tears before. "I know you."

"Of course you know me."

"From before. A long time ago."

"Dad?"

Ashley's feet padded on the floor behind him. "What's going on?"

"Nothing. Go back to your show." He put his hand on his belly, feeling the barrel of the gun. "You were there. When my son died."

She'd been watching as they pulled the bloody, boneless, lifeless body out of Dana — those huge closed eyes, frail, narrow shoulders. The limbs only half-formed. Dana crying. His own face frozen. And that nurse's aid, babbling mindless prayers just outside the door. Pushing her way into the room when it was over. She'd put those veined, bony hands on Dana's leg, spreading her fingers across the anemic orange blanket. *He gives life and he takes life.* She'd gripped Dana's leg with one hand, and tried to grab his hand, missing as he yanked it out of reach, succeeding only in pinching the tips of his fingers. She'd asked them to pray for another child. The gift of new life.

It flooded his mind, as if it were happening in front of him right now. All her ugly, hateful words. Dana crying, tears running down her face, turning her head away so he couldn't see her grief. Feeling his own tears, refusing to cry. Telling the aide to shut up and get the hell out of their room. Pushing the button to call the nurse.

When they were finally rid of her, Dana turned and looked at him. Her eyes were cold, the tears dried up. There was no shadow of redness to show she'd been crying at all. Her voice was firm. "I'm done. God gave us a daughter and she's enough. I'm not going through this again."

He'd wanted to chase after that aide and strangle her for twisting Dana in the wrong direction, for bringing god into it. God wasn't in charge. Human beings had the power to create life.

He'd gripped Dana's hand. "Now isn't the time. You need to calm down."

"I'm perfectly calm. And I'm done."

"You don't get to make that decision on your own."

"You need to stop trying to prove your manhood with a male child. It's my body and I can't take any more. I'm not going to create more children and watch them die."

"We'll talk about it later."

"I'm done, Bob."

After that, she wouldn't even speak when he brought it up. She just looked at him, or through him, until he stopped talking. For nearly a year they hadn't made love. She'd worn layers of clothes to bed and wouldn't let so much as the tip of his finger touch the skin of her stomach. He'd never cheated, he'd tried to take care of himself, but it was only satisfying for a moment or two. When he finally stopped talking about it, she gradually warmed to him again, but after that, sex felt like something happening outside his body.

He'd done everything god required and gotten kicked in the teeth. And still they kept coming. Preaching at him, telling him what to do, promising that god would answer prayers. Talking out of both sides of their mouths — *expect everything . . . accept everything.*

If it was a matter of passively accepting every insult and deprivation and sorrow god wanted to shove down your throat, what was the point of living?

He pulled the gun out of his waistband. He flicked off the safety, surprised at how easy it was, as if he was in the habit of handling a gun, equally surprised by the sensation that he was standing further down the hallway, watching himself, impressed that he was taking charge, excited to put a bullet in that woman's throat and shut her up once and for all.

"Dad!"

Ashley's feet slammed against the floor as she ran, plowing into him. "Don't."

He grunted and pulled the gun close to his side.

Ashley grabbed his forearm, her fingers like iron bands. He hadn't realized she was so strong. That was the disadvantage of being almost fifty instead of twenty — a female could get the better of you.

Melody pushed through the opening. She wrapped her hands around his face, half covering his eyes. He smelled her perspiration, musty and sour. She was praying, "Oh God, Oh Lord, Oh Jesus. Help him. Forgive him, heal him, touch his heart."

He yanked his arm with Ashley's fingers still wrapped around it. He shoved the gun at Melody's hip. He needed to get it higher. Right in the neck, that lumpy Adam's apple bobbing up and down, vomiting out senseless, stupid words. He strained his arm. Ashley pulled harder. God, she was strong. He felt a flash of pride.

The gun was higher now, near his ribs.

Ashley released her grip. She pushed him hard and he fell back. The door slammed into the wall under the weight of his body. The force drove the knob into his spine. He groaned. Melody's fingers tore at his cheeks as she fell with him, refusing to let go. Ashley had her hand on his now. She dug her fingers beneath the heel of his hand, groping to find the safety. Smart girl. Another rush of pride coursed through him.

He pressed the trigger and the gun exploded. It was so loud he couldn't hear anything for a moment. Then he felt something in his stomach, a warm glow. His knees gave way and he collapsed to the floor, falling on his hip, but there was no pain from the impact.

From far away, echoing around the explosion that seemed to be repeating itself deep inside his ears, he heard a female voice. "Call 9-1-1. Now. Don't just stand there like an idiot." It was Ashley. That woman was helpless to take charge of a situation.

He closed his eyes. Or were they already closed? The sounds around him seemed far away, voices, but he couldn't make out the words. Ashley was a great kid — he couldn't have asked for anyone better. A great kid and a perfect wife.

Dana's little smile. She'd known him better than he knew himself. She'd known why he was angry, and she'd loved him anyway. You couldn't be angry at something that didn't exist. And now he wasn't angry anymore, just tired. Blood flowed out of him. He thought he was supposed to be somewhere. He had an appointment. There was someone waiting for him, he just couldn't get his mind to focus on who that might be.

He was drifting to sleep. "Forgive me," he said. He let his upper body slide to the floor.

"Daddy. I love you, hold on."

Twenty-nine

ASHLEY SAT ON the back porch. She stared at the line of trees along the fence. It was dusk, the sky a lovely dark blue, the stars and the nearly full moon glowed softly. The whole canopy looked like an inviting lake of warm water.

She was alone. And it wasn't so bad. She was really a very independent person. There was no one she had to please or answer to. The whole universe opened up before her. Nothing would get in her way now. Her life was stripped clean, as if she'd been re-born.

With an excellent education, good references, plenty of money once the house was sold, she could go anywhere, create her own future. Everything she wanted was there for the taking. She'd always gotten what she wanted and there was no reason that would change now.

Hopefully it wouldn't be hard to sell the house, with that stupid church across the street. Maybe one of the members would be interested. She smiled. How convenient to be able to trip across the quiet street every other day of the week and stumble through those front doors. She shivered.

When she thought about it, what went on inside that dull little building was frightening — people working themselves into a frenzy. It was like some kind of orgy. Swaying and clapping, waving their arms and making inhuman sounds. It seemed as if they were trying to create a god out of the sheer force of their will — herd mentality, mass psychosis.

Before she moved, maybe she'd take Melody up on her offer to attend one of their services. She hadn't given up on her idea of recording something shocking, producing a video that would add to her digital resume, getting her name out there so job offers came to *her*. All she needed was a story that would grip and horrify.

She picked up her glass and took a sip of wine. It was crisp and cool. It spread across her brain, giving her a warm softly pulsing vision of her future.

WATCHING ASHLEY SHOOT her father had served as Melody's absolution. She and Ashley were both weapons of death. By accident, of course, but the girl's loss could no longer be blamed on Melody.

When the bullet went into Bob's stomach, the first thought that passed through Melody's mind was to place her hand on the wound, asking God to give her the gift of healing. All His children had gifts. She'd accepted she was not going to receive the gift of tongues. She refused to make a fool of herself again — not at Triumphant Life Tabernacle or any other church of its kind. She was done begging Him to notice her, to prove His love with the gift that was indiscriminately handed out to others. The ability to heal would be a terrifying and exciting gift. Then, as quickly as the thought and accompanying desire arose, it vanished. The potential for humiliation was even greater.

It wasn't that she'd lost her faith, but she was confident God was not the character those people made him out to be. Instead of stripping everything out of her life in a frantic search to make room for God, hoping He'd notice her unreserved devotion, it was time to add things back in. She wanted new clothes and a new car. She might want a more interesting job, even a mate. She definitely had to get rid of that car.

Ashley had sobbed, telling her father she loved him, begging him not to die. But as his breathing became thinner and the blood leaked out of his body, the tears dried from her eyes and a calmness spread across her lips until her face was serene. After that, she'd had only one thing to say — *You didn't really love me. But I loved you.*

Strange words for a dying father. They echoed Melody's thoughts, although in her case, the Father who didn't seem to love her was even more remote.

Melody's cell phone shuddered, plastic rattling against the tile. The number displayed on the screen was familiar, but she couldn't remember who it belonged to. It wasn't someone from Triumphant Life. She had all of their names on her call list. Gordon's brother, that was it.

She picked up the phone. "Hello?"

"Hi. It's Tim . . . Gordon Wilson's . . ."

"Yes, I know who you are."

"I heard what happened."

"The shooting?"

"Terrible," he said.

"It was."

"You're okay?"

"I think so."

"First the wife killed, now the husband."

"It wasn't my fault," she said.

"I didn't say that at all."

They were silent for a few seconds.

"The car accident . . . Sarah thinks it was . . . maybe you . . ."

"I didn't."

"Okay."

"Why did you call?" Melody said.

"You seem like a nice person. I was a jerk for what I did."

"Oh."

"Sarah went too far. I knew she was out of line."

"But you called me anyway?"

"If my brother found out I borrowed money from his wife, he'd punish my sister. But I told him about it. All he said was I'm weak. Like you said."

She thought about his muscular arms, the feeling of what it might be like to rest her head in his large, strong hands, his fingers caught in her hair. "I don't think you're weak. That was a mistake. You did what you needed to do for your sister."

"I think so," he said.

"It's true."

"I was wondering, can I invite you over for dinner?"

"Sure." Her instant agreement surprised her.

"Tomorrow?"

"Okay."

After they finished talking, she walked to the sink and looked out at the deck. The window was dirty and spotted from a winter of hard rain, a filmy coating on the inside. It was already May. She needed to do some serious cleaning. Wipe away everything. Like letting people walk all over her. Was that the kind of God she wanted? Was that who God was, expecting His children to become vaporous, faceless shadows? One thing she'd never figured out was why she was told to chip away every facet of herself, while others, like Elise, did as they pleased and declared it God's will. As if God's will was something that varied from person to person, twisted to suit your own agenda.

She was tired of trying to get God to prove His love. She touched the window and ran her finger along the glass, leaving a clean streak. Maybe it was more important to give love to other people, and to God, than to try to get it.

She grabbed her purse and went outside. She stood on the porch looking at the Buick. This was the last time she'd walk out the front door and see that enormous, ugly vehicle. When she drove to Tim's apartment, she'd be in her new Mini Cooper.

There was a fluttery feeling in her chest, like a moth's papery wings brushing against her heart. It could be God. Or something else.

THE END

About the Author

Cathryn Grant is the author of Suburban Noir novels, ghost story novellas, and short fiction. Her writing has been described as "making the mundane menacing".

Her fiction has appeared in Alfred Hitchcock and Ellery Queen Mystery Magazines, and been anthologized in The Best of Every Day Fiction. Her short story, "I Was Young Once" received an honorable mention in the 2007 Zoetrope All-story Short Fiction contest.

When she's not writing, Cathryn reads fiction, eavesdrops, and plays very high handicap golf. She lives on the Central California coast with her husband and two cats. Contact Cathryn through her website at SuburbanNoir.com or sign up for her quarterly newsletter to receive updates when new books are released.

www.ingramcontent.com/pod-product-compliance
Lightning Source LLC
Chambersburg PA
CBHW030548260626
47157CB00006B/2223